THE FAE SIDE OF FORTY

MAGICAL MIDLIFE MISADVENTURES BOOK 2

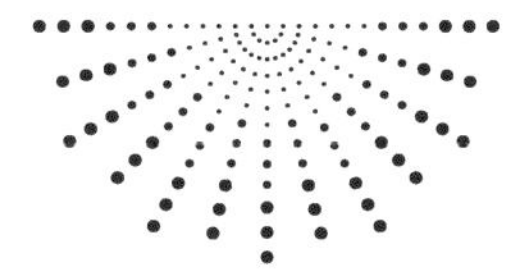

JENNIFER L. HART

ELEMENTS UNLEASHED

CONTENTS

THE FAE SIDE OF FORTY

Far Side of Forty, The
Hart/ Jennifer L.

1.Women's—Fiction 2. North Carolina—Fiction 3.
Paranormal—Fiction 4. Fae—Fiction 5. Time Travel—
Fiction 6. Humor—Fiction 7. Small Towns—Fiction 8.
Gymnastics—Fiction 9. American Humorous—Fiction 10.
Mountain Living—Fiction 11. Divorce— Fiction 12. BBW—
Fiction I. Title

ISBN 978-1-951215-49-1

THE FAE SIDE OF FORTY

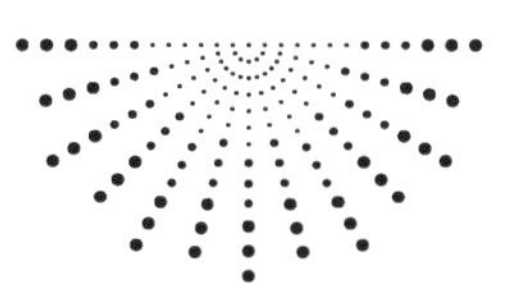

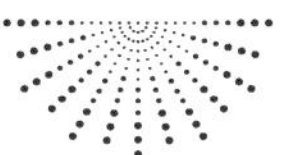

*"You know why they call a woman of a certain age a cougar? If you make her angry,
she'll tear your face off."*

-Notable quotable from Grammy B

Midnight. My pulse pounded along with the toll of the grandfather clock in the downstairs hall. The damning bong echoed through the darkened Victorian like a dirge. *Time's up, Joey,* it seemed to say. I was tempted to rush to my phone and double-check the hour, just to make sure. But technology wouldn't work if *he* was nearby. Technology and magic didn't get along, at least according to him. I sat on the window seat in my bedroom, still fully dressed, dry-mouthed, and on the edge of panic.

One month. He had vowed to return in exactly one month. And he had promised that when he did come back, we would be married. Well, *promised* wasn't the right word. I wasn't some eager bride waiting breathlessly for her beloved to return. It was more of a threat, really. Because I, Joey Whitmore, a middle-aged gymnastics coach, sat waiting on a fae prince who I'd screwed out of two and a half centuries worth of bargains.

Who knew I had it in me?

The tolling stopped. I stared around the darkened bedroom. Nothing. No sign of ensnaring sapphire eyes or gold and purple magic swirls. No irreverent voice laced with sexual innuendo. I shoved open the window, needing to breathe in a bit of the cool springtime mountain air, and let out a sigh of relief.

Are you relieved? Or are you...disappointed?

It was my inner voice, the one I had dubbed the sensible shrew. She relished adding her no-nonsense two cents to my inner turmoil. Wasn't it enough that my stomach had been churning all day and that I hadn't managed a bite of dinner on Taco Tuesday? Couldn't I just go downstairs for a midnight snack and then fall into bed for a few hours before getting on with my life without that bitch making a federal case of it?

Having Robin Goodfellow not drop back into my life like a chaotic whirlwind was a good thing. I refused to be disappointed by him. He wasn't some blind date who'd stood me up. Better if he had moved on without looking my way. I needed to take a page out of his book and do the same.

Resolve firmly mounted to the sticking place, I headed out of my room and down the second-floor hall. After having lived all my life inside the old Victorian, I knew where all the creaky boards were on the stairs and skipped them with ease. I didn't want to wake Dragon, my cousin who lived on the floor above or worse, my mother, whose room was downstairs. Neither of them knew about Robin, his magic, or why I'd been squirrely for the last few days. Though I wanted to tell them, I didn't know how to explain the predicament to anyone else.

You see, I sort of hated my life and promised a fae prince a favor if he would take me back in time to change the accident that had ended my gymnastics career. And after many misfire adventures, he decided that his price was my hand in marriage.

Nope, no way in hell could I say that without sounding crazier than an outhouse rat.

I pushed through the swinging door to the kitchen and flipped the wall switch for the Tiffany lamp that hung over the breakfast nook. The illuminated space was cozy, perfect for a cup of coffee while reading the news or an intimate family dinner. Or a late-night calorie-fest. My feet headed right for the fridge. I was hungry as a bear emerging from hibernation to forage. Never mind the six pounds I lost over the last month after being very careful to count fat grams and make sure I was fueling my sluggish forty plus metabolism properly.

I had *not* been dieting because of Robin. And if I decided to pig-out when he didn't show? Well, a woman was allowed to indulge herself without it having anything to do with a man.

Mom had made extra chicken for taco filling. Dragon— our resident vegetarian—ate only beans and my mother kept expecting that to change. I'd just snagged the leftover meat and put it on the plate to heat when someone knocked on the back door.

I shrieked and whirled around. My hand flew to my chest and I pounded on the spot a few times, to make sure my heart hadn't stopped.

Robin had shown up after all. Strange, he usually didn't bother knocking, just magicked himself right into my personal space where I couldn't ignore him.

"So close," I muttered and then squared my shoulders with military precision and headed for the door. If tangling with a fae prince was my destiny, I would meet him with my eyes open and my chin raised.

But it wasn't fate that stood on the concrete slab, it was my best friend. Darcy's pink hood was up, buffering her pixielike face against the wind. Her blonde hair shone almost white under the light of the full moon. She looked like the perfect mom caricature from a cartoon, an image that was obliterated whenever she opened her mouth. "Did the bastard show?"

"No." I gestured for her to come in. While it may be close to the spring equinox, we lived in the high country of North Carolina which meant the night air held a wicked chill. Perfect for easing a hot flash, but uncomfortable the rest of the time.

"And how do you feel about that?" After removing her coat, she went to retrieve the chicken from the microwave. "This is going to taste like a used rubber if you nuke it."

I raised a brow. "Eaten a lot of used rubbers, have you?"

She glared at me and headed for the toaster oven. "Answer the damn question."

"Relieved." Other than me, Darcy was the only person

who knew about Robin Goodfellow and our bargain. Anyone else on the planet would assume I was nuts. As a certified whacko herself, Darcy wasn't one to judge.

I didn't like the way she was scrutinizing my every muscle twitch or the flat note in her voice as she drew out the next word. *"Riiiight."*

I snagged some bagged salad from the fridge, even though I wanted a taco shell, sour cream, and extra cheese to go with that chicken. It was one thing to have a midnight snack, another entirely to hoover out the fridge in front of a witness.

Darcy retrieved two bowls—barely. She stood just shy of five feet tall and though our house was old and the cabinets were low, they were just high enough to frustrate my bestie's notorious killer bunny rabbit temper. "Maybe he forgot."

I scowled at her. "I'm his anchor to this realm. I seriously doubt he forgot about me."

"His anchor. You still haven't explained what exactly that means." Darcy snagged the cheese and taco sauce.

"Probably because I don't know myself, other than he needs me to help him stay here." I poured the salad mix into two bowls while Darcy scoured the fridge. "What are you looking for?"

"Open wine."

I snorted. "There's no such animal in this house."

Undeterred, she shut the refrigerator and headed to the built-in wine rack on the far side of the counter and extracted two bottles. "Red or white?"

"It's chicken." I pointed to the bottle of Moscato.

Darcy got two glasses and the electric corkscrew while I gathered my thoughts. When the timer dinged, I stuffed my right hand into an oven mitt, snagged the tray, and doled out the protein into equal portions onto our salads before dumping the hot pan into the sink. We each took a bowl and a glass to the tiny kitchen table.

"What about the sex?" Darcy asked. "You can't tell me you're not a little disappointed about missing out on some fae nookie."

I swallowed a gulp of the fruity Moscato. "Who said we were going to have sex?"

"Please." She rolled her eyes. "Like you weren't interested in making the beast with two backs with your magic man."

Heat stained my cheeks. "It isn't like that."

Darcy shook her head with mock sympathy. "Oh, Joey. Joey, Joey, my poor muddled and extremely naive friend. *Of course,* it's like that. It's always like that when there's an attraction between two hot and not yet dead people."

"I'm not naive." I might be a little bit naive. Savvy women don't get themselves indebted to fae princes.

Darcy raised a brow. "Look, my personal theory? Your boy Robin is not so good with the social skills. I mean, do you really have an unfulfilled bargain with him?"

I opened my mouth to say yes, we definitely had a bargain but then I frowned.

Darcy set down her wineglass and began to count. "Bargain one, you traded an open-ended favor for time travel. You cashed in your trips and then strong-armed him into accepting a BS favor. You know that worked because he disappeared, correct?"

At my nod, she held up another finger. "Bargain two was you committing to be his anchor in exchange for him saving a life. There was no open-ended favor."

I scowled and then nodded. "You're right."

"So he can't mystically force you to marry his sneaky-fine ass because say it with me, you don't owe him jack."

My lips parted. "How did you remember all that?" I'd spent the past month trying to sort it all out in my head.

"Mostly because hey, surprise, I'm not emotionally invested enough in the guy to not pay attention to the critical details." She winked and speared a piece of chicken with her fork.

I thought it through. "But what if he can control me because I'm his anchor? The last one he turned into a cat." And he'd had some sort of mental telepathic link with her. I kept that tidbit to myself. Darcy had a fear of all things psychic and telepathy might be a bridge too far.

And then the meaning of her words struck. "What do you mean *emotionally invested*? You make it sound like I'm hung up on him."

She tilted her head to the side. "Aren't you?"

"No." Even in my ears, the word sounded hollow.

Darcy gave me her patented, *who do you think you're fooling* look.

"Well, okay. He's a fae prince. He's gorgeous and smart and he has that killer Welsh accent. You know I like men who can actually string a coherent sentence together."

"That explains Georgia," Darcy muttered.

I glowered at her. "Bringing up the ex? Really? Low blow, Abrams."

Darcy leaned back in her chair, both hands wrapped around her wineglass. "Look, babe. I'm not trying to be a bitch about it. I'm worried about you. You have to admit that what happened with Georgia damaged you. And you've been carrying the hurt around ever since."

"You make me sound like a piece of luggage." The salad had become unappetizing and I pushed the bowl across the table and stared out the darkened window.

"Georgia hurt you. I know it and you know it. Even after the divorce, you supported her transition and you hid everything you were feeling. Isn't that why you're still avoiding her?"

My teeth sank into my lower lip. "Not as much as I used to. I invited her over for Margarita Monday."

Even in the warbly reflection, I could see her eyes narrow. "And were relieved when she didn't come. Don't deny it. It was written all over your face."

I fiddled with my fork. She was right. I'd resisted getting too close to Georgia even though she constantly made overtures of friendship. "It's not about Georgia. Not really. I don't trust my own judgment. Seeing her reminds me of all the bad calls I've made. Even in the other timeline, who did I pick? Cheating Pete."

"You're using past hurt as a shield around your heart and the only thing it's doing is blocking out your future happiness." Darcy reached over the table to clasp my hand. "I'm not saying the fae is the right guy for you. I'm saying you need to make peace with the past so you can truly move on. And who says you need a man to be happy?"

"That's right. We've got Taco Tuesday."

"Speaking of which…." Darcy frowned down at her salad. "You know what this needs? To be put in a damn corn shell and smothered in cheese and sour cream."

I was already up out of my chair and heading to the pantry. "You read my mind."

She shivered. "Don't even joke about that."

"Good, Mikala." I extended a hand over the edge of the foam block pit to the star pupil from the seven and eight-year-old class. After only a few weeks in the gym, it had become clear that the girl already had what it took to be an elite gymnast. She was a looker too, with dark brown hair and skin, and jade green eyes. Her plucky attitude sealed the deal. It was hard for me not to play favorites during her classes.

She flashed me a gap-toothed grin as she took my hand, allowing me to haul her out of the pit where she'd just landed. "Thanks, Ms. Joey."

Alina, the gym's owner, looked up from where she had been working with one of the other girls on the springboard. We had them practicing hitting the board in just the right place so they could get the feeling of being propelled into the air. Instead of clearing a vault or landing on a balance beam, the class was landing in a pit of primary-colored foam blocks. The exercise had been filled with shrieks and squeals of delight. Even stone-faced Alina had cracked a smile.

The scent of chalk and sweat, the sounds of the gym filled me with a rightness that I had all but forgotten. Every day since I had started working for Alina had been better than the one before. The reward of doing the thing I had been put on the planet to do after a long absence from it filled me with joy and appreciation.

Being a gymnast gave me poise. Now, settled into midlife, I was rediscovering that confidence by being the tempered sweet to Alina's sour. I offered gentle encouragement and tips where the Romanian bronze medalist demanded perfection of form. She was surprisingly good with the younger students though. Between the two of us, the gymnastics classes were booked six days a week.

The little bell over the front door jangled. From my position near the block pit, I couldn't see who had entered. Probably one of the parents coming in from the coffee shop next door. Newer parents sat in the uncomfortable plastic chairs that lined the wall behind the check-in desk. That usually lasted a week or two. Once they saw their children were in good hands and had all but forgotten they had parents, they drifted next door and spent the hour chatting with friends, catching up on their reading, or just sitting quietly with a peaceful cup of java.

The last student ran down the strip of red mat toward the springboard with less skill but more enthusiasm than Mikala had. "Go easy," I called out to her. "You want to make sure you land on the right spot."

It happened in an instant, the way accidents in the gym always do. She hit the board too fast, forgetting to jump. The momentum carried her up, but not high enough to hit the pit. She wasn't going to make it into the foam.

We had thick mats down but out of instinct, I lunged forward to catch her before she hit the mat and broke her nose. Having experienced that pain firsthand, I couldn't bear the thought of a young girl enduring the same. She screamed. I couldn't tell if it was the sound of unbridled enthusiasm or sheer terror. Did she realize what was about to happen?

I moved to catch her. My wrist wouldn't hold her weight at that velocity. I prayed for the best and then braced for impact. *I wish she would make it.*

It never came.

Defying all laws of physics, the girl lifted up into the air, high enough to clear the side of the pit. I saw a whisp of amber light as though she were nothing but an oversized butterfly being carried by the most powerful air currents on the planet. She landed amid the foam blocks with a soft plop.

"Emma, are you all right?" Her mother, one of the newbies, rushed over to the side.

Emma's eyes were wide and she stared at me and then nodded.

I forced a smile, hiding the adrenaline drop that made my knees wobble. "You need to slow down. At this point in your training, the technique is more important than speed."

She nodded even as her mother half climbed into the pit to scoop her out.

Alina stepped up to my side. Her Romanian accent was thick as she asked, "Time to call it a day, yes?"

"Yes." I nodded even as my mind whispered the truth.

He's here.

My stomach flipped and then face-planted somewhere near my groin. I'd seen those golden flecks of light before. Knew the source of them. And even though I'd been expecting him the night before, I wasn't ready to face Robin Goodfellow.

"Do you need a minute?" Alina scrutinized my face and

clearly mistook my anxious expression for being rattled over Emma's close call. "I can dismiss the class."

I nodded, grasping for the out she'd offered me. "Thank you. I'd appreciate that."

On unsteady legs, I headed toward the locker rooms where the older gymnasts stored their stuff. I headed to the nearest sink and braced my hands on either side of the cool, white porcelain. Robin waited outside. His fae ass was parked in a plastic chair in my freaking gym. It had been his magic that had staved off disaster. Would he claim I owed him a favor for that?

Despite Darcy's insistence that there was no way the fae could force me to marry him, I still felt like I owed him. If not for Robin Goodfellow and his interference, I wouldn't have come back to the gym. Would never have considered teaching. He had changed my life for the better.

"That doesn't mean you owe him the rest of it," I told the woman in the mirror. "So, march your lily-white hide out there and tell him how it's gonna be. You set the terms going forward."

Yes. That was how to handle the situation. Take charge and draw the line. I needed to give him boundaries. I was willing to be his friend but refused to fill the role of brow-beaten fae bride. And if he turned me into an immortal cat like he had my predecessor?

Well, one worry at a time.

I studied my reflection. Bloodshot blue eyes from too much premature celebrating. Broken nose from that long-ago car accident. Dark brown hair threaded with gray. Though I kept meaning to stop at the store and buy a box of dye or make a salon appointment, it hadn't happened. Six pounds didn't look like nearly enough weight loss, considering I was at least sixty over my goal weight. I'd start off the day okay with oatmeal or an egg white omelet and the gymnastics classes kept me moving throughout the day. I made big plans to steam broccoli and broil chicken for dinner. But inevitably, Grammy would stop at the bakery and insist I come over for a cupcake. Or Dragon would beg me to take her to the café for a slice of Kentucky pie. Even my mom sabotaged me by making homemade pizza or eggplant parmesan. Encouraging her to cook vegetarian to support Dragon meant she tended to use extra cheese on everything to make up for the missing meat.

Well, no sense fretting about it now. I looked like what I was. A middle-aged former gymnast gone soft who indulged in too much wine and tacos with her bestie in the middle of the night. I hadn't gotten much sleep lately and it showed in the deep purple bruises beneath my eyes. Although that was mostly his fault. If he didn't like it, he could bugger off.

Resolve firmly mounted to the sticking place, I squared my shoulders and headed for the locker room door.

Alina was in her office when I strode by. She looked up but didn't say anything. That was Alina's way. She spoke more with pointed, disapproving glances than with actual words. When I'd been a teen, she used to intimidate me but now I recognized her coaching style for what it was—ruthlessly efficient.

I tried to balance that both with the girls who soaked up praise like little sponges and their nervous parents. I chatted and praised and encouraged, doing my level best to share my love of gymnastics with the next generation. It didn't matter if any champions emerged from our studio, at least not to me. What mattered was the environment we created, one where girls felt safe and empowered and could form friendships that would stand the test of time. Like Darcy and me.

Darcy. I paused, wondering if I should shoot her a text to let her know that Robin had finally made an appearance. What if he abducted me? It would be good for someone to know what had happened. And knowing my friend, she would want to be updated on the latest.

I debated if it was a good idea to involve Darcy for so long that someone tapped me on the shoulder. A familiar lilting Welsh voice murmured in my ear.

"Lamb, are you almost done stalling? We're on a bit of a schedule."

I whirled around to face the fae prince. "Robin. You're here."

"For a limited time only." He inclined his head. "No need to thank me for saving the exuberant mortal imp from having all of her teeth knocked out."

"Because I should never thank a fae?" I asked.

"That's one reason. There is no sound more abhorrent than the scream of a human child." He studied me. "Is that what you're wearing?"

I looked down at my black and aqua hoodie worn over a black tank and black stretch pants. "What's wrong with what I'm wearing?"

"It's not exactly bride wear."

"That's because I'm not a bride." I put my hands on my hips and raised my chin until I could meet his gaze directly. "And from my count, I don't owe you a favor."

His sapphire eyes twinkled. "Is that so? Have you

forgotten that you thanked me, and, this is a direct quote, 'for everything'?"

My lips parted. "I didn't know you were there!"

He made a tsking sound. "Doesn't change the fact that you did exactly what I warned you not to do."

Damn it, where was Darcy with her distant logic when I needed her? Robin had me all tangled up in my underwear. "That doesn't mean I have to marry you."

He continued as if I hadn't spoken. "Plus, there's also the small matter of you agreeing to be my anchor."

My hands flew to my hips. "If you're planning to turn me into a cat—"

He held up a hand. "That was Clara's idea. It became easier for her to blend in. Remember, in her time, women who didn't age were burned at the stake."

I wasn't sure if I was more horrified by the idea of women being burned at the stake or the reason behind it. "Are you telling me that I'm not *aging?*"

"Forever forty-something. At least as long as you are a fae's anchor." he sighed and then pulled an old-fashioned pocket watch from the liner of his jacket. "We really must be going, especially since you'll want to change."

"Going where?"

"Why, to introduce me to your family, of course." He said it so matter of factly. As though it made perfect sense to take a fae prince home to meet the parents and I was the nutcase who was being obstinate for no reason.

I stuck a finger in his face. "You better leave them out of this."

He sighed as though I was exasperating him. "Honestly.

I'm beginning to think you have no idea how the mortal concept of marriage works."

"That's because we aren't getting married!" My shrill voice echoed off the rafters.

Those sapphire irises focused on me and his irreverent humor seemed to melt away. "Joey, listen to me. My mother has to believe that we are engaged. Even now, she has spies in the mortal plane."

"Believe? As in pretend?" My tone was skeptical.

He nodded in confirmation. "For as long as it takes to accomplish what I came here to do."

"Which is…?" I prompted.

"My business," he flashed me a grin. "Come on, lamb. Please. I need this."

Pretend I was engaged to Robin Goodfellow. Could I pull it off? I had upended his life. Undone years of his hard work making deals with mortals and gaining power and influence in the fae court. One bargain had changed his fate as much as it changed mine.

I was better off. But my guess was Robin hadn't been so lucky.

You aren't actually considering this! the sensible shrew shrieked. I made a face. She had a point. "One condition. You don't tell my mother or grandmother or Dragon that we are getting married."

"I'll have to concoct another reason to be around you, for their benefit." He sounded as though he were considering the possibilities.

He didn't ask why and for once in my life, I didn't offer an explanation. Fae used information about mortals to their advantage. And though I wanted to help Robin, I sure didn't trust him.

"So, it's a bargain?" He raised one golden blond brow and stuck out his hand.

My heart raced and I wiped my damp palm on my pant leg before grasping his. "A bargain well struck."

He grinned, magic swirled, and the world faded to black.

CHAPTER TWO

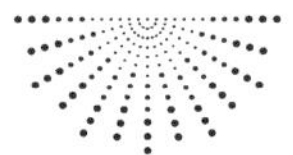

"Not everything is about you."

-Notable quotable from Grammy B

"Joey? Are you hurt?"

The concerned voice had a familiar Romanian accent and roused me from sleep. I blinked and looked up at Alina. "What happened?

She shook her head. "I am not knowing. One minute you stand here and then you were sprawled on the floor. Are you ill?"

Slowly, I sat up and then shook my head. Looked around. No sign of Robin.

"Did you see a man?" I gripped Alina's arm and let her

pull me to my feet. "A handsome blond man with a devil-may-care smile?"

She scowled down at me as though I was an idiot. Her standard expression. "I am seeing no one. Do you need me to call someone? A doctor perhaps?"

I shook my head and released her arm. My gaze drifted to the clock on the wall. Three oh five. "I need to go. Dragon is waiting for me."

Alina didn't look convinced that all was well so I forced a smile, hoisted my gym bag, and then headed out the door. My baby blue VW bug, freshly sprung from the impound lot, was parked across the street, not far from my father's law office. Normally I stopped in to chat with dear old dad after my last class, but after making another bargain and being knocked out I didn't feel up to talking to anyone. I turned the engine over, checked the road, and then pointed the VW toward the school. The final bell wouldn't ring for another twenty minutes or so, but there were already a few parents in line. My mind hummed as I tried to sort through everything that had happened.

Had it been real? Did I really strike yet another bargain with Robin Goodfellow?

I replayed it all. Maybe I should go to the doctor, get an MRI or something. Because not only had I hallucinated Robin's presence, apparently, I hadn't learned anything from my last encounter with him.

Dumbass, the sensible shrew sniped.

Another bargain. Pretending to be Robin's wife. Horror filled me as I realized that the bargain had no set end date. He would hang around for as long as it took to do whatever he had to do. And I hadn't asked anything from him, other than he did not tell my mom, Dragon, or Grammy B. Oh god, what had I done?

"Joey." Dragon rapped on the driver's side window, startling me out of my fae PTSD trance. "Can I drive?"

I nodded, glad that I didn't have to. Dragon—whose given name was Diedre which she hated and thereby had taken on a fiercer and more fitting handle—had gotten her learner's permit the week before. She hounded me to drive at every opportunity, eager for her license and the freedom that came with it.

She'd admitted that she hadn't been interested in driving when she lived in Baltimore. But moving to the country where there was no public transportation or really much of anything within walking distance, had been the motivation she'd needed to take the next step.

"How was school?" I did my best to sound normal and not on the verge of losing my shit as I clicked the seatbelt on the passenger's side and waited while she checked her mirrors and readjusted the seat so that her long legs weren't all scrunched up by the pedals.

"Fine." She glanced over her shoulder to check her blind spot and then headed out into traffic. "It's just school, you know?"

Her expression was carefully neutral. I worried about her sometimes. Dragon was a hard person to get to know. For one thing, the only color she ever wore was black. Correction—she only wore black clothing, right down to her scuffed combat boots. The right side of her dark hair had deep blue streaks while the left side was completely shaved. Today, she wore ripped black skinny jeans and a black muscle shirt with a black hoodie on top. Her default setting was standoffish and prickly, mostly because my aunt had been giving her grief about her sexual orientation. Dragon was a lesbian, a fact that had caused a rift between her and her mom and resulted in the latter shipping the former off to the middle of nowhere. Aka my hometown. After withstanding a rejection like that, it was no wonder Dragon didn't open herself up to many people.

"Hey, what's he doing there?" Dragon had turned out of the school lot and headed back toward home.

"Who?" I swiveled my gaze and almost screamed as I saw Robin Goodfellow standing on the corner, thumb out in classic hitchhiker fashion.

I hadn't paid attention to what he was wearing earlier, I'd been so nervous about seeing him again. He wore the same black and white checked flannel coat and well-worn jeans as the first time I'd seen him. Golden stubble coated his sharp chin. Unbidden, a memory shoved itself to the front of my mind.

I got tired of the whole rugged outdoorsy look.

"I like your rugged outdoorsy look," I said and then clapped a hand over my mouth. "That just slipped out."

His eyes flashed and he leaned forward. Planting his fists on either side of my hips, he invaded my personal space with a predator's stealth and skill. "Do you now? And here I thought you were angry with me. Shall we kiss and make up?"

Dragon put on her blinker and the sound pulled me from my reverie. Her intentions were obvious.

"Don't stop," I hissed.

She frowned at me. "Why not? I thought you guys had something going on?"

That was one way to put it. Robin got my blood pumping,

my ire up, and he made me doubt my sanity. "It's complicated."

Dragon curb checked the tire, forcing him to jump back to avoid being clipped by the front bumper.

"Sorry!" she called out.

He reached for the rear door and then climbed inside. "First day behind the wheel?" he asked.

"Third, actually." Dragon checked her mirrors, threw the car into reverse, and then shifted into drive. It was a good thing all of her focus was on the road. Mine was split between the student driver who had barely graduated from parking lots to the actual road and the fae prince who had discarded me like trash on the gym floor.

It had happened. It was real. And because of that, I was thoroughly pissed off.

"And where are you ladies off to on this fine spring day?" Robin's melodic voice rolled over me like a wave lapping at the shore.

"None of your beeswax," I snapped.

Dragon shot me a look and I pointed out the windshield. "Pay attention to the road. You're drifting too close to the shoulder."

She refocused, knuckles turning white as she jerked the wheel. That didn't keep her from commenting, "So, Robin. I haven't seen you around much lately."

"Dragon," My tone held a warning note. I could feel his presence in the backseat. He'd snuck under my guard before. But I was back on my own turf and not going to take any of his faery crap, bargain or no.

"I haven't been around for more than a few minutes at a time," Robin admitted.

"Work stuff?" Dragon glanced in her rearview mirror, more to look at Robin than the road.

"Mostly family stuff. Though my life here has gotten somewhat…complicated."

I snorted. Master of the understatement.

"What do you mean?" Dragon asked.

"Well, first of all, I don't really have a job anymore. And I lost my house, through no fault of my own." His tone was deceptively mild.

I could feel that sapphire gaze on the back of my neck. My shoulders grew tighter and tighter until I was sure my spine would snap. That had been my fault, him losing his magic tree house full of treasures.

"That's terrible." Dragon glanced at him in the rearview mirror.

"Turn right up there," I pointed, my knuckles turning white as I gripped the oh-shit handle.

Dragon swung the car wide and almost sideswiped a Subaru that was waiting at the intersection. The driver leaned on her horn but Dragon remained unfazed. "So, you're homeless then?"

"In a manner of speaking," Robin acknowledged without pinning himself in with the truth. Sly fae bastard.

What was he doing? I wish he had discussed his plan with me before he started weaving his tapestry of misinformation.

"Hey, Joey. Why can't Robin stay in the guest cottage?"

My lips parted in shock. The guest house was little more than a one room canning shed at the rear section of the property. It had been used for storage for most of my life but held a world of potential if we cleaned it out and spiffed it up. It was one of those things we intended to do several times over the years but had never seen to fruition.

Dragon shrugged. "Well, I heard you and Aunt Prudence talking about fixing it up and renting it out. Why not to Robin?"

Because he was fae. Because we had some sort of fake engagement going on and because the more time that I spent around him, the more things spun out of control.

"What do you think?" Dragon's gaze shifted to the rearview mirror.

I could feel his breath on the back of my neck as he spoke the words. "That's the best invitation I've ever had."

"It's not—" I began, hunting for the best way to kill the idea before it took root.

"It'll only be for a little while," Robin said. "Until things are…settled."

My stomach dropped. Settled. What did that even mean? I didn't like the way his tone caressed the word as though it held a world of promise. Robin's "job" had been to bargain with mortals in exchange for favors. Favors that oftentimes ended up with the mortals winding up as slaves in the fae realm. Personal reasons aside, there was no way in hell's half-acre that I could shelter him on our property knowing he was going out every day to do that.

Warm fingers curled around my shoulder. "I have a little set-aside. I can pay your family for taking me in."

I shook my head. "We'll have to talk to my mom about it."

Knowing my mother, Prudence Whitmore would take one look and Robin Goodfellow and toss him out on his sexy fae ass.

"WHAT A WONDERFUL IDEA!" My mother clapped her hands and beamed up at Robin in utter delight.

My mouth hung open and I wondered if I had somehow slid into an alternate reality. That was my mother that stood in front of me. The dove gray slacks and black twinset showed off her still trim figure. But she must have lost her mind.

Was really willing to entertain this…well, the term *harebrained scheme* was the only term that came to mind.

Prudence Whitmore began her classic thinking and pacing shtick, wearing a path on the black and white linoleum while fondling her pearls as she sorted through all the details. "We were just talking about fixing the place up. You'll have to stay in the room across from Joey's, at least until we can get electricity out there."

"What?" I exploded out of my chair.

Three sets of eyes focused on me. As though I were the insane one in this little grouping.

Through clenched teeth I muttered, "Mother, may I speak with you for a moment?"

"Of course." She spun on her heel and gestured to the Santa tin on the counter. "Dragon, why don't you see if there are any of those oatmeal raisin cookies left for our guest?"

I'd made those cookies. It shouldn't bother me that my family was being so hospitable to Robin. But they didn't know who or what he was. Or what he had done. Of course, that was my fault because I hadn't told them.

My mother led me into her studio, which once upon a time had been the conservatory. The stained-glass windows let in enough ambient light that it kept the space illuminated throughout the day, but diffused the bright Southern sun from blanching the color out of the hardwood flooring. My mother's ceramics projects were scattered over every horizontal surface. The subject, male genitalia. A tumult of trouser snakes in every color of the rainbow. I had yet to determine if she had intentionally chosen to model her art after dicks or if it was as Bob Ross claimed, not a mistake but a happy accident.

Either way, it wasn't the ideal setting for a serious conversation.

"Mother, what are you doing?" I hissed the second the door was closed.

She frowned at me. "Well, we can't put him out in the guest house as it is, now can we?"

Normally, no. There was running water attached to our well, but no electricity. Which wouldn't matter to a fae, because magic could easily replace technology. But I couldn't tell her that.

"I thought Dragon said he was a friend of yours?" My mother raised a brow. "Why are you so against the idea of renting to him?"

What to say? How to explain to her that this went well beyond doing a favor for a friend. "Well, for one thing, Robin…isn't like other guys."

"Why not?" Prudence Whitmore's gaze narrowed. "Is he a criminal?"

"No." Morally bankrupt perhaps but sadly, that wasn't illegal.

She moved closer and lowered her voice to a whisper.

"Are you afraid of him for some reason? Did he threaten you?"

Her and her notions. "Nothing like that."

"Abandon his family? Sell drugs or run guns?" Her gaze probed my face as she hunted for the truth.

No, he merely changed my life, made me immortal, then convinced me to fake a secret engagement for a reason he's unwilling to explain.

Somehow, I couldn't seem to make it sound as bad as it actually was.

She threw her hands up. "Then, what's the problem, Joey?"

How much should I tell her? It sounded incredible, even in the confines of my head. Nothing about faeries or magic or trips through time. She would think I had lost my ever-loving mind. Instead, I focused on the one thing that was guaranteed to get a rise out of her. "He wants to marry me."

She blinked. "Really?"

I scowled at her. "You don't have to act so surprised."

Her gaze narrowed. "But you told him that wouldn't happen, right? After all, you tried marriage in your rebellious youth, and look at how that turned out."

I flinched.

Oblivious to the blow she'd just dealt me, my mother pushed on. "So, you set your boundaries. Then everyone will be on the same page. I don't see any reason why he can't rent out the cottage as long as your relationship is clearly defined. Like me and your father for example."

My parents had an undefined relationship. They weren't married because my mother believed marriage was a trap to ensnare strong women and bind them to an unjust societal construct. But they were monogamous and saw each other a few times a week. My dad lived above his law office in a dinky little apartment and he did it all for her and her strong beliefs.

"We could desperately use the income." She added.

My mother was by no means a drama queen. She didn't fling around words like desperately without cause. "What do you mean?"

She sighed and sank down onto the three-legged stool that she used while sculpting. "Look, I didn't want to worry you about this, but we're not doing so well. Financially speaking. Tourism is way down and your grandmother's medical bills are piling up. If things don't turn around for us soon, we're going to have to make some tough calls."

"How tough?" And why was this the first I was hearing about it?

She shook her head. "Well, this house has a lot of upkeep. As does your grandmother's. And we really don't need both of them."

There wasn't enough room at Grammy's to fit all four of the women in our family under her roof comfortably. "But, that land has been in the Whitmore family since before the Revolutionary War." A fact I had learned thanks to Robin and our original bargain.

"I know." My mother let out a defeated sigh. "But times are tough all over. We're lucky we have as much as we do."

"What about dad?" My father ran a real estate law practice in town. Surely he would help the love of his life and his only daughter make ends meet for a bit.

"His business is down too. Besides, I don't want to drag Paul into this." Her eyes, the same shade of blue as mine, flashed with pride and stubbornness. "And I don't want you to bring it up to him either."

I had learned the hard way that interfering with their relationship was asking for trouble. "How long do we have?" I asked instead.

Her shoulders bobbed up and down in a helpless shrug. "If things don't change, maybe through the summer. And only if your grandmother's health remains steady. If she needs tests or treatments, it could be less."

Stunned, I sank onto the long bench seat across from her. "Why didn't you say anything to me before?"

"Because you've been so happy with your new job. I didn't want to upset you. But if that fellow out there is at all handy, well, maybe this is the solution to all of our problems." Her tone grew lighter and she got to her feet. "Now, why don't you take him out back and show him the guest house while Dragon and I prepare the upstairs room?"

I swallowed and then nodded, still too shocked to process all that she had told me.

"It will all work out, Joey. You'll see." She patted me on the shoulder and then left me alone to digest all she'd revealed.

Like it or not, my mother thought we needed Robin. In her mind, it was settled. The fae prince was going to be our houseguest/ renter. Giving him more opportunity to mess with my head, to coax and cajole me into whatever game he was playing.

Well, I just needed to strengthen my resolve. For my family's sake, I would have to draw the line between myself and him. We needed his money and maybe a little bit of his help.

But there was no way I would bargain with him again. Lesson freaking learned. The mental and emotional toll that came with magic was too damned high. I would just have to keep my guard up and draw the line. We were partners in deceit and nothing more.

The sound of two sets of footsteps on the stairs jolted me into motion. Chin set at a stubborn angle, I marched back into the kitchen. I could do this. I could take him on. No problem.

Robin's bright blue gaze was intent on the dented tin as he poked through the oatmeal raisin cookies. "So, it's all settled then?"

Planting my fists on the table I leaned in until my gaze was locked on this. "The only thing that is settled is that my mother has agreed to let you stay here. There will be no more bargains with me or my family. Understood?"

"Why, lamb. I'm hurt by your insinuation." The smirk on his handsome face belied his words. "I would never take advantage of such giving and selfless females."

My eyes narrowed on him.

"You know I'm unable to lie to you," he pointed out. "Besides, I'm not here to make bargains."

"Then why are you here?" I asked.

Instead of answering, he snitched a cookie then rose from the table. "These are exceptional."

I looked into the now empty tin. "They were."

He flashed me a grin and then popped the last bite into his mouth. "I'll make it up to you. Show me this guest house I will be renting. I can't wait to see it."

I blew out a breath. "Only if you promise not to make any pithy comments about how mortals live."

"I vow it." He gripped my hand in one of his and then, using my index finger, drew an X over his heart. "What is it you mortals say? Cross my heart and hope to die?"

I searched his face, wondering what his game was and if I could trust him at all. My gut told me that was a big, fat hell no.

So instead, I stepped back, needing away from his heady scent and mesmerizing sapphire gaze. This was bad. I couldn't help but be reminded of our one kiss, the shared moment in time that had kept me up at night, wondering what it would be like to do it again. To touch my mouth to Robin's when we weren't in the middle of a crisis. To let that slow drugging melding of our lips lead to more touching, deeper caresses.

Damn middle-aged hormones gone berserk.

The sun sank low to the west creating long shadows across the yard. I breathed in the scents of spring as we picked our way around the side of the house and through the back gate.

"Impressive," Robin said as he studied the winterized garden beds on either side of the flagstone path. "Who's the gardener?"

"Me, mostly." I stopped and waited as he studied the rich, dark soil that held the promise of life yet to be birthed.

"You enjoy growing things then?" he murmured. "Getting a little down and dirty?"

"Stop," I croaked.

He moved closer and his hand raised to my cheek. "I adore the flush of your skin when you're embarrassed. Or aroused."

Why did my stomach flip at his words? Was it a faery

thing that got me all hot and bothered every time he opened his mouth? Or maybe it was his scent, a potent combination of cedarwood and male spice. Having him so close to me was a piss poor idea. Robin's innuendos and my libido were on a collision course to a full-tilt disaster.

I gripped his hand in mine and pulled it away from my face. "Just tell me what it is you want from me."

"I already told you. I want you to be my wife. Why won't you believe me? You know my words are true."

"You want me *to pretend* to be your wife." Important distinction there.

He tipped his head to the side. "Is trust really so hard for you?"

"You keep secrets and twist the truth until it suits your end game. I've been on the receiving end of that, Robin. It's not a great position."

"Speaking of positions, I'm curious which is your favorite?"

My jaw dropped. "I can't believe you just asked me that."

He shrugged. "It's something a husband ought to know."

"It's none of your business."

That grin turned wicked. "Maybe I ought to guess? Shall we play charades?"

I narrowed my eyes on him. "Stop toying with me."

"Oh, lamb. I haven't even begun toying with you." Something hungry moved in those sapphire eyes. It made me press my thighs together in response.

I took a deep breath, trying to steady myself. "What are you doing here? Is this is some sort of revenge because I tricked you?"

He studied me, gaze roving over my features. "Maybe I simply missed you. Did you ever think of that?"

Damn my stupid traitorous heart. It squeezed at his words. But I hadn't missed the maybe part of his statement. Maybe changed the meaning. If he had simply said *I simply missed you,* I would have bought it. But he hadn't and I knew better.

I lifted my chin. "Maybe I didn't miss you. Maybe I had hoped I'd never see you again. Did you consider that?"

Direct hit. Pain flashed in those blue eyes, there and gone so fast that if I hadn't been looking for it, I would have missed it. He dropped his hand and stepped away. "I thought you were going to show me this guest house of yours."

I turned, offering him my back. "This way."

Golden hour burnished the molten strands of Robin's blond hair as we approached the structure. Forcing my gaze away, I studied the cottage. The roof was in decent shape, as was the small front porch. The white paint was chipped and peeling, but that was an easy fix. The door creaked as I pushed it inward, but in more a charming way than a haunted house.

I extracted my phone from a back pocket and shone the light into the dim interior. Stacks of Rubbermaid bins were pushed up against the back wall. An old sleeper sofa sat under an ugly green and yellow floral sheet. I reached for it and dust motes took flight, sparkling in the late day sun.

I coughed a little and turned away. Not too bad. Mom was right. With some elbow grease, the place would fetch a pretty penny.

Robin walked around the tight space, examining every-thing. I tried not to stare at his ass in those faded jeans that cupped him almost lovingly. If he caught me, I knew we would go another round of him digging for my secrets and me blocking him as best I could. I fervently wished I wasn't attracted to him.

Then again, I didn't know a single woman who would say no to all that.

He dipped into the bathroom, which was really just a shower stall, sink, and toilet. The steady *drip-drip* of the faucet in the bathroom, that we kept running to prevent the pipes from freezing enunciated the uncomfortable silence.

"Well?" I shifted from foot to foot. "What do you think?"

He looked at me. Didn't say anything. Did he hate it? Feel that it was beneath him? Sure, it was no faery palace or hewn tree house. But it was warm and dry and in relatively good shape.

My shoulders squared off and I tried to fight the urge to defend the place. "Now that winter is mostly over, we'll get my mom's car out of the garage and stow this stuff in there."

"No electricity?" Robin asked as he studied the walls.

"No. That's why we haven't tried to rent it out yet. Besides, you'll just do your magic thing, right?"

He shook his head.

Something wasn't right. "Why not?"

He met and held my gaze, his words landing with the impact of a lead balloon. "Because I am no longer able to wield magic."

CHAPTER THREE

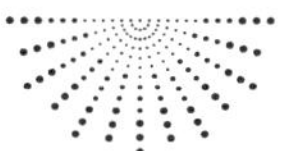

"You can't fix stupid. But you shouldn't have to clean up after him either."
-Notable quotable from Grammy B

"What do you mean he can't do magic?" Darcy yelped. "He's a frigging faery prince. What good is he if he can't do frigging magic?"

I made shushing motions, unsure if my mother and Dragon had opened the upstairs windows. They'd been cleaning out the spare bedroom for Robin to use and the room was directly above the side porch where the two of us sat in the white wicker furniture enjoying a bottle of sweet red wine which paired well with emotional upheaval and mayhem. "Keep your voice down. You're the only one who knows who and what he really is."

Her blue eyes narrowed. "Are you sure he's not just feeding you a bullshit line so he winds up in a better position to get to the goodies?"

I shook my head, even as my heart raced at the prospect. Right across the hall. Robin Goodfellow was staying directly across the hall from my bedroom. Would be sleeping there until we got Dan Fogle out to rig electricity up to the guest house. "He can't lie. He said flat out that he can't do magic."

Both her blonde brows went up. "And you're sure *that's* not a lie? Because men have been known to tell a few tall tales in pursuit of the promised land."

I twirled the stem of my wineglass between my thumb and index finger. "I'm not sure what exactly his game is. What happened to him or his magic or why he's insisting on a fake engagement. But no, I don't think he's lying about losing his magic. What would he have to gain?"

Darcy mulled it over. "Your trust back for one."

"That's so not happening. I will never trust him." Some deep-seated instinct warned me not to.

"But you're letting him move in." My bestie shook her head.

"It's not really my decision to make." While the Victorian had been my home for most of my life, it was my mother's house. "If it were up to me, he'd be on the next bus back to the fae realm."

Darcy absorbed the words and then plunked her glass down and got to her feet. "Introduce me."

"What?" I stared up at her, my fierce friend who looked like a china doll and took neither shit nor prisoners. "Why?"

Her hands went to her petite hips. "Because he's important to you. He is going to be living with you and your mom and Dragon. And because I don't trust your judgment where this rank bastard is concerned. You've always been a moron about pretty men."

"I have not," I puffed up in indignation.

She started counting on her left hand. "Bill Tate. Pete Green. Robin freaking Goodfellow and his freaking bargains that you keep making even though you know better. Should I go on?"

"I think you got all of them." No one could shine a truthful light on your foibles like a lifelong friend. A sigh escaped and I slumped in defeat. She was right, I made garbage choices when handsome men were involved.

"So, let me size him up and see if I can take him."

For an instant, I got a mental picture of Darcy, wearing a baby blue tank top and shorts and sporting rhinestone-encrusted boxing gloves circling around Robin, who was equally ridiculously garbed like they were reenacting the final scene from *Cinderella Man.* Then Darcy snapped her fingers in front of my face and I blinked.

"Come on, Joey. I'm out of wine. It's illegal to be out of wine on Wine Wednesday."

"Is not."

"Is too." She considered it and then added, "At least it should be."

"Fine." I knew when I was beaten. Though I kept hoping that Robin would grow tired of whatever game he was playing and poof back home so my life could go back to normal, he looked to be settling in for the long haul. And while I didn't want to admit it to myself, I was kind of curious about what my bestie would think of him.

Mom and Dragon were just exiting through the kitchen

door as we approached. "We're going over to pick up Grammy." Mom's tone was light and easy.

"You mean you are going to drive her here?" Typically, we just brought dinner to her either before or after we ate.

My mother shook out her coat. "Yes. It's been forever since the whole family gathered for a meal."

I read between the lines. Much like Darcy, Grammy B had insisted on having a peek at Robin. Grammy B was a force to be reckoned with and when she had her heart set on something, there was no weaseling out of it.

"Wait, it's Dragon's turn to cook!" I called to my mother's retreating back.

"No worries, lamb. I offered to make a meal for everyone." Robin's lilting voice carried out from the kitchen.

"That's him?" Darcy felt around her crotch. "Sweet baby Jesus and a bag of chips. For a second I was worried I'd wet my pants."

I squared my shoulders and marched forward to where he stood over the stove. A skillet was poised on the front burner and he was adding avocado oil to the pan. "You know how to cook?"

"I've picked up a few things here and there."

I rolled my eyes. "What would it take to get a simple yes or no answer out of you?"

"Yes, lamb. I am an accomplished chef. I find people are much easier to deal with when they are well fed."

"Fattening them up for the slaughter," I grumbled.

"You know me so well." He tossed me a saucy wink and then glanced over his shoulder and fixed his attention on Darcy. "And will you be joining us for dinner as well…?" The words trailed off, waiting for either Darcy or me to make the introduction.

I waited for a beat for my opinioned bestie to step forward and have at him. But she stood oddly mute beside me. The silence stretched out like the elastic in my yoga pants after Taco Tuesday.

Though there had been no formal introduction, Robin had once admitted that he had spied on me and Darcy while we were hip-deep in Margarita Monday's mindlessness. He had even gone as far as imitating her voice in eerie precision. But he waited as though he had never seen her before or heard some of her more colorful statements. And Darcy had apparently gone mute so I filled the silence as a proper Southern woman had been bred to do.

"Robin, this is my best friend, Darcy Abrams. Darcy, meet Robin Goodfellow."

"The pleasure, I assure you, is all mine." Robin turned from his meal prep and swept a courtly bow. Darcy tittered like an idiot school girl. I didn't want to hear another word out of her about how I was a moron around handsome men after her display.

"So, dinner?" Robin quirked a brow.

"No, thank you," Darcy stammered. The woman who had once told the mayor to "freaking grow a pair already," at a town meeting actually stammered.

Robin winked at her and then popped open the door to the oven. A delicious aroma of cinnamon and cooking apples wafted out. For an instant, I imagined we were in a cartoon and the scent alone made the two of us levitate off the ground.

"It smells wonderful though," Darcy spoke in this weird breathy voice. "What is that, apple pie?"

"What's wrong with you?" I hissed in her ear. "You sound like you're working for a 900 number."

She didn't respond though she stepped to the side as though putting some distance between the two of us.

"Dutch apple pie." Robin shut the oven door and then turned to face us. "My favorite. It will go well with the pasta primavera I'm making. Tell me, Darcy. What is your favorite spring vegetable?"

Her gaze appeared frantic for a moment before landing by the freshly washed green stalks in my canary yellow colander. "Asparagus."

I narrowed my eyes on her. "What are you talking about? You *hate* asparagus. You say it makes your pee smell funny."

She bared her teeth at me before refocusing on Robin. "I…I'm sure whatever you make will be delicious."

"What's happening here?" I asked the room at large. Robin said he was cooking but I suspected the only thing he was conjuring was pheromones. And Darcy looked like she had died and gone to boy band heaven.

"You worry too much, Joey. You need to learn to relax more. Here, have another glass of wine. You, too, Ms. Abrams. It ought to be illegal to run out of wine on Wine Wednesdays." Another wink at Darcy.

My tough as nails bestie, who had been all set to make mincemeat out of the faery prince, blushed to her blonde roots. "Exactly what I said."

"Smart as well as beautiful. Aren't you two a pair? Go on, sit outside, and let me finish dinner."

Getting Darcy away from Robin sounded like a prime

idea. Clutching my wine glass in my left hand I looped my right arm through hers and then dragged her back out onto the porch. I nudged her down to sit on the step, took the wineglass from her hand, and then set them both down out of her reach.

Darcy blinked as though coming out of a deep trance. "What was that?"

"I'm pretty sure he was enthralling you." Another few minutes and Robin's essence would have ensnared her into mindless servitude.

"Huh?"

"He didn't do it on purpose. It was part of his fae defense mechanism. Put your head between your knees," I instructed.

Darcy obeyed. "He's…potent. I feel all tingly and tight all over. And in desperate need of an orgasm. Is that what it's like for you?"

Wordlessly, I nodded.

She blew out a breath. "Then I guess you're right. He doesn't need to lie to get into a woman's pants. He just needs to exist."

She rose and then shook her head. "I'm sorry, Joey. I wanted to, I don't know, defend your honor, threaten to make him sleep with the fishes or some such but I don't think I can go back in there without climbing him like a jungle gym."

"It's okay," I soothed. "He's my mess and I need to clean him up."

She eyed me. "That sounds filthy as all get-out. Especially since he's in there elbow-deep in pie."

I shook my head. "Go home, Darcy. Your husband is

probably tied to a chair while the kids are trying to set fire to the living room rug by now."

She threw her hands up. "The fire department gets called once and you'll never let me hear the end of it."

"It was twice." I hollered and watched her walk down the street, making sure she didn't weave in front of oncoming traffic.

A car drove by, a sedan with tinted windows. It wasn't one I recognized. The driver gunned the engine and blew through the stop sign. At least Dragon wasn't the worst driver on the street.

I collected the wine glasses and headed back inside, ready to give Robin a piece of my….

Pie. I stopped dead in my tracks.

Robin was bent over the oven, extracting the Dutch apple pie from the heated depths. That man had an ass that defied reality. And he freaking baked.

Give me strength. Climbing him like a jungle gym sounded like a stellar idea. How long had it been since I had sex anyway? It was probably a bad sign that I couldn't remember. Before my marriage ended because I hadn't been with anyone else since.

Which may have been a tactical error.

Robin straightened and then set what looked to be the world's most magnificent dessert on the waiting trivet before turning to face me.

"Before you ask, no, I wasn't attempting to enthrall your friend with my fae essence. Much like you, she is a surprising lightweight. I have developed a theory about that."

"Oh?" The word came out as a sort of croak.

Robin stalked toward me slowly and took the wine

glasses from my hands. "Yes. You see, the more sexually frustrated a mortal woman is, the more susceptible she is to faery enthrallment."

I frowned. "That makes no sense. Darcy's not sexually frustrated. She's the most sexually liberated woman I know."

One golden brow quirked up. "She has how many children now? Four?"

"Five. All boys under the age of ten."

He made a low, tsking sort of sound. "And you think that isn't a recipe for sexual frustration? I bet she's been too exhausted to have more than a quicky for months. And a woman in her prime deserves long, lazy days filled with sensual massages, hot baths, and a lover attuned to her every wanton desire."

Was I drooling? All control over my body had vanished. I licked suddenly dry lips. "But I'm immune to you, right?"

"You're immune to my essence." His gaze scorched the skin along the column of my throat like he had stroked over it with a sizzling brand that promised all sorts of wickedness "Not to your own cravings. And believe me, lamb, I've *never* had any complaints when it comes to pleasing a lover."

A horrible thought occurred. "You haven't enthralled my mother, have you? Or Dragon?" I couldn't even bring myself to mention Grammy B.

He shook his head. "No. I've granted immunity to all the members of your family."

That was…unexpected. "But you said it was a defense mechanism. That it kept mortals from trapping you. Why would you give that up?"

Instead of answering, he returned to the cutting board

where he had been slicing carrots for the pasta primavera. "Any dietary restrictions I ought to be aware of?"

His consideration was oddly touching. "Dragon is a vegetarian and Grammy needs to limit her sugars."

He nodded.

"Robin?" I circled the countertop so we were facing each other once more. "Why would you give up your ability to enthrall us?"

He looked up and our gazes locked. There was heat there but also shadows. His secrets had always seemed so playful before. But there was an edginess to him now, a wariness. In a flash of insight, I knew that whatever was there, it had come about because of the way I had tricked him. Trapped him.

And as sexy as Robin was before whatever had happened to him, now I felt…drawn to him on a more primal level. I wanted to coax that darkness forth, to soothe it and wrap it around myself to help dispel the coldness that lurked there.

So not a good idea, the sensible shrew piped up.

Robin refocused on his veg prep. "Would you mind setting the table? The others will be back soon."

He wasn't going to answer, that much was clear. Sighing, I went to where he put the wine glasses and knocked them both back.

Clearly, it wasn't a night to bother with counting calories. And as Grammy always said, waste not, want not.

My gaze slid to the fae prince who was adding diced veggies to the sizzling skillet. Who would be sleeping right across the hall from me.

I wanted. Desperately. Hungrily. And letting him sleep alone felt like a total waste.

❄

HALFWAY THROUGH DINNER, sense returned. Maybe the delicious meal helped soak up the alcohol. Or it could have been that I had Grammy seated to my left, my mother to my right, and Dragon directly across the table. Maybe it was the way Robin flattered the women in my family, telling amusing stories about his siblings and their various love interests. Aka, the mortals they had enslaved and swapped like trading cards around the fae court.

"Sounds to me like you have one of them incestuous families that are always squabbling on TV." Grammy B helped herself to a second slice of pie, ignoring my mother's pointed glower. "All them young folks hopping in and out of bed with one another. A mighty fine way to spread the crotch crickets if you ask me."

I choked on my own saliva.

"Agreed." Robin's gaze twinkled with mischief, probably because his youngest family member was centuries older than Grammy. "It's a game to them. Take what another has, just to see if you can. Then discard it when it has served its purpose. It's one of the many reasons I can't stand being around them for long. Are you enjoying the pie, Joey?"

His sapphire gaze swung to me, pinning me like a bug under a thumbtack. It took all of my concentration to keep from squirming. "It's delicious."

"I'll bet it is a flavor unlike any other," he murmured.

My gaze dropped to the plate that I had all but licked clean so I wouldn't make eye contact with my family. I felt dirty somehow. In a very thrilling way. There were so many layers to his words, the innuendo dripped like syrup from every syllable.

God, what I could do to him and a bottle of syrup.

Bad hormones! Bad, naughty, evil hormones!

"Hannah called today," Grammy's words broke me out of my lusty stupor.

"Who is Hannah?" Robin's gaze slid to my face.

"Dragon's mother." My gaze slid to my cousin who had grown quiet. As far as I knew, Aunt Hannah hadn't been in touch with her daughter since she came here. I had a few choice names for the woman and most of them ended with er.

"Oh?" My mother, ever the diplomat asked. "What's new with her?"

"She'll be coming for a visit this weekend." Grammy reached for the pie, clearly intending to serve herself a third piece. "Said she was going to stay with me."

Silence. Beneath the table, I tapped Dragon's foot. When she looked up, I gave her a reassuring smile. The kid needed to know that she was wanted, even if her mother blew her off.

Robin reached for Dragon's plate to collect the dishes but my mother jumped up and made a grab. "No no. We'll get that."

"It's no trouble," Robin held on to the plate and for a wild moment, I thought Prudence would tear it free and whack him over the head with the dish to drive her point home.

"In this house, when you cook, you don't need to clean up," Dragon recited.

"If you insist." Though he didn't look happy about it, Robin released his hold on the plate.

"So, Robin, what is it you do for a living?" Grammy could always be counted on to cut to the chase.

"I used to make investments." Robin watched as Dragon and my mother began stacking dishes before swinging that penetrating blue gaze back to Grammy. "But a lapse in judgment took me out of the running for a leadership position. After that, I lost my taste for the trade."

My heart pounded. The vague words meant nothing to anyone who didn't know that Robin used to enslave those he bargained with. I, however, did possess that knowledge. Could he really turn over a new leaf, just like that? "So, you don't do what you used to do at all anymore?"

Holding my gaze he gave me the most straight-forward answer sans flourishes and embellishments that he ever had. "No, lamb. I've left that life behind."

"Why do you call her lamb?" Dragon asked as she returned from the kitchen to collect the linens.

That wicked grin stole across his face. "Inside joke."

The inside joke was that Robin had caught me in the bath and thought it was funny that I was swathed in white froth like a little lamb. Of course, that hadn't really happened. Or had it? Alternate timelines made my head hurt.

Grammy B nudged me in the ribs and whisper-hissed loud enough that the neighbors could have heard over tap dancing gorillas. "Psst, I think you've got a live one there, Joey."

Again with the fevered blushing. Robin didn't need to enthrall me with his fae essence. He just needed to open his mouth and say whatever was on his mind. And if he didn't, my relatives would give him a boost.

"Come on, Mom. I best be getting you home." My mother

had abstained from drinking so she could drive Grammy back to her place. I had seen her eye-humping my wineglass and knew I'd better refrigerate another bottle for her return. "Joey, I put a load of towels in the dryer. Make sure you fold some for your guest."

It was on the tip of my tongue to tell her that no way no how was he my guest. For one thing, he was more like a party crasher than someone I'd invited over. But I held my tongue. It was my fault he was in our house in the first place and until I figured out how to shed a two-hundred-pound fae parasite, there was no way to tell my family what was up.

I wish he would just disappear. The thought bounced around inside my skull. As I sashayed into the laundry room and stooped to retrieve the clean linens from the dryer, I stubbed my toe on the corner of the washstand. "Ouch, son of a six-fingered goatherd."

I hopped up and down, irritated at the pain, my own clumsiness, Robin, and his unnerving effect on my willpower. Once the throbbing subsided, I huffed out a breath and retrieved a basket for the towels, and began folding. The small domestic chore soothed my ruffled feathers. I had a weird fixation about warm towels. They lined up so neatly, corner to corner, and I'd watched a YouTube video and learned how to roll them into neat fluffy sausages that would stand up in a basket as well as stack on a shelf. Neat and precise, one of the very rare things in my life that fit that description.

Seriously, how had people learned to adult before the internet?

Folding accomplished, I returned to the dining room

with my basket of terrycloth sausages and looked around. "Robin? Where did you go?"

No answer. Setting the basket down on the hall table I backtracked into the kitchen where Dragon was loading the dishwasher. "Do you know where Robin went?"

She shook her head. "Did you check upstairs? Maybe he went to his room."

"Does he even know where it is?" Of course, this *was* a fae prince we were talking about. The Victorian may be large but it was hard to believe he would get lost in it.

Dragon smirked, indicating how ridiculous my statement was. "He's not a toddler missing at the mall, Joey."

"Right." Still, his sudden exodus was a tad unnerving. "Can't wait to see what penis paraphernalia your Aunt Prudence left for him to discover in there."

Dragon grinned and returned to the dishes and I headed for the second floor, to the room two doors down from my own. No stiffies, thankfully, but also no Robin. Weird. He had been hanging around all afternoon and now he just poofed out with no warning. I should enjoy the reprieve for however long it lasted but I couldn't shake the feeling that he was plotting something terrible.

To distract my paranoid brain, I took in the room, which was barely big enough for the full-sized bed and nightstand. Until a few hours ago, the space had held all that remained of my brief stint as a married woman. The china I had picked out and my dad had bought us off the registry. A silver picture frame with our wedding photo. A blender and a few pots and pans. Curtains that Darcy had made out of some pretty blue sparkly fabric. The folding card table we had used in place of a dining table until we could afford one.

Sheets and a patterned quilt that didn't fit any mattress in the Victorian. We had indulged in a king-size bed and after we split up, I had let Georgia keep it. Standing lamps with funky shades and the smushy reading chair I had bought to replace the window seat in my childhood bedroom. Everyone deserved a special reading spot.

Guilt needled me that I'd left my mother and Dragon to deal with all this stuff. After all, it was my past. I ought to have been the one to clear the space and put it to rest. But I'd been too busy brooding and resenting the reason for the hustle. I wondered where they'd stashed it all. Probably the garage. Between my stuff and whatever we lugged out of the canning shed, we'd be lucky to get the door closed.

We ought to have a yard sale. Whatever didn't work in the cottage or the house should go. Maybe I'd roll up my sleeves and tackle Grammy's house too. That might help a little with the money issues. As would Robin's rent.

Speaking of which, where the hell had he gone? The window overlooking the side yard was open and I could just see the outline of the cottage as the sun silhouetted the small structure. I would breathe easier if the sexy fae who wanted me to pretend to be his wife was staying outside of the four walls of my home. I would have to call the electrician from work tomorrow and get him on the job, asap. Damn it, I wished the place had electricity already.

Lights flicked on inside the cottage.

I jerked so fast that my head cracked against the window frame. Stars blurred my vision but didn't diminish the cheery glow that blazed from the small structure. I blinked, rubbed my eyes but the light stayed put.

"No magic my ass," I snarled and then stormed out to go

confront the fae. If he could lie, there was no way I would let him stay so close, bargain, or no bargain.

"Joey?" Dragon had just set the big metal pasta pot in the drainboard as I passed through the kitchen. "What's wrong?"

"Nothing," I snapped.

She flinched and I forced myself to moderate my tone. Dragon hadn't done anything to deserve my wrath. Other than suggest Robin stay with us. Which he had manipulated her into doing. "Nothing for you to worry about. I've got to go outside for a few. Just leave the rest of the dishes and I'll get them later."

"Are you sure?" Her blue-gray eyes searched my face.

"Yeah. Sorry I snapped. It's been a beast of a day." I bobbed my head and winced at the throbbing in my skull.

"Okay, I have a bunch of homework anyway." She dried her hands and I watched her go, trying to leash my temper before I pushed out into the early evening air.

The cottage stood like a bright haven from the gloaming. Something about it reminded me of a storybook house. Darcy's curtains would look magnificent over those windows. And the reading chair could replace the couch. I wished I could get little solar lamps festooned along the winding footpath through the garden. It would be magical.

My foot snagged on something and I went down, landing palms first in the gravel. "Ouch. Son of a—"

"Lamb?" A voice said from behind me. "Are you hurt?"

"Only my pride." I rolled over and glared up at the fae. "Robin? Did you just trip me?"

"Don't be daft." He held out a hand and after a moment's hesitation, I took it, allowing him to pull me to my feet.

"Then what did I…?" My voice faded out as I stared at the

dislodged solar lamp that had somehow appeared between one thought and the next. A few steps ahead, another one glowed. Then another. They trailed around the walkway just as I'd imagined. "That's funny, I was just thinking that getting some of those lamps would be neat."

"Were you then?" Robin's gaze narrowed. "Were you thinking or were you wishing?"

"What's the difference?" I frowned up at him.

He took my hand in his and then examined my scraped palms. "Thought might be something idle, a notion there and gone. But a wish…a wish takes vision, imagination. If you can see, it can be."

My lips parted. He'd said that to me once before, back when I'd been trying to become my own faery godmother and learning how magic worked. "So what, you're reading my thoughts somehow?"

He shook his head. "I don't have that power."

Darcy would be relieved to hear that, as was I since I'd been lusting after him all evening. I thrust my index finger toward the lit cottage. "Then how do you explain that?"

He took a deep breath and forced out the words as though they hurt him to say. "Lamb, I don't have my magic anymore, because you have it."

I blinked. "It?"

"My magic. All of it." He waved at the glowing cottage, the solar lamps. "Out of the two of us, Joey Whitmore, you're the only one who could have made this happen."

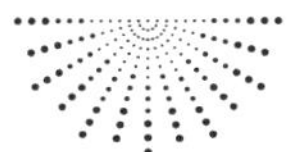

CHAPTER FOUR

"The hurts on the outside never smart as much as the ones we can't see."
-Notable quotable from Grammy B

I sat at the kitchen table, head aching from where it'd hit the ground, hands throbbing from where they'd scudded across rocks to break my fall. Damn, I was going to be no help to Alina tomorrow if I had a concussion and hands that couldn't guide miniature gymnasts. Tomorrow was supposed to be my first day working on my yoga instruction certification too. I had signed the gym up so we could host classes for that to help pad the gym's income. Alina hated the idea but said if I wanted to waste my time teaching fat old women to do yoga, I could. All in all, not a great time to be injured.

Robin stood by the stove, his back to me. He hadn't spoken a word since we came inside. Neither had I. It was as if by tacit agreement, we'd decided I needed to process his unbelievable revelation. And it was absurd.

He said that he couldn't do magic. And that I could.

Implausible. Totally and completely out of the realm of possibility. I was a middle-aged gymnastics instructor. The one time I had attempted to use magic I'd almost gotten myself killed.

"What about earlier? At the gym?" I asked him. "The girl who almost crashed onto the floor?"

"Alas, that was also you," he admitted.

"But you said…?" My brow furrowed as I recalled his exact phrasing. Robin had said there was no need to thank him. And there wasn't because he hadn't freaking *done* it. A growl escaped. Lying without actually lying was his forte.

"Where is everyone?" Robin's sapphire gaze slid to the kitchen door.

I sighed. "Dragon went upstairs to do homework and my mother took the wine bottle into her office where she will drink and create more of the same." I gestured toward the penis sculpture nestled obscenely between two upside-down blue bowls. Dragon had put the bowls there the other morning and I had snorted coffee out my nose when I'd seen.

His lips twitched in amusement.

The kettle started to hum, steam billowing upward. Robin reached for the knob and turned the heat off, then lifted the kettle and poured the boiling water into two earthenware mugs. He plunked Chamomile teabags into each mug and then carried them over to the table and set mine down in front of me.

In my mind, I couldn't help but compare the scene to the first time Robin had made tea for me. No heat, no stove to boil water. He'd magicked the tea into existence.

I stared at the mug and thought, *go away.*

The mug stayed where it was.

"I wouldn't recommend that." Robin lowered himself into the chair across from me and took a sip from his own mug.

"What?" I asked.

"Trying to use magic again so soon. It always comes with a price, you know."

"What do you mean?" Though I didn't really like chamomile, it was nice to have something to wrap my chilled palms around and let the heat seep into my cold depths.

Of course, I hadn't anticipated the sting of the scrapes. I jerked back and made a sound like bacon cooking on a griddle.

He set his mug down and then reached for my hands. He didn't touch the tender spots, but I could feel his heat as it ghosted over my tattered flesh. "This for example."

I frowned at the damage. "My skinned palms? I'm not following."

"Magic always comes with a price," Robin's tone was low, almost careful, as he repeated the phrase. "The stronger the magic, the higher the price."

"You never told me that before," I hissed. "You let me use magic to try and prevent a car accident!"

He shook his head, his tussled golden hair falling every which way in a most charming manner "That was different. It was magic used in pursuit of fulfilling a bargain. The bargain itself is the price."

My lips parted. I couldn't think of a damn thing to say though.

"But you no longer have that protection." His tone was serious. "I am no longer gifted with magic."

"But I am?" I stared at him. "How is that even possible?"

He shook his head. "I'm not sure. All I know is, that bargain we made, for you to become my anchor, created a bridge between the two of us. A connection. For centuries no one knew what it was or why I was unable to cross to the mortal plane or make a bargain with a mortal."

"Because I hadn't been born yet."

He nodded. "And that meant our bargain was one-sided, at least until you grew into the woman I had met and traded with. And when that happened…no more magic."

I shook my head. "But that can't be true."

He made an exasperated noise. "Lamb, pretending something is untrue because you don't want it to be true is very different from it actually being untrue."

"But why not tell me this earlier?" I tugged my hands free and set them in my lap.

He stared into the depths of his mug. "Honestly? Because I don't trust you any more than you trust me. Not after what happened. I misjudged you, badly and it cost me much. But we need each other. And more than that, we need to keep the truth from my mother."

"Why would she care?"

"Faeries have magic. Mortals have far greater numbers. If it were discovered that mortals could wield magic outside the confines of a bargain it could mean the end of our people. There would be panic in the fae realm and could spark a war. My mother will do anything to prevent that."

He shuddered and then took a breath. "By claiming you to be my mortal bride, we bought ourselves some time."

"Time?" I shook my head, not comprehending. "What do we need time for?"

"To set things right. You, Joey, are a human female who possesses magic. The queen will not let that stand."

My lungs seemed to freeze. "You're not saying, she'll kill me?"

"You, me, and anyone else who knows that this sort of power shift is possible."

"But you're her son."

The darkness returned to his gaze. "She would do anything to protect the fae realm and her standing within it."

I shook my head. First a fake engagement and now I had to worry about a phony mother-in-law? "Then why tell her we're getting married? Why tell her about me at all?"

"She would have discovered you eventually. Her spies are everywhere. And I need a reason to stay close to you so we can figure it out. You need to be very careful what you wish for because you truly will get it. And you will pay for it in whichever way fate decrees."

"But we're not getting married," I pointed out.

"Not in the traditional mortal sense," he confirmed.

I threw my hands up in exasperation. "What other sense is there, Robin?"

"Marriage is a union. A partnership. And that's what we have. If others have taken it to mean something else, how is that my fault?"

Tricksy damn fae. "But you can't lie. Or is that a lie?" My eyes narrowed to slits as I studied him.

"I'm still fae even if I am inconvenienced with no magic at the moment. The fae can't lie, that hasn't changed."

"But I can lie." I was fairly certain anyway but needed to hear him say it.

He nodded in confirmation. "Just one of the many reasons why the queen would view you as a danger. And why we need to figure out a way to unpick this tangle of thorns we've been ensnared by."

I let out a breath. "Why is nothing ever easy with you?"

He smirked. "Funny, lamb. I was thinking almost the exact same thing about you."

My jaw cracked on a yawn. "This is just…too much for one day." Every day with the fae prince felt like a lifetime.

"Perhaps you should go to bed." His gaze turned hot. "Want me to tuck you in?"

"No," I snapped.

"Liar," he purred.

I let out a breath and went to scrub a hand over my face, only realizing when my palms started to sting that it had been a bad idea. "Okay, I am old enough and wise enough to know better than to play pretend. Am I attracted to you? Yes, I am."

His expression turned smug.

I leaned forward and pushed the next words out before he could interrupt. "You know it and I know it. Do I plan on doing anything about that attraction? Absolutely not."

"Why?" he asked. Maybe it was just my fatigued mind but he sounded almost hurt by my steadfast refusal.

"Because, Robin. I don't trust you."

His blinked. "But you know fae can't lie."

"That doesn't mean you're honest," I pointed out. "Or that you can give me what I want."

"And what exactly is that?" He folded his arms over his chest, the picture of belligerence. "Do you even know?"

My chair creaked as I scraped it back from the table. "Goodnight, Robin."

"Joey?"

I paused at the door and hazarded a glance over my shoulder at him. "Yeah?"

That sapphire gaze roved over me and if I had to name his expression, I would call it yearning. The shadows were back. Dark nooks that he kept hidden behind witty banter and seduction. I wanted to know that man, that secret fae prince who hid behind all the masks and quips. I wanted to have him open his heart to me.

For a long moment, I thought he was about to reveal one of those heartfelt truths that would alter the course of both our lives.

But that wasn't Robin's style. "Sweet dreams."

"You too," I escaped up the stairs, shut and locked my door, though I wasn't sure if it was an attempt to keep Robin out or myself in.

We needed to un-switch the magical mishap fast because wishing for more with Robin Goodfellow felt almost inevitable.

And I sure as hell didn't want to pay that price.

Light reflected off of every surface in fractured rainbow prisms. I turned in a slow circle, taking in the high ceiling that came to a sharp angle. Hard, transparent walls on three sides and an hourglass cutout on the fourth. A fluffy bed sat in the middle of the floor, dominating the space.

Looking at the bed made my female parts tingle.

I studied the far wall. Transparent but not. It looked almost like a lake that had frozen over with layers of frost obscuring the direct view to whatever lay beyond. The light didn't come from fixtures, but rather little balls of floating amber that drifted as though on a current. The entire room looked as if it had been carved from ice. The ambient temperature around me was at least seventy degrees though.

My heart thundered in my chest as I asked "What is this place? And why does everything look frozen?"

No one answered.

I moved to the large hourglass-shaped cutout that served as a window. Or maybe a door. The sill was low and I stepped through to the oblong deck that stretched out into a foreign world. Night blanketed the icy structure and above me, hundreds of thousands of stars glittered in the obsidian sky. My palms began to sweat and my stomach fluttered. I really was in another realm.

To my left, I saw the sparkle of what looked to be a frozen waterfall. To my right, more balconies like the one I stood on. Beneath me lay a heavy layer of clouds that obscured whatever might dwell beneath. Clouds. I stood on a structure that reached above the clouds.

How high up were we? The air wasn't sharp or thin. It was spiced with the scent of pine and fresh snow, but nothing like I expected to find at an elevation so high. More magic.

I shivered and turned back to the crystal room. The wall

opposite the bed was a solid block of ice. I could see a few dim shapes moving on the other side but couldn't hear a thing.

"Hello?"

"Here."

I turned to find Robin, dressed in a tuxedo and holding a single red rose.

The sight of him made me want to sigh.

"Where are we?"

"We're in the palace." Robin had moved to a large ice blue wardrobe. "Which one?"

From the wardrobe, he extracted two blue gowns. One was fluffed up by what looked like miles of petticoats that didn't do a thing to flatter those of us with a little junk in the trunk, as Grammy B would say.

The other…

"I think I'm in love," I breathed and stared at the sparkling blue gown. A backless number with a sweetheart bodice that seemed to sparkle as the light caught it. The skirt would be a tight but flattering fit around the hips and there was a long slit up one side that would reveal leg to mid-thigh and allow for easy movement.

"Excellent choice." Robin draped the dress over the back of a stiff-backed crystal chair and then returned the other to the wardrobe. "Try it on."

I blinked up at him and from one moment to the next, my body had gone from wearing flannel pajamas to the gorgeous gown that fit like a dream.

"This isn't real," I sighed.

He strode forward and brushed a strand of hair away from my ear. "Now I know you must be nervous."

"Not nervous," I corrected. "Terrified. Agog. Completely out of my depth. But not nervous."

"Not nervous." He grinned down at me with amusement. "What if I told you that I am?"

"Why?" I asked.

Instead of answering he extended his hand. "Dance with me."

My left hand slid into his and my right went to his shoulder. He stepped back, I moved forward. He led me around the room until it began to swirl around me.

The space around us melted away until we danced on a layer of clouds beneath a blanket of stars.

"This is incredible." A laugh bubbled up from my chest.

He paused and stared down at me. "You're so beautiful when you are happy."

My heart pounded and I knew from the way his gaze fastened onto my mouth that he was going to kiss me.

"Robin," I breathed his name through parted lips. "I wish this was real."

He smiled then. "So do I. Too bad you're going to die."

I was so lost in the spell that it took a minute for the words to register. "What?" Then I fell through the cloud. A scream tore from my lips. Too fast the ground was coming up. Above me, I could see Robin's sapphire eyes boring into me, filled with regret and that same longing.

But he couldn't help me.

I turned in midair and saw the Earth beneath me as I fell to my doom. My eyes squeezed shut and braced for impact.

Right before I struck, I jolted upright in my bed, heart racing after my near-death experience. What a nightmare. You didn't have to be a shrink to figure out what my subconscious was trying to tell me though. If I let myself fall for Robin, there would be spectacular things, wonders I could hardly imagine. And I would get hurt.

"Message received, self." I turned on my side and stared at the closed door to my room, trying very hard not to wish things were different.

"WHAT'S on your agenda for the day, lamb?" Robin, freshly showered and looking far too scrumptious, waited outside my door with a coffee mug extended. Sin on a stick, that's what he was. Something about his stance brought to mind the image of the way a cat might corner a mouse.

Ignoring the offered mug I skirted around him. No time for a back and forth. "Can't talk. I'm late!"

"Late for what?" he called as I raced down the stairs.

"Work." I barked and then hopped on one foot, stuffing first my left foot and then my right into a gray sweat sock. They hadn't always been gray. Once upon a time, they had been pure white. Sheer laziness prohibited me from separating my laundry. Socks were nowhere near as interesting as towels.

"I thought the gym didn't open until ten?" From his position on the landing, Robin checked the face of the grandfather clock. "It's not even eight."

"Shoes, shoes, shoes," I chanted, scurrying around the coat rack in a desperate attempt to locate my sneakers. Way behind schedule. My digital alarm clock and my cell phone had both died at some point during the sleepless night. It had to be a coincidence because I couldn't make myself believe that I had magic that shorted the gadgets out. I found one sneaker wedged beneath a chaise in the front parlor, but where the hell was the other?

"Joey?" Robin had crept up behind me.

I sat up and bashed my head on the corner of an end table and let out a string of cuss words that would make even Darcy pause. "What, damn it?"

His blue eyes sparkled with sheer mischief as he proffered my missing sneaker. "You're not avoiding me by any chance, are you?"

In fact, I was. I couldn't look at him without remembering the way he had held me in the dream. "No. I have a yoga training class that starts at nine. And unless I get out of here in the next few seconds, there is no way I am going to make it down the mountain, through traffic, and to the class in time."

The next task was to find my damn keys. Gym bag? No, I hadn't taken one the day before. Coat pocket maybe. Now, which one had I been wearing? I began rummaging through the closet.

Robin followed, the picture of ease. "You must have hidden them in your vault."

Huh? "I don't have a vault."

"Of course you do."

With one hand in the pocket of my blue parka, I spared a moment to glare over at him. "Is that some sort of euphemism for the old prison purse?"

"Nothing so crude," he moved closer. "All of the fae have what amount to traveling storage units. If you want to keep something nearby, you simply will it away when you are through. It stays with you without having to physically carry the object."

My lips parted. "Are you serious?"

Robin nodded. "It's where a faery stores his or her hoard so no one can steal from it."

I'd seen his faery hoard. Things like a hairbrush that restored my hair to its youthful glory and that accursed hourglass full of the sands of time. "Are you saying being a temporary magic wielder means I become some sort of supernatural hoarder?"

He shook his head. "No, the space is limited. Small items like a hat or basket can go in the vault. Not a car or a house. Nothing much larger than a toaster, unless you are fae royalty."

"I see," I said even though I didn't.

"Try summoning the keys to you," he prompted.

"I'm already late," I huffed.

He stood there and folded his arms over his chest and waited.

"Fine," I huffed and then closed my eyes. A moment later they opened and I glared at him. "I have no idea what I'm doing."

"If you can see, it can be." He repeated the phrase he'd spoken the night before.

A dreadful thought surfaced. "I'm not going to get beaned on the head with the keys am I?"

"Calling in a stored object is different from making a wish. Just like opening your eyes is nowhere near as arduous as climbing a mountain."

"Okay," I said slowly and then let my lids slide shut. I imagined the keys and held out my hand. Nothing happened.

"Robin, I really don't have time to—"

"Just try again, Joey," he insisted.

It was easier to do what he wanted than to argue. Maybe if he saw that I couldn't do the stuff he claimed I could he would get past the notion that I had somehow stolen all his magic.

"You have to believe you can do it," Robin whispered in my ear. All the small hairs on the back of my neck stood on end and I barely stifled a shiver.

"Easier said than done," I muttered.

"You believed you could do gymnastics, didn't you? That you could be a champion? Envisioned the end result?"

"That's different," I protested.

"How?"

"It just is."

"No, it's not. The two are exactly the same. Right now, magic is new to you. You've seen me do it, have made a few attempts yourself. But just like the first time you saw someone else take to the mat and accomplish amazing things, you are unfamiliar with how and unsure of your next move. The more you practice, the more your confidence will grow and the more adept you will become."

I huffed out a breath. "Okay, I'll try again. But if I don't get it this time, will you please just help me find my keys?"

"Deal," Robin said. "Now concentrate."

My eyes slid shut again. I took a deep breath and then held out one of my scraped palms.

And something plopped into my hand, making them burn. "Ouch." My eyes snapped up and I stared at the ring of keys.

Robin rested his chin on my shoulder. "See? I told you that you could do magic."

My lids lifted and I stared in disbelief at the keys. No way. No freaking way. "You did this," I said to Robin.

He shook his head slowly, never breaking eye contact. "No, I didn't."

"You *must* have."

"Lamb, you look paler than usual. You'd better sit down." He began steering me into the front parlor. I didn't resist as he pushed me onto the antique chaise lounge.

After that unsettling dream, I had told myself over and over that Robin was just pulling one of his elaborate pranks on me. Like a weird and petty sort of vengeance. Messing with my mind. There was no way that I, Josephine Louise Whitmore, a middle-aged gym assistant who still lived with her mother, could do magic.

But the evidence was gripped in my battered hand.

I could do magic. And if the faery queen—aka Robin's mom—found out….

I started to hyperventilate.

"Is this a hormone thing?" Robin crouched in front of me.

I shoved at him with both hands, a move that didn't budge his solid form at all. "How could you let this happen?"

"You make it sound as though I had a choice in the matter. I assure you, I didn't."

"So, what are you saying? That this is my fault?" Oh hell no. Panic gave way to temper and I stood up. "You're the one that poofed into my life and started making promises. If you had just left me alone none of this would be happening!"

Without giving him a chance to respond, I snagged my

parka and stormed out the front door, steam practically billowing from my ears.

The day was cold and gray, which suited my mood perfectly. I stalked to my VW, threw open the door, and flung myself behind the wheel before I remembered where I was supposed to be going.

"Frick." I grumbled

"Joey, wait," Robin called. "I have something for you."

He held something in his hand, something that glinted in the sunlight.

"A pocket watch?" I frowned but rolled down my car window.

"Not just any pocket watch," Robin bent down and extended his hand until the watch dangled on a golden chain before my eyes as though he planned to hypnotize me.

"Look, I know you are stressed and I apologize for my part in it. That isn't my intent."

"Really, Robin, I don't have time for—"

"With this, you'll have all the time you need." His lips twitched. "Consider this an engagement present."

I frowned at the object. "What do you mean?"

"Wind it backward."

"Robin, I really don't have time for—"

He lowered the chain and let it slip into my hand. "Just trust me, this will help you."

I let out a sigh. "Fine."

I fumbled the watch in my grip and my thumb spun the dial counterclockwise. Robin said something unintelligible.

"What?" I looked up sharply, but his gibberish continued. I watched Robin take a step backward and then call out something else. He continued to walk in reverse to the house and then shut the door behind him.

"No way," I breathed when, a moment later the door opened and Robin repeated, "Joey, wait."

I waited with my hand wrapped around the small pocket watch.

Robin strode to the car. His brows pulled together and he blinked down at the object in my hand. "That watch—"

"Reverses time?" I croaked.

"How did you know?"

"Because I just did it," I explained what had occurred. "Is it like the hourglass?"

"It's a little more complicated than that," Robin shook his head. "You can't return to another point in the river of time. No taking yourself backward or forwards."

I thought about what I had just seen. "It shuffles other people around?"

"What it does is create time loops. It lets the bearer hold her place in time while others move around her. The scope is limited to you. But you can change things."

"So like say if a conversation is dull, I can just fast forward my way through it?" As much as I was dead set against using magic in any way, the idea of fast-forwarding through the next time my father's ancient assistant cornered me at the coffee shop to tell me about her sciatica, her deadbeat son and her two awful grandchildren was tempting.

"I've used it exactly that way on numerous occasions," Robin winked. "See why I said you wouldn't have to worry about missing your appointment?"

I blew out a breath. "Thanks, but no thanks." I offered him the watch back.

Robin scowled. "You don't want it?"

"Didn't you just tell me that magic always comes with a price?"

Blue eyes flashed. "This is different."

"Well then the term always doesn't really apply, does it?"

His lips parted and then he scowled. "You know, I believe you are right. In any event, hold on to the watch. It is a highly sought magical artifact."

There was no sense arguing with him. It would only make me later for my yoga class. "Now, if you don't mind, I have to go."

Robin nodded and popped the car door. "Have a good day, lamb. I'll see you when you get home." The words were domestically cozy. And wrong on every level.

He shut the door and I shook my head before heading to my class.

Yoga sucks. The thought went on repeat in my head as I struggled to move gracefully from downward-facing dog into a high lunge. The trouble stemmed from getting my left foot up between my palms because my left hip didn't want to cooperate. The instructor said it was all right to grab the reluctant foot and drag it into place. However, doing so put too much of my weight on my bum wrist, never mind my scraped palms.

Though I'd been flexible in my youth, years of drudge jobs and a sedentary lifestyle had robbed me of the fluid grace I was trying to attain. Did I look as ridiculous as I felt?

What was I trying to prove anyway? Alina was dead set

against holding yoga classes in her gym. I'd shown her numbers, even going so far as to run a Facebook survey around town to drum up interest. It was there, women of all ages were eager for yoga classes that they didn't have to drive an hour round trip to attend. But there was no way I would be in shape to be the instructor and Alina couldn't hire anyone else. So much for our extra income.

"You're doing great, Joey." The pretty earth mother instructor, Pam, had stopped by my side. Judging by the crow's feet around her warm brown eyes she was at least sixty, but beneath her flowy overshirt that covered her leotard, her body was smokin'.

I forced a smile. "I don't think I'm any good at this."

"Sure you are," She encouraged and then moved on to the next student, who was already in the high lunge.

"You have to say that or I stop paying for lessons," I grumped. My palms hurt like hell. For a moment I considered wishing myself into the pose. But no, I refused to screw around with magic. It only made things worse. Look how dependent Robin had become on it and how absolutely lost he seemed to be without it.

"Stay in this moment," Pam called out. "This is as much a mental cleansing as it is a physical pose."

How did she always know? It was like some well-honed yogi instinct. I reigned in my wayward thoughts, admitted defeat, and let my knees move to the yoga mat until I was in table pose. Then I got to my feet and, feeling like a cheater of the worst order, fell into the lunge alongside the rest of the class.

From the lunge, we returned to downward dog and then moved forward to plank pose. Again, my knees hit the mat well before the rest of the class. I couldn't wait for corpse pose, the one where I could lie on my back and not try to contort my plus-sized frame into all sorts of unnatural shapes.

My gaze slid to the gym bag that sat beside me. The watch was in there. Maybe I could do that little fast forward thing, just this once.

No! Bad Joey, the sensible shrew barked. *You know better.*

I did, but temptation lingered. I was in my forties. It was time to work smarter, not harder, right? And if I had the means to make my life a little bit easier, maybe I ought to at least consider doing so.

But hell, talk about a slippery slope. Where would it end? Would I fast forward through paperwork, or driving, or dishes? Sure, those things were tedious, but if I sped through all the dull bits to get to the fun, I'd end up like Robin— seeking pleasure at any cost. And look where that had got him.

Somehow, I slogged through the rest of the class and then took my five-minute rejuvenation in corpse pose, trying to ignore how much more I sweated than all the other students, most of whom hadn't yet hit thirty.

It took me longer than it took them to get up, roll my yoga mat, and head out the door as they chatted and laughed and talked about going out for green smoothies. I wasn't invited. If it had been Darcy, she would have included herself with the group out of spite, then won them over with her wit. I had to get my happy hide back up the mountain in time for the pre-lunch gymnastics class.

Sometimes adulting just sucked canal water backward.

There was a text from Dragon waiting on my phone. *Can we get a dog?*

Where had that come from? I sent back a series of question marks.

She must have been sitting on her phone because she wrote back, *it would be good protection for you and Prudence.*

Those didn't sound like my cousin's original thoughts. Protection? We didn't bother to lock our doors most of the time. I suspected a certain fae prince was somehow responsible for the sudden interest in canine companionship. Reason enough to tread carefully.

Dogs are a big responsibility. Someone will need to feed it and walk it and clean up after it.

Three little dots flickered across the screen, indicating that my cousin was typing a lengthy reply. When it finally popped up it said, *Got to go. Class is starting.*

Curiouser and curiouser. Stowing my phone in my gym bag, I headed to my car, cranked the classic rock station up high, and did my best to drown out all the crazy thoughts that cluttered my head.

Which was why it took me until the turn back into town to realize that I was being followed.

CHAPTER FIVE

"Ain't nothing stronger than female intuition."
-Notable quotable from Grammy B

The vehicle that had been tailing me was a beige SUV with tinted windows. I had first noticed it on the steep incline as the highway snaked up the mountain. Normally, a car like that would have moved into the left lane and blown past me and my battered VW that could barely handle the slope without redlining. The fact that it hadn't wasn't unusual on its own. What roused my suspicions was that it had exited the highway exactly when I did, heading toward my dinky town instead of out to the Blue Ridge Parkway or toward any of the resort hotels.

The clock on my dash read 12:08. Anyone who had business in town should have already been in place. The vehicle was new enough that it would have been the talk of the town if any of the residents had purchased it. High country folks bought cars and drove them until they died and you were lucky if they didn't let them sit tire-less on cinderblocks for parts for the next three decades. Grammy's diesel truck, which she had named Earl, came fresh off the line a year before I was born.

Why would someone be following me? My stomach flipped and flopped like a fish swiped from the river by a hungry bear. I debated my options. I could go to the gym, park in my usual place, and see what the SUV did. Perhaps I was overreacting. Gut instinct told me that wasn't the right call. I could drive to the police station. That was what the hefty security officer who'd taught self-defense at the community center last year had advised to women who thought they were being followed. But what if whoever was tailing me wasn't human? Did I really want the authorities involved in faery shenanigans? Robin had cautioned me that the fae queen might have her minions watching me.

Robin. Thinking about him convinced me to head home. For one thing, if there was going to be some sort of magical confrontation, our property was more remote than either the gym or the police station. The fae prince knew how to use magic, even if he couldn't access it at the moment, and he was the only being who could possibly help if the SUV did hold a load of fae assassins.

My palms sweated as I navigated through the familiar streets. The SUV stayed several car lengths behind me. Had my imagination run away with me? After all, the fae didn't know that I had somehow ganked Robin's magic. And no one else had a reason to tail me. Just a coincidence. Any minute the SUV would turn off. Any second….

It didn't and by the time I took the sharp left onto my street, the VW was practically up on two wheels. I screeched to a stop at the curb, wrestled with the seatbelt which somehow seemed to have gotten twisted. The struggle knocked my bag onto the floorboard. Something glittered in the sunlight that streamed through the windows. The pocket watch. I scooped it up and then threw myself out of the car and sprinted for all I was worth toward the house.

Tires screeched to a stop behind me. A man got out. A shiver went up and down my spine as I felt his gaze land on me. Fae for sure. Jet black hair, bright green eyes fringed with ebony lashes. Tall and broad. His dark hair was cropped close to his skull, but he had the bone structure to pull off the severe look. He possessed that same unearthly air as Robin that went beyond physical perfection. Way too pretty to be mortal.

My instincts were screaming that I needed to run, to hide, to get away from him. He strode toward me with predatory grace and I had no doubt that he knew what it was like to watch life leave someone's eyes.

Time. I needed more time to barricade myself inside and warn Robin so we could form a plan. I fumbled with the watch. As I'd done earlier, I wound the watch back. Five minutes. The man looked surprised for a moment as he saw what I held, but then the watch's effect caught up to him. He walked backward, climbed back inside the SUV. I didn't draw breath until I saw it back up the street and turn the corner.

Then I ran for the house.

"Robin?" I bellowed even as I slammed the front door and threw the deadbolt. I doubted the cheap lock would stop a fae with ill-intent but it made me feel a little better once the door was secured.

There was no answer to my summons, but from outside, I heard the screech of tires. He was back already? I crept to the window in the front parlor and pulled the lace curtain aside. My eyes went wide as I saw the driver reemerge. Did he know what had happened?

If so, we were in deep shit.

A hand landed on my shoulder. I shrieked and whirled around to stare into amused sapphire eyes. "A little jumpy aren't you, lamb?"

I gasped for breath but before I could regain it, a knock sounded on the front door.

Robin moved toward it.

"Don't," I hissed and gripped his arm.

He scowled. "Whyever not?"

"Because," I wheezed. "He's been tailing me."

"Who?"

I shook my head. "I don't know. I spun the watch back just to make it inside and from the looks of him, he knows it."

"Describe him." All the amusement had left Robin's gaze.

I did, haltingly, doing my best to make it a cold and clinical description, like I was talking to a police sketch artist.

"Andreas," Robin grumbled. "Do you still have the watch?"

"Right here." I nodded and showed it to him.

Robin stepped back. "Keep your hand on it, just in case."

In case of what? Magical attacks? "You said it's only good for me."

"That's right. If Andreas tries anything, I want you to promise to wind the watch back and get yourself to safety."

And leave him to whatever the fae intended? "But—?"

One blond brow went up. "Worried about me, lamb?"

"Yes." The word slipped out before I thought better of it. "You can't do magic."

His expression softened and he lifted his hand as though to stroke my face, but lowered it without touching me. "It won't come to that. The fae don't want mortal authorities asking questions. And I doubt he's here for a fight."

"Who is he?" I asked.

"My brother."

"You never told me you had a brother."

"That's because he's a miserable son of a bitch." Robin sighed. "Everything will be fine. Trust me."

I really wished he'd stop saying that. Trusting him was up there with sticking a fork into an electrical outlet to see if it worked. Foolish with the potential for extra crispy disaster.

And now there were two of them on my property. How had the other fae even found me?

Before I could ask, he opened the door. "Andreas."

"Robin." The fae male studied Robin for a long minute, his gaze unwavering. "Aren't you going to invite me in?"

"It's not my home," Robin blocked the door with his body.

"Ah, but it will be soon. Since you're betrothed to the lovely Josephine." Those brilliant green irises swept over my body, and I had to stifle a shiver of revulsion. "Imagine my surprise when I spotted her out and about without you. And she has grandfather's watch."

"A token of my affection. And Joey is her own woman who will come and go as she pleases." Robin smiled, but there was no warmth in the expression. "Thank you for seeing her safely back into my care."

There were more layers of subtext between the fae men than I could interpret. Did Andreas suspect there was more to Robin's story than some sort of whirlwind romance? I seriously doubted he had accidentally stumbled across me. While the words were pleasant enough, I couldn't shake the feeling that Andreas was digging for the secrets Robin was burying.

Secrets that could get both of us killed.

Andreas gave us a slow nod and then turned away from the door. Then he paused and called over his shoulder, "You know, you two don't behave at all like a soon to be married couple."

With that, he walked away.

Robin shut the door. His shoulders slumped forward and his gaze trained on the floor.

I sagged against the oversized doorframe between the parlor and the hall. "What was that? No apology for scaring the crap out of me. And what does that mean, that we don't behave like an engaged couple?"

"We don't," the fae prince murmured and then looked over at me. "And if Andreas can sense it, then my mother will as well. She has incredible instincts."

"And no soul." Not if she sanctioned enslaving desperate humans as servants.

"We all use the gifts that we've been granted." Robin lifted his gaze to meet mine.

My hands landed on my hips. "Okay, I have had enough

of your cryptic bullshit. Do you agree with your mother's practice of keeping humans as slaves?"

He slowly shook his head.

Some knot inside my chest eased. "But you enthralled humans? Took some of the ones you bargained with back there to serve?"

"I did," Robin agreed. "And before meeting you, I didn't think anything was wrong with that."

I huffed out a breath. There was no getting through to him. "I need to go to work. Alina will have my hide if I'm late."

My intention was to stride past him to the door but he caught my arm before I could escape. "You must try to understand. I was born a fae and learned how to survive in that world. I never had a moral compass nor anyone else to show me right from wrong. So how is it fair for you to hold me to the human standard you have held for your whole life when I have only known for a month?"

I tugged my arm free. "Some things are just wrong, regardless."

ALINA MADE me pay for my tardiness by doing the paperwork. Quarterly and year-end taxes were fast approaching and I had to slog through spreadsheets until my eyes ached from the strain of a gazillion tiny little numbers crammed into cells and rows that all looked the same.

After an hour, I got up and headed into the break room for a coffee. Alina was in the middle of a class and with just the two of us, I had the space to myself. The pot stood empty.

Alina wasn't much of a coffee drinker, though she indulged in a cup if I went to the trouble of brewing it. Usually, I just brought a coffee in with me so I didn't have to listen to her lectures on the evils of cream and sugar and what my drug of choice did to my body.

The filters and coffee had been crammed onto the top shelf, just out of reach. Probably my boss's passive-aggressive way of making me work for something I wanted. Feeling a pang of sympathy for Darcy's height-challenged self, I dragged one of the blue chairs over to stand on. It was one of the cheap kind that had a molded metal frame instead of four sturdy legs and it wobbled precariously as I clambered onto it. My teeth sank into my lower lip. This was probably a piss-poor idea. I should find another chair. Or maybe just give up on the idea of having coffee. Or run across the road and see if my dad had any already brewed in his office. But I was tired of second and third guessing every damn decision. It seemed like the only thing I had been doing since Robin came back into my life.

Robin's words had chased me throughout the day. Was he right? Did I blame him for things he couldn't control? It had been a long time since my high school sociology class and I hadn't been in the best headspace to absorb all the information. But I recalled enough to understand that diverse cultures operated in different ways. And while I knew slavery was abhorrent, could I really judge him when no one had taught him otherwise? When he grew up in a culture that promoted and elevated those who did the enslaving?

Bad enough he had invaded my home and somehow foisted his magic on me. Now he was taking up valuable real estate in my head. Maybe he was doing the best he could with what he had been given. Maybe he was struggling with a new understanding of right and wrong. And maybe I just needed some damn coffee and to get my happy ass back to work and deal with Robin's mischief later.

An image flashed through my mind, of the fae tied to my bed frame to keep him out of trouble. I stumbled and caught myself at the vivid mental picture. If I can see it can be…

No, bad Joey! Don't picture it.

I shook my head hard.

Setting my gaze on my target, I braced one foot on the seat of the chair, one hand on the cabinet, and hoisted myself upward. The chair wobbled, but I balanced and then snagged the can in one hand, the filters in the other. Victorious, I turned in place, prepared to step down.

Crack!

The plastic seat on the chair split. Instinct had me shifting away from the weak point. The chair overbalanced. I dropped the coffee and filters, arms pinwheeling as I struggled to keep myself from falling on my face and breaking my nose again.

I wish Robin was here.

The thought flashed through my mind and an instant later, the fae appeared directly in front of me. Just in time for me to land smack on top of him.

His arms went around me even as I crashed into him, sending us both careening to the floor. He broke my fall well. No impact on my bad wrist and I didn't break my nose again. Robin took the full impact of the crash.

"Oh, hell," I gasped. I wasn't exactly dainty and he had no time to brace for the hit. "I'm sorry, I didn't mean to—"

"Are you hurt?" His arms were like steel bands around me, those sapphire eyes intense.

"No." My heart raced and I took a steadying breath, only to inhale the spicy wild scent of him. I wanted to bury my nose in the crook of his neck and just breathe him in. Desire pooled low in my belly. I licked my lips and his gaze dropped to them.

Bad idea, the sensible shrew cautioned.

"Lamb," he brushed the hair away from my face. "Let me kiss you."

"That's not a good idea."

"Then tell me you don't want me. Tell me I disgust you and that I ought to leave and never come back." His eyes were so intense, almost pleading for me to do exactly that.

"Is that really what you want?" I whispered.

"I want to know what *you* want."

My lips parted but no sound came out. Our eyes locked. "I don't know."

His thumb ran along my cheekbone. "You do. You're just scared to admit you feel it too. The pull between us."

I shook my head. "It's just attraction. Chemistry."

"It's so much more than that." He lifted his head to mine and pressed a soft kiss to the corner of my mouth. It would be so easy to just turn my head a little and really kiss him. To lose myself in the feel of him if only for a little while.

He was wrong. I wasn't just scared. Terror coursed through my system alongside blatant desire whenever I thought about us. This had to end. Right now, before I did something incredibly stupid. I scrambled back, intending to put some space between our bodies, but in my haste, planted my knee between his legs and racked him. Hard.

That made him let go. With a groan, he curled over on his side like a shrimp.

"Ohmigod, I'm so sorry." I patted the air between our bodies. Not that it was doing much good. Poor Robin. I'd magically extracted him from wherever he had been, used him as a landing strip, and then kneed him in the family jewels for good measure. Was I trying to torture him?

"You could have just said no," he grunted.

"I'm sorry." It bore repeating.

He made a motion with his hand, gesturing for me to back away slowly. The profusion of apologies continued to spill from my lips, but I did give him some space.

"Josephine?" Alina had appeared in the doorway. "I thought I heard a scream."

"We had an…incident." Massive understatement.

Her gaze went from where I stood, to the curled form on the floor. "Should I call the police?"

"No. It's fine. He was trying to help me." And had almost seduced me before I'd kneed him.

She stood there, eyes narrowed, arms crossed, clearing wanting more.

I sighed. I hadn't excluded my boss from our ruse. "Robin, meet Alina. Alina. Alina, my fiancé, Robin Goodfellow."

"A pleasure," he croaked but didn't offer a hand since he was still clutching himself.

Alina eyed the two of us and then decided we weren't worth any more of her time as she strode back to the gym.

After a long minute, he sat up and took an audible breath. "What just happened?"

"I fell." I gestured to the cracked chair.

"Yes, I realize that. What I mean is, how did I come to be

here?" He frowned and then looked around the small space. "I was helping your mother relocate boxes from the canning shed. She wishes to sell the garage this weekend."

"You mean a garage sale?"

He nodded. "So how did I get from there to here?"

"I sort of… wished you were here. It was an accident." Unsure of whether I meant the fall or summoning him like a genie from a lamp, I clamped my lips together.

"Did you now." He studied me and I prayed that he wasn't going to say anything about the heated moment of intimacy.

"It was an accident," I repeated.

He nodded. "An impulse."

And how odd was it that I had wished for him in that moment of sheer terror? Just like I had headed for him when I was being followed. Almost like he was home base and I would be safe if I were with him.

Don't be an idiot. The sensible shrew snarked.

Slowly he rose to his full height and then extended his hand to me. "Your magic is growing exponentially. And far too quickly. At this rate, you'll expose yourself to the fae before we can figure out how to transfer it back to me."

My head bobbed in agreement. I hadn't meant to use magic, hadn't meant to make the wish. It had happened between heartbeats. This wasn't like getting up early to exercise or saying no to a jelly doughnut. All the willpower in the world couldn't keep a catastrophic idle thought from exposing my secret. And with Andreas lurking around….

I swallowed hard. "What should I do?"

"First off, we need to siphon off some of that magic."

"How?" I asked.

"Easy. You need a familiar."

I shook my head. "Oh no. I'm not enslaving anybody."

"I'm not talking about an anchor. I'm talking about an animal companion. You need a living creature to keep you grounded in the world. Didn't Dragon mention something about getting another pet? It would be a perfect cover."

Wait a second… I narrowed my gaze on him. "And how the hell did you know that Dragon asked about getting a dog?"

It might have been the shadows from the outer window playing across his face but I could swear the fae prince blushed. "We may have discussed the topic this morning."

I groaned. "Damn it, Robin. You can't just talk to a teenager about getting a pet. Especially since she's missing the stray cat that was hanging around."

That stray had been Robin's former anchor and my many times great grandmother. And a bit of a bitch if I were being honest. But it was like Grammy B always said. Bitches get things done.

"Did you set this into motion so that I would be forced to get a familiar?" Nothing was beyond Robin when he put his mind to something.

He held his hands up. "I swear to you, Joey. Dragon was the one who brought it up. The girl is lonely and wants a companion." That devilish glint returned to his eye. "Is she the only one?"

No. It wasn't a pet I wanted but a partner. Though I didn't dare say a word about it, not after that moment. I blew out a breath. "And this won't hurt the animal? Being my familiar?"

Robin shook his head. "It shouldn't. Mortal mages use familiars all the time and no harm ever befalls them."

I decided not to touch that bit about mortal mages. I was

already in it up to my ears with fae and magic and bargains. The last thing I wanted was to invite more chaos into my orbit.

"Fine, I will talk to my mother about it." Though I didn't hold out a ton of hope that Prudence Whitmore would block the way. She'd let Robin move in, for the love of grief.

Robin smiled. "All right. Well, since I can't magic myself away, you are going to have to drive me back to your home."

I raised a brow. "Um, maybe you want to try that again, sans the snarky attitude?"

"What do you mean?" He frowned at me.

I blew out a breath and then bent to retrieve the coffee and filters from the floor. "Look, I decided earlier that maybe I was being a little too harsh, expecting you to see things the way I do. But," I added hastily when his Cheshire cat grin appeared. "That only applies to the past. Because ignorance isn't an excuse that I'm willing to tolerate for long. If in doubt, ask me."

"What would Joey Whitmore do?" He winked. "Well then, since you are such a paragon of virtue, how would Joey Whitmore go about getting herself home?"

"It's the middle of the day. Joey Whitmore needs to work so she can't take you home right now." I was already skating on thin ice with Alina, what with being late and then Robin's unexpected arrival. "And you need to leave before you get me fired."

Robin appeared distinctly put out. "Then what am I supposed to do until you are finished with your work?"

I gave him a palm's up gesture. "I don't know? Get a job."

He stared at me for a full minute, expression incredulous. "A *job*?"

"It's not a dirty word."

"I know that. I like those." He glowered at me. "Are you serious?"

"You wanted to know what a mortal male would do? He would go find a way to earn his keep."

"But I have currency," he protested. "Things of value. Why should I work?"

After filling the coffee pot at the tiny sink, I poured the water into the machine and pressed the button. "Look, it's just what we do. Mortals need a purpose in their lives. If we are going to figure this whole magic swap out, I need you to at least pretend to blend in here. Because having you pop in and out all day is too distracting. I can't focus on my life and this magic problem and give you all the attention you so desperately crave."

His lips parted. "I don't think anyone has ever spoken to me that way before."

"Maybe they should have." I glanced at him over my shoulder. "Because, Robin? I don't know how things work where you're from. But you're here now. You should at least try to fit in with us, even if you hate us."

He shook his head. "I don't hate you, Joey."

"Maybe not. But what about Grammy B? My mother or Dragon? Can you honestly say you don't hold them in contempt? That you wouldn't bargain with them if you were in any position to?"

I turned my attention back to the coffee. His eyes were fixed on me, the intense concentration bore invisible holes into my skull. Maybe I had gone too far.

"Robin, I didn't mean—" I turned around.

But he was already gone.

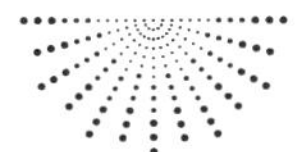

CHAPTER SIX

"What doesn't kill us makes us stronger. And madder than a bear with a bee stinger in his rump."

-Notable quotable from Grammy B

Dragon leaned against an ugly statue that had been put up by the school district nearly two decades ago. I wasn't sure what it was supposed to be other than an eyesore. Her hands were tucked under her armpits and her head was bent as she waited. The picture of teenage dejection. She climbed into the passenger's seat her eyes fixated on something only she could see.

"Dragon?" I asked. "Is everything all right?"

"Fine." The terse reply held no emotion.

"Did you want to drive?"

She shook her head. I was batting a thousand today.

After maneuvering back out into traffic, I hunted for the right thing to say to my cousin who was so clearly struggling with something. Did it have to do with school? Or maybe her mother's impending visit? Aunt Hannah was a harridan who had all but abandoned Dragon to her poor country relations when she went off galivanting to the UN to rub elbows with important people. That had been bad enough. But what was worse was the fact that she hadn't acknowledged her daughter's sexual orientation, had called her girlfriend back in Baltimore a bad influence.

Thinking about that connection gave me an inkling as to what might be plaguing her. "Is it Tasha?"

"She broke up with me," Dragon said as we turned off the main street and headed back to the Victorian.

Shit. Long-distance was tough. At least, that's what people told me. Having never attempted a long-distance relationship myself, I wouldn't know. Unless you counted Robin being off in the fae realm for the last month. But that had been more of a relief than anything. Somehow, I doubted that Dragon would relate well to that.

"I thought if I could get my license, I could drive up to see her." Dragon's words were so low that I could barely hear what she said. "I thought she would wait for me."

"But she didn't." It wasn't a question.

A tear fell. "She didn't even tell me. I just saw pictures of her and this new girl up on her Instagram."

"Maybe it's not...." I trailed off as she sent me a black look.

"She hasn't even called me. Or tried to come to see me." Dragon shook her head.

"I'm sorry." What else could I say? How rough it was, being a teenager. One day you're going along and everything is fabulous and the next the rug gets yanked out from under you. Of course, it's the same way for the middle-aged too. We're just more used to the seismic shifts life dealt out. Plus, we have more cushion on our backsides to help pad the landing.

Thinking about my well-padded posterior, I knew what we had to do. Dragon scowled as I made an illegal U-turn. "This isn't the way home."

"We're going to the diner," I told her. "It's Thursday, which means Kentucky pie and homemade vanilla ice cream."

"I'm not…" Dragon began.

"Not what? Hungry? Because I know that's a lie. I remember being sixteen and I was always starving." Of course, that had to do with the strict diet I had been on to improve my chance of becoming an elite gymnast.

I held my breath. If Dragon insisted on going home to sulk, I'd take her. Even though I really wanted a reason to avoid Robin, who was probably pissed that I had made him find his own way back to my house.

After a long moment, she leaned back in her seat and closed her eyes. As close as I was going to get to teenage approval.

The diner was more of a greasy spoon café perched on the outside of town close to the highway and directly across the street from the recycling plant. I'd worked there for all of three weeks over the winter, right before I'd met Robin.

It seemed like a lifetime ago.

The lunch rush had slowed to a trickle. Harry Flanders

from the hardware store and Maggie Simmons, the retired school nurse, sat at the counter sipping coffee. An elderly gentleman I didn't recognize sat in a booth playing solitaire while he waited for his early bird special. Ignoring the please wait to be seated sign, which only applied to tourists so that the townies could gawk at them, I made my way to the booth on the far end. Normally, Dragon and I would eat at the counter. But if her hunched shoulders were any indication, she was feeling exposed and vulnerable. Sitting with one's back to the room never helped that condition.

The waitress, June Mott, sauntered over to us. June was a pretty young thing in her mid-twenties with boobs that still defied gravity and legs for days. She'd been my replacement and had proven herself to be a decent waitress, even if she held a grudge. I stifled the groan at the craptastic luck that had her working the afternoon shift.

"What can I get you?" The words were acid, the smile pure menace.

We'd had a run-in when June had tried to pick Robin up under my nose and he had insulted her. Loudly. In front of half the town. And even though I had come back later to apologize and give her a hearty tip, she was still barely civil. And I was pretty sure she spit in my food whenever she got the chance and the manager wasn't looking.

"Nothing for me. But my cousin here would like…?" I trailed off and waved at Dragon.

"A hot fudge sundae," Dragon decided.

"No pie?" I asked, disappointed that I wouldn't be able to snag a taste of hers. At least having June as a waitress helped me stick to my diet. Much easier to cut back on carbs when there was the potential for phlegm.

Dragon shook her head. June rolled her eyes and left.

"About the dog." I fiddled with the sugar packets on the table. I wasn't OCD, not like my mother anyway, but the fact that I was the only person in the history of this place to dump out all the sugar packets and arrange them by color instead of just cramming more into the container irked me.

"Did you talk to Aunt Prudence?" I'd managed to pique her interest at least.

I nodded. "She's onboard." Yet another unexpected compliance from my mother. Maybe she was mixing medications. I knew for a fact Benadryl made her loopier than three glasses of wine.

"That's fantastic," Dragon perked up, but then deflated.

"Something wrong?"

"It's just…I really wanted a dog just so I'd have something cute to put on Instagram. So I didn't look like such a loser."

All for the 'gram. Sigh. I should have known it was something like that. "Having a dog is a big responsibility," I scolded, then paused, wondering when my mother had body-snatched me. Joey Whitmore didn't scold. Well, I scolded Robin, but that was different. Someone needed to straighten his cocky fae hide out.

"I know."

"So, do you not want to get one now?" And what would I do about a familiar if she said no?

"No, I do." she hurried to say. "What kind should we get? I was thinking maybe a corgi."

I barely stifled a grimace. Purebred corgis cost upwards of $1,500 each. And while I agreed with Dragon, they were freaking adorable—there was a reason I knew the cost—we had medical bills and property taxes to pay. "Maybe we should check out the shelter tomorrow after school."

"Can Robin come with us?"

"We'll see." Damn, I was getting good at that non-committal answering. I'd thought it was a mom thing but apparently, it was a skill one developed after spending enough time with a teenager. "And you're not a loser. You're only a loser if you stop playing the game."

Dragon's ice cream was delivered and I tried to ask non-invasive yet interested questions while ignoring the daggers a certain server cast my way via her eyeballs. I paid, leaving a hearty tip on the table, though I doubted it would help with my PR.

Ice cream and the talk of getting a dog had perked Dragon up enough that she agreed to drive home. There was only one close call where she braked a good twenty feet before the intersection and Harry McCrae almost rolled over the top of us in his eighteen-wheeler.

Dragon pulled up in front of the house and I was surprised to see the garage door up and my mother wearing her grubbies. Aka the one pair of jeans she owned and an old concert t-shirt that she'd probably snitched from my dad. To my knowledge, Prudence Whitmore had never attended a concert unless there was a string quartet involved.

"What are you doing?" I extracted myself from the car and made my way across the lawn to her. The temperature was cooler than it had been the day before but still warm enough for shirt sleeves, as long as the wind didn't pick up. The garage smelled a little like mildew, which didn't bode well for all the cardboard boxes filled with miscellanea.

"Sorting through all this junk to see if there's anything

worth selling." She set down a box and beckoned me forward. "Robin hauled all of this from the cottage and the spare bedroom? He's a good egg."

I made a noncommittal sound even as I poked through the contents of the box. "Would you look at that?" I shook my head as I pulled out a collection of beanie babies. "They're still in pretty good shape, too."

"If we get all this organized, maybe we can pull off a garage sale. That is if it doesn't rain. The temperature is supposed to be in the upper fifties." Mom moved on to the next box.

"Practically a heat wave."

"Hmm?" She was frowning as she sorted through a stack of National Geographics. "Why on Earth would we keep all of these?"

"You said they were full of diverse cultures and that if I was going to travel the world after winning a gold medal that I would need a decent baseline so I didn't put my big fat foot in my mouth and add to the ignorant American stereotype," I recited dutifully.

My mother shook her head. "I'm sorry, Joey. It's amazing you are as well-adjusted as you are with me for a mother." To my horror, her eyes filled.

"Mom, what's the matter?"

"Your father asked me to marry him," she sniffed.

My parents had a bizarre relationship. They'd been exclusive since before I was born, but my mother was an uber feminist and thought marriage was a tool of a patriarchal society. My father went along with her, mostly because she hadn't given him any other option. If Paul Blackthorn wanted Prudence Whitmore, he had to take what she offered. He lived his life, she lived hers and they got together a few times a week to go out to dinner and…stuff. I loved them both but it was a strange arrangement.

"When did this happen?"

"This afternoon," she sighed and shook her head.

"Was he joking?" My dad had an offbeat sense of humor and it was entirely possible that he had maybe made a joke and my mother had missed the punchline.

"No, he's serious." she sniffed. "Oh Joey, what am I going to do?"

"Dad?" I called as I let myself into my father's law office. His receptionist, Edith, was conspicuously absent. Not that she was much of a watchdog since she had a tendency to fall asleep at her desk when things were slow.

The door to my father's cubbyhole office stood ajar. I poked my head in and saw the usual mess of file folders, books, and old coffee mugs. Edith wasn't allowed to tidy up his clutter. I was just about to hustle upstairs and check his apartment when the sound of male voices filtered from the conference room door. He must be with a client.

I took the opportunity to visit the bathroom. Still no sign of Edith. Maybe she'd gone home for the afternoon. Mom had said things around the office were slow. I leaned against the sink and my hand went to the pocket of my hoodie, where the golden watch lay. It was tempting to spin it back and see the interaction between my parents. What on earth had prompted my father to propose after all the years of their…arrangement?

It made me nervous. In the other timeline I had visited, my mother had consented to marry my father and they'd wound up divorced. At the same time, I knew Paul Blackthorn wasn't content with his life. He'd given up a lucrative career as a big city lawyer to be a country real estate attorney and stay near my mother and later on, me. But he was nearing retirement age. I knew he harbored regrets and wanted more for his golden years than the same old same old. Perhaps the proposal was a way to sus out whether he and my mother had a future together?

I needed to know where his head was at. My dad and I had always been close and I was surprised and a little bit hurt that he hadn't confided in me about his intentions before he'd blindsided mom.

The sound of footsteps approached and I emerged from the bathroom, still unsure of how to broach the subject when I caught sight of the man shaking hands with my father.

"Robin?" My jaw dropped. "What are you doing here?"

"Taking your advice." Robin strode toward me and draped an arm over my shoulders. "Your father was kind enough to offer me a job."

"He did what now?" My gaze swung to my father's.

"Just a trial run, to see if the law is a good fit for your young man." Paul Blackthorn tucked his hands into his pants pockets and then rocked back on his heels. "Robin told me he's been searching for a new direction for his career. He's going to operate as my assistant for a few weeks and then perhaps train as a paralegal."

"After all, I need a way to support my wife." Sapphire eyes sparkled with mischief.

I made a strangled sound. Before I could string together a

coherent sentence, Robin pressed a finger over my lips. "Now now, I know you said I couldn't mention our engagement to the women in your family, but I felt it was only right that I formally ask for your father's permission."

"Which I granted of course. Joey, are you feeling all right? You look pale." My dad frowned.

"I need to sit." The words slipped out.

Robin guided me over to Edith's vacant chair and eased me into it. "There now, it'll be all right."

But it wouldn't. Because my father thought Robin and I were to be married. Mom had said money was tight for him. And he had only extended the job offer because he believed he was doing a solid for his future son-in-law.

How had things gotten so complicated?

"What have you eaten today?" Robin asked me.

"None of your beeswax," I huffed.

He turned to my father and confessed, "She's terrible about skipping meals."

"She's been like that since she was a teenager," Paul Blackthorn—the traitor—nodded in agreement. "I got in the habit of stashing snacks in the glovebox of my car so she didn't gnaw her own arm off."

"Don't talk about me like I'm not here," I huffed.

They ignored me.

"I think there might be a few oranges in my fridge." My father continued. "I could go up and check."

"Allow me." Robin double-timed it up the stairs.

"Dad, I…" My throat clogged.

My father pulled out the chair across from me so we sat eye to eye. "It's all right, Joey. Robin explained everything."

"He did?" I was almost afraid to ask.

"He said that it was a fairly recent decision, but he's never been surer of anything in his life. He's an impressive young man and seems to be smitten with you." The lines around my father's eyes crinkled as he spoke. "I'm happy for you sweetheart. And if I'm honest, maybe even a little envious."

It clicked. "Is that why you asked Mom to marry you?"

He glanced away. "I've been thinking about it for a while. You know that."

My head bobbed. "I do. But dad, she's in a state over it. Now is not a great time."

"It's never been a great time." My father looked sad. "But I'm not getting any younger. I need to know where we stand. Can you appreciate that?"

Considering I couldn't hold my footing with Robin, yeah, I could understand the need. The sly fae was weaving himself into every aspect of my existence and it was driving me batty.

"The oranges were molding," Robin said as he reappeared. "Perhaps I should take the two of you out to dinner instead?"

"Thanks, but I have plans with Prudence," my father said.

"Joey?" Robin asked.

I shook my head. "I have an evening class. Plus, it's my turn to cook."

"If your mother is going out, we can pick Dragon up, bring her with us. We can collect your grandmother, too. Let's grab a pizza. I promise to have you back in time for your late class."

He'd thought of everything, neatly dismantling my protests one by one before I'd even uttered them. I huffed out a breath and relented.

My father saw us out to the car. Robin plucked the keys from my hand, unlocked the door, and saw me settled. He murmured something to my father that I couldn't hear but made the older man laugh.

"Can you even drive?" I asked as Robin slid behind the wheel.

"It's not that difficult." He shrugged and threw the car into reverse and braked so hard the momentum threw me back against the seat.

"So," he shot me a sideways glance as he pulled out into traffic. "Come on, let me have it."

"It?" I asked, my arms braced against the dashboard.

"How angry are you?" Without bothering to use the blinker, Robin made a sharp left.

My shoulder thudded against the door. "Not angry. Afraid for my life but not angry. Slow down, please."

"Immortal, remember?"

I kept forgetting that part. "Doesn't mean I can't feel pain."

He lifted his lead foot a bit. "I thought for sure you'd be upset."

Something in his tone snagged my attention. "Are you trying to upset me?"

He shook his head. "No, but it was necessary. Your father wouldn't have offered me the position otherwise. And I needed to be there, close to where you are during the work day."

He made a right, cutting off a minivan and merging onto the road that led to the Victorian. I flinched but he merged smoothly with traffic. Once my heart slowed to a more normal speed I asked, "And why is that, exactly?"

"So I can get to you quickly," Robin's expression sobered. "Without my magic, I must travel in conveyances such as these. By the time I get to you, it might be too late."

Cold dread pooled in my stomach. "Too late for what?"

He released a deep breath. "My mother has crossed to the mortal realm. And she's hunting for you."

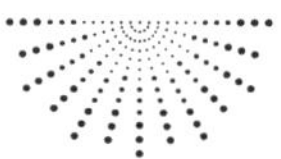

CHAPTER SEVEN

"Animals eat their young to prevent one thing. Teenagers."

-Notable quotable from Grammy B

"I have to hand it to you, Joey. He's a keeper." Grammy B reached for her third slice of pizza. "You better nail him down soon."

I had just taken a sip from my unsweetened ice tea and nearly choked. "You barely even know him."

"What else do you need to know?" She gestured to where Robin and Dragon stood playing Ms. Pacman. "Every woman in the place has been staring at him. Not only is he a good cook and a fun person to be around, he's a looker too."

I shook my head. "It's more complicated than that." Like the fact that his mother was a psycho and was lurking around the mortal realm, possibly hunting for me. Robin had dropped that little nugget in my lap but refused to say anything more about it, other than that he needed to stick close to me.

One wrinkled hand lifted and batted at the air. "Complicated, bah. You're a woman in your forties. It's time to stop wasting time letting men make the first move. God knows they cock it up nine times outta ten."

Several patrons glanced our way with raised eyebrows.

"Grammy!" I leaned forward and lowered my voice. "Volume control."

"I'm old, no one listens to me anyway." She waved it off. "Just crawl into his bed in the middle of the night, grab him by the dumbstick, and let nature take its course."

I had no idea what devil prompted me to ask, but the question escaped like it was making a jailbreak. "Is that what you did with Grandpappy?"

"You bet your ass it was." She narrowed her eyes on me. "Don't be such a prude, Joey. You sound like your mother."

I blanched. "Low blow, Grammy." It was my fault for asking. I could admit that.

We sat in silence for a moment before I murmured, "And what made you so sure that Grandpappy was the right man for you?"

Grammy picked up the red plastic cup full of sweet tea and then set it down on the table, making little rings with the condensation. "I wasn't, at least at first. In fact, I did my level best to keep him at a distance."

"Really?" My grandparents had been the perfect married couple so hearing that Grammy had ever had doubts surprised me.

She nodded. "You see I'd had my heart broken once already. And I was gun shy."

"Really?" Grammy B and the word shy in the same sentence? Who would have thought?

Her focus was lost in the past. "Phillip Grant. We were high school sweethearts. Everyone thought we'd be getting married as soon as we graduated, myself included. Well, about a month before we were due to graduate, his dad had a heart attack. Phillip was the oldest and he had to provide for his mama and two younger brothers. So, we decided to wait for a while. He enlisted in the army and left right after graduation. And he never came back. I heard from his mama that he met some woman in the Philippines and eventually they had eight kids together."

My lips parted. "How did I not know about this?"

She shot me a pissy look. "Like I said, no one can be bothered to listen to old people."

She was extra feisty tonight and it was hard not to smile as I cleared my throat and brought the focus back to her story. "So, Phillip broke your heart. How long was it before you met Grandpappy?"

She shrugged, her frail shoulders bobbed up and down. "Oh, I knew who he was all along. He was a year behind me in school. And you know how boys always seem younger, even when they are the same age as a girl? Well, he was one of those idiots that seemed like he couldn't find his ass with both hands."

I snorted.

"He was like that. Making lewd comments and wolf-whistling at the girls. Because of that, I'd never paid him much notice. I only had eyes for Phillip."

The man she was describing sounded nothing at all like my grandfather. "What changed?"

"After Phillip shipped out, I got a job at the local hospital as a receptionist. One night your grandfather came in with his baby sister. She was maybe five at the time. She was all banged up and so was he. I checked him in and asked what happened. He refused to tell me or the doctors. They assumed it was a car accident. While the doc was setting her bones, I approached him and asked if I could call his parents. The look he gave me…" She shook her head. "I knew right then, I wasn't dealing with a boy, but a man who had someone to protect. That was when I started seeing him in a different light."

My grandfather's parents had been long gone by the time I came around. "Did you ever find out what happened?"

She sighed. "Not for months. After that night he insisted on coming to the hospital after my late shifts. To see me home safely. It took a long time to get him to trust me with the story. He was like a wild animal. It took time to develop any measure of trust. I told him about Phillip leaving and how disappointed I was. I trusted him with my truth and eventually, he trusted me in return."

My gaze slid to where Robin and Dragon played. Was that what he was doing, trusting me with tiny pieces of his truth?

Unaware of my wandering thoughts, Grammy continued. "You see, his father was a drinker and unbeknownst to me, his mother had run away, leaving the two of them behind."

I let out a shaky breath. "Holy crow, Grammy."

"Yeah, I was floored by it. I told him that he ought to go to the cops. He said he was worried that they'd take his sister away and he would never see her again. He was only a few months away from his eighteenth birthday and he fully intended to raise her himself. They just needed to get by for a few more months and then they would be safe. He was going to drop out of school and get a job so he could support her."

"And?" I was leaning forward in my seat, desperate to hear the outcome.

She shook her head. "It didn't work out the way he wanted. A few weeks before he turned eighteen his father beat him bloody. The neighbors called the police. His sister was removed from the house and taken into foster care. He searched for her, but by the time he found her, she'd been adopted by a new family and he knew she would be better off there than she would have been with him."

"Wow," I shook my head. "That's incredible."

"Your grandfather was an incredible man. I knew that after that first night when he brought her in. He had so much weight on his shoulders, such a burden but he never once complained about what he had been through. If I hadn't been so broken-hearted about Phillip, I probably would have made my move sooner. As it was, it took me another six months to accept that Phillip was never coming back and another two months of his constant asking before I pulled my head out of my keister. Kinda like you should do with Robin."

My heart was racing. "It's not so simple."

She sat back. "Joey gal, nothing worth having ever is. Now I need to tinkle."

I watched as she got up and shuffled toward the ladies' room. Wow, what a tale. I had no idea that my grandfather had lived through all that. No wonder he had radiated such quiet integrity, that he looked after the women in his life. It was a pattern of behavior because of his sister. What had happened to her after she grew up? Had they stayed in touch? Did my mother know anything about this?

The server, a girl who looked to be Dragon's age, set the pizza down in front of me. "Here you go, Ms. Whitmore."

I saw her shoot a glance to where Robin and Dragon were focused on their game. "Do you want as I should go get them for you?"

Great, another waitress hellbent on flirting with the fae. "That's okay…Jillian," I said as I read her name tag. "I'll do it." I needed a break to absorb all that Grammy had told me. Damn, you think you know people but in reality, even with your closest loved ones, you're barely scratching the surface.

I slid out of the chair and wound my way through the tables to where Robin and Dragon were screaming at two-dimensional ghosts and a bow wearing eating machine doing her level best to avoid them.

"Bloody hell," Robin exclaimed as Blinky careened into his Ms. Pacman, costing him a life. "Those bastards are fast."

Dragon laughed and shoulder checked him. "My turn. Let me do as I do."

I touched her shoulder. "Pizza is on the table."

"Cool, I'm starving." Game forgotten—Dragon turned away.

"I demand a rematch," Robin called after her.

"Glad you found something you enjoy." I moved toward the table but Robin caught my arm and dragged me into the shadowed hallway that led to the restrooms.

"What is it?" I glanced around, nervous. Was his mother nearby, poised to strike?

"I was thinking about what you said, earlier."

My brow furrowed as I studied him. "You'll have to be more specific."

He inhaled. "About whether I would bargain with a member of your family for power. And I decided that no, I wouldn't."

"Because it's wrong?" I prompted.

He shook his head. "No. I still don't comprehend the right or wrong bits you are so adamant about. But, I…enjoy them each on their own merits. They are as unique as snowflakes. And I wouldn't want to see them enthralled. Or worse, broken."

I swallowed hard. "What do you mean, broken?"

"Forget I said that. We should go eat." He slipped past me and I was left there, reeling.

Broken. Did he mean physically? Or mentally? Or some combination of the two? By untangling two and a half centuries of Robin's bargains, I had saved countless people from that fate.

But if magic always came with a price, what had that price been?

I thought about my grandmother's story. About how she had seen my grandfather as being a goof. Right up until the moment that the veil had been ripped away and she'd witnessed for herself that he was more than what she'd believed.

I stared at Robin for a long moment, then put those thoughts aside.

They were too dangerous to my peace of mind.

T HE LEVEL ten gymnasts were my least favorite to instruct. Sure, they had the skills. Not just any gymnast would reach level ten. It took years of sacrifice and dedication. There were only four currently enrolled in our program and they were as hardcore as I had been at the same age.

Total cutthroat bitches.

The competition at their stage was fierce. The pressure made many a gymnast give up long before level ten. I had lived it. I knew what it was to have a level ten mindset, and frankly, it wasn't all that healthy or fun to be around. The stress mounted and at their age, every mistake felt like the end of the world. They sniped and snapped and tore each other down to make themselves look better and all of it was just a release valve for the pressure they were under. Not all level tens got that bad. Some of them rose above the pettiness and were in it for love. But at the end of the day, even an elite gymnast is only human.

Alina usually took the reins with this crew. After all, she was the one still in great shape, what with her body being a carb-free, sugar-free, booze-free temple and all. But she had some dental work scheduled so it was on me to handle the mean girls.

And the parents. Oy. Level ten parents were a unique breed of pain-in-the-ass crazy. They expected to see their darlings rise to elite status, to be the next Simone Biles. They demanded perfection for all the countless hours they had spent hauling their cookies to practice and competitions. They were type A's who wanted to see results and threatened to "fire my worthless ass" if they didn't get them.

Never mind that I didn't work for them or their precious darlings.

And kill me now because one of them was my archenemy, Ursula Green.

Many moons ago, the two of us had been friends. Ursula had spent years in gymnastics with me, made her own way up to level ten. She hadn't made it to elite though and had resented me because I had. Add some boy drama and our relationship had never truly recovered.

I'd made overtures to befriend Ursula in recent weeks, extending the invitation to join me and Darcy for Margarita Mondays or Wine Wednesdays. She'd blown me off with a cloud of sneering derision, clearly not ready to put our tumultuous past behind us.

I watched with narrowed eyes as Tammy Wentworth and Ursula's soon-to-be step-daughter, Veronica St. John, snickered as Allison White staggered on the beam. Allison righted herself but their pithy commentary could be heard from across the gym. I saw her cast an embarrassed glance at her spectators, her confidence clearly rattled.

The best thing to do was to separate them. "Veronica, go work the uneven bars. Tammy, do your floor routine please."

"Veronica needs to work the beam."

I turned to discover Ursula had left the designated parent seats, kicked off her shoes, and joined me on the mat. She wore a long turquoise sweater dress that hugged her trim figure and set off her red hair which had faded with age but was still brilliant. She narrowed her green eyes to slits and then added, "A real coach would know that."

"Veronica needs to wait her turn." It took some work to keep my voice calm and level.

"This place is a joke," Ursula looked around with obvious disdain scrawled across her face. "I told Henry that we should hire a private coach for Veronica. It's the only way she'll improve."

I bit my tongue. It wasn't my place to tell Ursula that the best thing Henry St. John could do for his daughter was to find a better female role model for her than Ursula. "Practice is what she needs to improve. The only thing she's been working out tonight is her mouth."

Ursula did a quick once over my body, taking in my cheap yoga pants and hoodie, and raised her voice so that it echoed through the space. "Like you're one to talk."

I didn't respond to her baiting. Even so, Veronica paused in chalking up her hands and Allison hopped off the beam to stare at the two of us. *I wish...*

I slammed the door before the image could manifest. Can't use magic. I could not let my petty desires get the best of me. Even if I did crave nothing more than seeing Ursula take a long walk off a short pier.

"When was the last time you did a full routine anyway?" my nemesis pushed. "Or did anything other than waddle your fat ass from the fridge to the couch and back?"

I rounded on her. Bad enough that she took potshots at me in a neutral setting because of her moldy old grudge. But this was my place of business and those were my students. "Look, Ursula. If you have a problem with me, you can talk to Alina about it, but I would appreciate it if you would show me the respect an elite gymnast deserves in front of her students. Otherwise, I'll have to ask you to leave."

Her hands went to her barely-there hips. "Are you kicking me out?"

Damn it, why did she have to be so difficult? A sick part of me wondered if she had gotten herself engaged to a level ten's father just to torment me. But no, that was crazy.

I moved closer to her and lowered my voice. "These girls need to work. Their parents pay for them to receive the best training they can afford, not to watch the two of us bicker. So yes, if you continue to disrespect me in front of my students, I will have no choice but to ban you from the gym."

Her green eyes narrowed and I saw a flash of something…predatory. It was gone before I could name it. She stepped back and then called out loudly, "I'll be sure to let Alina know what a no-talent hack you are. Come on, Veronica. We're leaving."

"You're not my mom," Veronica shouted.

Despite everything, I felt a moment's pity for Ursula. Much like me, she hadn't had any children of her own. Learning to parent in your forties was no cakewalk, especially when you got saddled with a teenager who wasn't about to let you in without a knock-down-drag-out.

Ursula's nostrils billowed out and I wouldn't have been surprised to see a puff of smoke emanating from them. With a final glare at me, she retrieved her shoes then stalked out of the building and crossed to where her shiny new black Lexus was parked. The vanity plates read, Beeyotch1. Fitting.

I did my best with the level tens for the remainder of their practice time, but my heart wasn't in it. A seed of self-doubt had been planted in fertile soil. I had been good—

that wasn't in question. But was Ursula right? Maybe I was nothing more than a has-been gymnast pretending to know more than I actually did? I wasn't like Alina. I couldn't live and sleep and breathe gymnastics anymore. The drive and determination from my younger years had evaporated. Too many things distracted me, ate away at my focus, tempted me to make choices other than the ones I knew I should make.

I'd eaten too much pizza. I hadn't meant to. But it had been so nice to be out with Grammy and Dragon and even Robin, once he'd stopped talking about the danger his mother posed. It had been such a roller coaster of a day. One slice had turned into three before I'd made a conscious decision to overeat and now all the gooey cheese had congealed in a hard lump in my belly.

I didn't blame my past choices for all the things that had gone wrong anymore. But being my best self in the present was harder than I thought it would be. I didn't want to forgo life's small pleasures the way Ursula did. The way Alina did. I didn't want to be like them because neither of them seemed all that content.

So, what was the answer? How did I manage to work on improving my own beam routine when everything in my life was so decidedly imbalanced?

"Lamb?"

I started and realized that I had been standing alone in the middle of the gym for several minutes. Long enough for the level tens to change and head out and for Robin to appear.

He tilted his head to the side, studying me. "You look pale. What's wrong?"

How to answer that without giving in to the tears that pricked my eyes? Stupid hormones. It had to be some sort of perimenopause action. Nothing else would explain the urge I had to walk over to him, lay my head on his shoulder and sob my heart out while he held me in those strong arms. Because I knew Robin would make me feel better. He always helped me regain perspective, even when he was yanking the rug out from under me.

Instead, I squared my shoulders, lifted my chin, and asked, "Any sign of her?"

He ran a hand through his already disheveled hair. "No. I've circled the town several times. It's so damn frustrating, I can feel her presence nearby. But she's the fae queen for a reason. She can hide who and what she is when it suits her. I just wish I knew what she was doing here."

"Looking for you?" I suggested.

"Andreas would have told her where I am." His eyes narrowed and he looked around the studio. "Are you almost through here?"

"Let me just grab my bag and check the back door." I headed into the office. The door to the rear was always secured, but I triple checked the lock, hit the overhead lights, and then returned to where Robin waited.

He held my bag for me as I locked the front. His sapphire gaze roamed up and down the street. A light mist had begun to form, as the warmth from the ground merged with the steadily dropping ambient temperature. By sunrise, there would be a dense fog covering the town. The streetlamps had come on, helping dispatch the gloom. He led me over to my car and opened the passenger's side door.

"So, what do we do now?" I asked as he settled himself behind the wheel.

"This." Without warning, Robin's hand snaked around the back of my neck and pulled me to him.

Too startled to move, I held still, feeling more like prey

than a woman in the throes of passion. His lips seared mine almost as though he were branding me. It was a hot, intense sort of kiss, much less tender than the first time when I'd gently brushed my lips over his in a delicate exploration. He was hungry for me, and as the shock faded, I responded to that hunger. Matched it with my own. He felt and tasted like an element I'd been desperately missing. The intensity of passion and magic writhed and danced between us like a flame.

His fingers threaded into my hair, untangling it from the loose ponytail until it slipped over my shoulders. His mouth moved on mine and if not for the gearshift, I had the feeling that he would have dragged me onto his lap. Damn gearshift.

His lips left mine long enough for me to gasp in a breath. He nuzzled the side of my face and whispered in my ear, "We're being watched."

"Huh?" My brain was foggier than the ground outside and I didn't have time to process the words before his mouth covered mine once more.

So much pent-up desire, so much need. It bubbled within me like a pot about to boil over. I craved him more than all the sweets, all the sinful pleasures the world had to offer. True, he wasn't good for me, but that only made me want him more. A taste of the forbidden.

Slowly, his words registered. Being watched. Either by Andreas or perhaps the fae queen herself. Someone was out there and the abrupt kiss was only part of the cover between a tricksy fae and his supposed fiancée.

It's not real. My heart squeezed even as my body gave in to the searing pleasure of having Robin smooth his thumb along my jaw as his tongue tangled with mine. He didn't mean the kiss, not really. Just another game.

Well, at least I knew that we were putting on a show. He'd told me. So what if his kiss was not genuinely ardent and possessive? He was protecting me from people who would kill me if they found out I had absconded with his magic. Plus, it felt amazing. It had been a very long time since I had been kissed this way.

Let's face facts. I had never been kissed that way.

I decided to take advantage of it. My hands were busy where they fumbled with the buttons of his shirt, needing to make the fabric part so I could get my hands inside. I had to touch his hot skin, felt drugged by the need for more. *Wish I could feel him.*

There was a series of pinging sounds and Robin jerked back, stared down at his now buttonless garment. "What did you do?"

"What I wanted to." Gripping him by the lapels, I pulled him back to me.

"Joey, stop." He caught my hands before I could lay them on his skin. "There's something you need to know about—"

Someone rapped on the window. I jerked back, my breaths coming out in ragged gasps.

"Who?" Robin's gaze was locked on mine. The windows had fogged up and I could only imagine what whoever was outside of the car would think to find a middle-aged woman and her supposed fiancé necking in public like a couple of randy teens.

"Start the car," I said even as my focus fell to his kiss reddened lips and my tumultuous hormones cried out for more. Delicious. Robin Goodfellow was utterly scrumptious.

And I did have that itty bitty problem with self-denial.

"Do you have the watch?"

"In my gym bag." I reached for it just as the rapping started up again.

Taking a deep breath, I rolled down the window.

And stared at my doom.

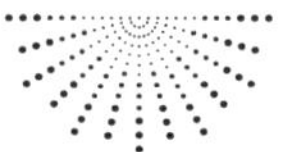

CHAPTER EIGHT

"Trust is more fragile than an egg. An egg can be cooked, but trust, once broken is no damn good to anybody."

-Notable quotable from Grammy B

"Necking in a parked car on Main Street?" My mother paced the length of the kitchen in front of me. My father, having driven her home, sat by my side.

"I didn't think anyone was watching," I flat out lied. Even to my ears, it sounded lame.

She rounded on me. "Is that how you were raised? To make a spectacle in public with a man you barely know, who is gallivanting all over town telling people you are engaged?"

She made that reality sound like a fate worse than a low-carb diet.

"Now Prudence, be reasonable," he said. "Just because you have a chip on your shoulder about marriage doesn't mean the same is true for our daughter. Joey is a grown woman, I'm sure she knows what she's doing."

That makes one of us. I put a hand over his and squeezed. While I appreciated my father's show of support, I did not have the first clue what I was doing. I felt the watch in the pocket of my hoodie and the urge to spin it backward until I could return to that all-consuming kiss was almost too great to withstand.

At the very least, I wanted to fast forward through this awkward conversation.

My mother thrust an accusing finger at me even as she rounded on my father. "She was behaving like a teenager! I expect this sort of behavior from Dragon, not you."

"Dragon is much too classy to make out in a parked car," I interrupted.

"Not helping," my father muttered. Then he got to his feet and gripped my mother by the shoulders. "Sweetheart, if we could speak in private—"

"There's nothing to discuss," my mother huffed and folded her arms over her breasts. "Joey tried marriage and it didn't take."

I flinched.

"Now, Prudence." Dad gestured to her art studio.

His tone took me aback. My father was mild-mannered and usually never pushed my mother on anything. She called the shots and he went amicably along. I looked to her to see how she would react. She gaped at him. Clearly, I wasn't the only one surprised by his tone. My mother opened her mouth, then closed it again, shook her head, and stormed ahead of him. He gave me a wan smile and then followed. The door shut and I heard the snick of a lock.

I grimaced. Not wanting to hear whatever it was they were about to say—and do— I slipped outside and sat on the back steps. A moment later, a figure emerged from the shadows.

"Hey," I said. "I was wondering where you scurried off to."

Robin seated himself beside me. "Family arguments are not in my wheelhouse. I thought it more prudent to make myself scarce."

"I would have done the same if I could." I smiled and shook my head. "Sometimes it's easy to forget that I'm an adult. Especially when those two are in the room."

A steady spring breeze that smelled of damp moss picked up and I shivered.

Robin turned to face me, a frown on his face. "Cold?"

When I nodded, he doffed his coat and draped it around my shoulders. The heavy wool smelled clean and woodsy with just a hit of the spice that made up his unique scent. I wanted to bundle myself up in it and fall asleep, breathing him in.

He sighed. "Are they going to insist that I leave?"

"What?" I raised a brow. "Why would they?"

"They seem upset." He looked out into the night. "They really care about you."

"Of course they do. They may be melodramatic nutjobs, but they're my parents."

"You say that like it's so easy." He shot me an indecipherable look and there was no hint of his standard amused tone.

"Like you can just take their love and caring for granted. Like nothing you could ever do would cause it to end."

I studied him for a long minute. "Robin, that's how real love works."

He picked at a hangnail. "In our training to make bargains, we—the fae children— we're taught to use a mortal's loved ones to our advantage. Love is a weakness for us to exploit and use to trap humans into accepting our bargains."

I shivered and it had nothing to do with the cold. "Don't your people love their children?"

He shook his head. "It's not the same. Offspring are supposed to siphon power for the tribe. Make better trades, win better slaves."

I flinched.

He cast me a sidelong look. "I know that aspect troubles you."

"I don't like the idea of being used. Or of using others. It's wrong." Frustration filled me. "Can't you see that?"

"I'm beginning to." His brow crinkled. "When I think of another fae tricking you or your grandmother or Dragon under their thrall or making a bargain… it's not a pleasant feeling, Joey."

A lump formed in my throat. "That's what it's like when you care about people."

He'd come so far. The spoiled fae prince who'd lived for nothing more than his next bargain and the power it brought him. He was making friends. Entangling himself in my life and seeing his past behavior differently.

He was silent for a time. "Are you sorry?"

I blinked in surprise. "Sorry? About what?"

"That your parents discovered us in a compromising position."

I snorted. "Believe me, my parents have enough of their own drama to dwell on." As if to punctuate my words something broke inside. "Another ceramic dick bites the dust."

He frowned at the house. "Aren't you going to stop them?"

"Dear god no. This is only the prelude."

When he looked at me quizzically, I added, "They are only fighting for an excuse to have make-up sex."

Robin grinned. "And you know this…why?"

I clapped my hands on my knees and stood up. "Oh no, there are some childhood traumas I am not going to share."

After removing his coat, I handed it back to him. "No worries, you haven't worn out your welcome. So don't skulk around out here all night, okay?"

It was on the tip of my tongue to invite him to my room. So we could finish what we'd started. But the lust was banked once more and it was so much easier to get carried away with his hands on my body than it was to just proposition him.

Besides, it was all an act because someone had been watching. Not genuine desire. No wonder he had stopped me when I tried to touch him. He hadn't been lost to sensual pleasure the way I was. Maybe I should be embarrassed about that, but I wasn't.

He was beautiful, sensual and the way he made me feel was utterly addictive.

Robin took the coat then looked up at me. "About before—"

I held up both hands. "I know, it was part of the cover story. No genuine emotional attachment."

His lips parted and he appeared stunned. "And that's what you believe?"

"That's what it is." I shrugged. "Night."

I ran a cool shower, doing my level best to calm my raging hormones. It didn't work, not entirely. Part of me wanted to take Grammy's advice, to slip into his room, between his sheets.

What would he do if I did? Would he insist that I leave? Or would he kiss me for real?

I shut off the water and slipped into my bathrobe. I paused in the hallway outside his door. There was no light visible beneath it. Maybe he was asleep. Or maybe he was lying there, wishing that I would come to him and finish what we had started. Heart pounding, I turned the knob and pushed the door inward.

The bed was neatly made with no sign of Robin. He must have gone back out to patrol for his mother.

Disappointed, I shut the door and padded down the hall to my bedroom. It was probably for the best that I hadn't found him there. We wanted different things. Robin wanted his magic back and me....

I wanted to be loved. Cherished. The same way my grandmother and mother were by the men in their lives. Flaws and all. Not used because of some magical bargain gone awry.

I slithered into bed and shut off the light, too exhausted to think.

The dream consumed me whole. In it, I still wore my fleecy PJs with the clouds on them. The colors were just as vivid as they were in real life. I was the only speck of color in any direction. There was no sound, no hum of climate control, no feel of wind or scent of anything. Yet I sensed a presence. All around me the world was gray and shrouded in fog. No breathing or sounds of footsteps and yet I could feel eyes on me. I turned in a circle and called out, "Hello?"

Then the fog parted and she appeared. A gown that seemed to be formed from the mist itself swathed her lithe body. Strands of colorless spiderweb silk rippled with her movements. The gown wrapped around her throat and slithered over her pert breasts, down over perfectly rounded hips, and then split at the juncture of her trim thighs. Little dewdrops clung to the ethereal fabric, barely preserving her modesty.

Her blonde hair fell in a waterfall of molten gold from the crown that seemed to be made from glittering stardust. And her eyes….

Sapphires. But instead of the amused heat, I recognized in Robin's gaze, hers were icy. Cold.

My heart pounded a frantic tattoo. An early warning system. This could only be the faery queen.

She walked around me in a slow circle, the mist parting for her every step. She was shorter than me by several inches yet it felt as if she loomed over me. When she spoke, her voice tinkled like the chime of silver bells.

"You are the human woman who ruined my son." Her tone left no doubt that she found me less than impressive.

I licked suddenly dry lips. "He came to me. Made me a bargain."

"And yet somehow, you have managed to ensnare him. Tell me, mortal, what magic do you possess?"

My heart rate increased and I balled my hands into fists to keep from wiping my sweaty palms and displaying my nervousness. I wasn't sure what it was about her that unsettled me so. Maybe the outfit, maybe the demeanor. Maybe the fact that she had nothing but sneering disdain for me.

"I have no magic."

"Liar," she purred. "Just because I cannot speak a lie doesn't mean I will fall for one. I can sense an untruth even as it leaves your lips. You do have power, I feel it, even here. Are you a mortal witch? Have you ensnared my son through one of your crafty traps?"

"Robin is with me because he wants to be," I said, ignoring the fact that she had called me a witch. "And because I want him to be."

She tilted her head and for a moment I thought she would call me a liar again. Instead, she spoke a soft promise. "I will have all of your secrets, Josephine Louise Whitmore. And when I do, I will have my son back where he belongs. This I vow. A little token, to remember me."

Her hand slashed out and only at the last second did I see that her nails had morphed into silver and black thorns. I flinched back, raising my arm up to cover my face as she made a swipe that could have taken my eye….

A scream tore from my throat and I rocketed up out of bed, gasping and fighting for breath.

A tapping sound on the door. "Joey? Is everything all right?"

Robin. It took another minute for me to suck in enough air to croak, "Yeah."

A pause. "Can I come in?"

Moving on shaky legs, I made my way over to the door.

Robin stood in the hall, one of my recently folded bath towels wrapped around his hips. Another was in his hand, which clearly he had been in the process of using to dry his hair. Any other time, I would have goggled at the sheer perfection of his body. Not an extra ounce of fat anywhere. Nothing but smooth, tan skin. But dark circles had formed under those sapphire eyes and his shoulders drooped with obvious exhaustion.

"Lamb?" He made a move to come closer. "What's wrong?"

I blocked the entrance with the door. "Nothing. It was just a nightmare."

His gaze studied my face. "Are you sure?"

I forced a smile. "Positive. Too much weirdness plus too many carbs. That's all."

His lips parted and he looked as though he wanted to say something.

And I couldn't hear it. Because I desperately wanted to drag him into my room and have him comfort me until I stopped shaking. So I murmured, "It's late."

Again he probed my face. "In that case, I will see you in the morning."

He moved away toward the guest room and I shut the door, then turned my back on it. My knees gave out and I sank to the floor, my body trembling from my gray and brown roots to my chipped red toenail polish.

Slowly, ever so slowly, I held my left arm up in front of my face. Five deep gashes had rent the blue and white flannel to shreds. Blood oozed from the scrapes in my skin until it dripped in silent condemnation onto the hardwood floor.

"Shit just got real," I whispered.

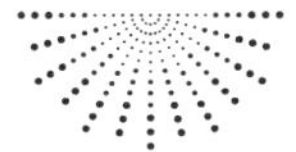

CHAPTER NINE

Men and women are different. Forget that at your own risk.

-Notable quotable from Grammy B

I headed down to breakfast, sore and spooked, and more than just a little bit cranky from my sleepless night. At least there was no yoga to torture me.

I found my mother in the dining room, looking more relaxed than I'd seen her in a while as she put price tags on items for the upcoming garage sale.

"Morning," she said. "Coffee's fresh."

I peered around the kitchen door. "Where's Robin?"

"He went into the office with your father." She bobbed her head.

"About last night," I hedged.

She held up a hand. "No, I'm sorry. It was wrong of me to take out my frustrations on you. If he truly makes you happy, you should be with Robin. Though a little more discretion is in order."

And what could I say to that? I paused at the stack of old records. "Do we even own a record player anymore?"

"I think it was broken. These were my father's."

"I remember." Grandpappy had a massive record collection. When I'd been young, I had curled up on his lap and listened to Black Beauty almost every Sunday after church.

She sighed. "Things like this are the hardest to get rid of."

"Then why do it?" I asked. "Keep stuff if it makes you happy."

She shook her head. "No. it really doesn't. I wish it did. I wish I cared enough to get the player fixed, but if I'm honest, I will go into it with the best of intentions and then never get around to it. It's just someone else's belongings."

"Maybe you're right." Still, I snagged Black Beauty out of the pile. "I'm keeping this one."

She nodded and I took my record into the kitchen to get some liquid life, aka coffee. Mug full, I headed out to the porch. The day promised to be warm and sunny with temperatures promising to top out around sixty. The perfect spring morning did little to help me past the awfulness from the night before. Had I been dreaming? And if so, how had my arm gotten scratched?

I pulled up the sleeve of my hoodie and stared at the red marks. They hadn't bled for long, but that didn't make the encounter any less unnerving. It was said if you die in your dreams, you die in real life. I wanted to go to Robin, to show him what had happened, but at the same time, I didn't think I could handle any more surprises without a total mental breakdown.

My cell chirped and I fished it out of my back pocket. Darcy's face flashed across the screen. I swiped and then held the device to my ear. "What's up?"

"The whole town is talking about you getting married." Darcy's high-pitched voice had hit a new octave. "Are you out of your ever-lovin' mind?"

A slow steady throbbing had started behind my left eye. "You know I'm not. It's part of the whole Robin ruse thing."

"And what about you making out in public? Irma Getz told Mike that your parents caught you getting hot and heavy with a certain out of town hottie in your car."

Crap. "We were being watched."

"Yeah, you were. The way I hear it, more people were digging you getting busy on Main Street than the total viewership of Disney Plus and Netflix last night. So, is he circumcised?"

"*What?*" The word came out louder than I intended. Across the street, Old Man Tate paused in his steady back and forth rocking chair action to glare at me.

Darcy had no shame. "Well, you know, being that he's from a magical land and all. Inquiring minds want to know if he was born with perfect bait and tackle or is his trouser snake sporting a sweater?"

"Robin has a theory that women who are sexually frustrated are more susceptible to being enthralled by the fae." Don't ask me what devil provoked me to say it. Other than I didn't want to speculate about the wardrobe choice for Robin's pants python with her. It was way too early and I was way too sober for such a discussion.

Silence on the other end.

"Darce? Hello?"

Then a quiet sniffle followed with, "Mike and I haven't had sex for a month."

"What?" I frowned. No way. Darcy and her hubby had an amazing sex life, which she told me about in excruciating detail. There were days I had trouble looking Mike in the eye because the vivid picture Darcy had drunkenly painted had seared itself into my gray matter.

"I don't think he wants me anymore," she sobbed.

"Oh honey, you know that's not true. Mike worships the scorched Earth you stride over in your do-me boots."

"Well, why isn't he doing me then?"

I scrambled for a valid reason that would soothe her. "Maybe he's having performance issues. You know men are stupid and secretive about that."

Her voice had regained its cutting edge. "And you know this, how? From all the middle-aged men you've been shagging?"

I ignored the barb. "I read. And quit changing the subject. You won't know unless you talk to him about it."

"Talk is one thing. I need action before my lady bits shrivel up and blow away in a stiff breeze." She sighed theatrically.

"Get a sitter," I suggested. Darcy had a digital database full of babysitters she employed regularly to help watch her kids while she worked from home.

"A sitter comes *here*. Where my bed and lube are located. I need someone who will take the boys away for a few so I can get my freak on."

"It's not…" I trailed off as a familiar SUV pulled up behind the house. "Crap, Darce, I need to go."

"No, Joey, wait a—"

I cut her off and then stowed the phone, rising to meet the fae male who emerged from the SUV.

"Robin's not here," I told Andreas.

His green eyes glittered like newly polished emeralds. "Actually, I'm here for you."

No, that didn't sound ominous at all. "What can I do for you?"

His grin turned wicked as he perused my body. "I wanted to apologize for frightening you yesterday. I was curious, you see. You aren't Robin's usual type."

"What is his type?" Damn my knack for speaking without thinking. I didn't want to know.

"Pretty much what you would expect. Leggy, young, and empty-headed. The opposite of you."

"Thanks?" It came out as a question because I wasn't sure it was a compliment.

"I can definitely see the appeal of a more…seasoned mortal. Especially one who radiates such a curious mix of experience and insecurity. You're brimming with passion and power Josephine Louise Whitmore and I find I am drawn to both." He took a step closer to illustrate his point.

My heart rate kicked up. Not the way it did for Robin, but out of self-preservation. I stumbled a few steps, putting distance between us and raising my hands in the universal stay back motion. Warding off one fae's advances was plenty. Andreas was the bridge too far. "I really wish people would stop using my full name."

"Who else has?" Those emerald eyes drifted to my

scratched arm, which I had forgotten to re-cover. When his gaze locked with mine, I saw the knowledge there. "So, you've met *her*." The last word was coated in bitterness.

I didn't speak, afraid anything I said or did would give Andreas more insight that he would use it against me and Robin.

He studied me for a beat, seeming to make up his mind about something. "Our mother is evil incarnate. And for the last two hundred and fifty years, Robin has been her whipping boy."

I flinched and Andreas noticed. "Do you know anything about this?"

"He never said anything…." my words trailed off. No, he hadn't really. But he had hinted that his childhood was far from picture-perfect.

Wait a second. "Did you say two hundred and fifty years?"

He smirked. "Right around the time, you agreed to be his anchor. In a way, all of the abuse he's suffered—the scorn, the rages because her most powerful son and heir had been trapped and unable to bargain for what we needed—was really your fault."

My mouth had gone dry and I shook my head. "That wasn't my intent."

His tone was cold as he murmured, "Magic always comes with a price. Someone has to pay up."

"Stay back." I took another step toward the safety of the house. If he was planning to exact some sort of revenge, I wouldn't hesitate to wish him off a cliff, price be damned.

Andreas put his hands up. "I'm not going to harm my brother's little mortal. I'm here to enlist your help."

"My help?"

"Yours and Robin's. After all, any mortal who can outfox a fae prince is clearly worth the trouble." Again with that sensual once over.

Robin looked at me the same way, as though he saw something when he looked at me that was brave and powerful. Even before I had his magic. Being a middle-aged, overweight woman, I'd gotten used to being overlooked by society, especially by handsome men. Having gorgeous fae princes size me up like they wanted to strip me to my skin and sex me up for hours on end was a heady rush.

But that thrill was what got you into trouble in the first place, the sensible shrew piped up.

I hated when she was right. Kicking my wayward thoughts back into the gutter where they belonged, I refocused on his request. "And what exactly is it you need our help with?"

"Overthrowing the queen." His eyes were clear and steady, all signs of seduction gone. "You don't know what it costs me to say that. Or what the penalty would be for me if she knew I was here."

Recalling those cold, pitiless eyes I had a decent image in my head of how dangerous a failed insurrection might prove to be for Andreas.

"We've wanted to be rid of her for hundreds of years now. But she is too powerful and has a way of dividing and conquering. With a mortal anchor and soon to be bride, Robin is out of her grip. No more bargains are required to keep him free of her. He can help me. If you can convince him to do it."

My lips parted but before I could decide how to respond, Andreas bent at the waist in a courteous, old-fashioned gesture. "Just think it through, Josephine Louise Whitmore. Talk to Robin. I will check in with you later."

He turned and climbed back behind the wheel of the SUV, backed up until he could turn around, and drove off.

My shoulders slumped in relief as the SUV's taillights disappeared. Too many fae. And me with no idea how to deal with any of them. What had once been a quiet mountain town was now brimming with supernatural beings who wielded magic.

And I was one of them.

ALINA DIDN'T SAY anything to me about the run-in with Ursula the night before. Clearly, my nemesis had not brought the altercation to my boss's notice. It should have made me feel better but I worried that Ursula had something even worse up her sleeve. The morning classes went by in a flurry of activity. I was just finishing up with the pre-K group when the bell over the door jingled. I looked up to see Robin approach. He carried a paper sack and the scent of garlic and herbs wafted enticingly from it.

"Your father told me Italian is your favorite," Robin smiled. "I thought we could have a picnic lunch since it's so fine out."

I looked to Alina, who nodded. "Just be back for the after-school lessons."

After snagging my coat and bag, we headed out to the town greenway which sat about a block away from the gym. Several people walked dogs along the paved trail and I greeted each one by name as we wound our way through the battered picnic tables by the duck pond.

No ducks today. But the ice had melted and sunlight sparkled on the water. Someone was fishing on the far end. Ignoring the benches, I lowered myself onto a flat-topped rock. After a moment's consideration, Robin copied my movement.

He passed me the bag and I peeked in to find two meatball subs, one with cheese and one without. My father really had divvied up my preferences.

"This is nice," I said, unwrapping my cheese-free sub. "Thank you."

He nodded and we ate in silence for a time, watching the wind ripple the surface of the water. I didn't want to kill the tranquil moment so I stalled. "What's it like, working with my father?"

Robin frowned and thought about it. "A bit tedious. So much paperwork and pointless phone calls. But overall it's not an unpleasant way to spend a few hours. And I do enjoy finding all the legal loopholes."

"You would." I grinned and touched his arm lightly to take the sting out of my words.

His hand crept up and lay over the top of mine, entwining our fingers. A glance at his face stole my breath. He stared down at our joined hands, his eyebrows pulled together tightly.

"You look baffled."

"Explain this to me," he all but ordered.

"What?" I asked, a bit breathless. That electrical connection flowed between the two of us yet again.

"This need I have to touch you." He frowned. "It's not

sexual. At least not entirely. But it's a want that I find I can't ignore. And when I do touch you like this…."

I held my breath, almost afraid to hear what he was going to say.

"It eases something within me." He looked up. "Can you explain what it is?"

"It's companionship. Caring. Affection." I bit my lip. "Don't you ever just enjoy being with someone, Robin?"

"Just you," he murmured. "Only ever you."

A puff of air escaped. He was centuries old. How had he never shared a sweet and tender moment with anyone before?

The look in his eyes was intense. He watched me closely, not in that predatory way, but more of a thoughtful manner. As if he were weighing the possibility of kissing me again.

Extracting my hand, I put a little distance between us. "I need to talk to you about something."

"If it's about last night," he began.

"No, yes. Well, it's not what you're thinking." I pressed my lips together to stop the inane flow of babble.

He reached for my face and swept his thumb along my cheekbone. "Tell me what's on your mind, lamb?"

I wanted to come clean. To tell him about my freaky dream that had ended in bloodied scratches and what Andreas had said. But I also was afraid of spoiling the moment. Robin appeared peaceful, his sapphire eyes had lost the wariness, the cold detachment that had always banked his heat. It did my heart good to see him relax for a change.

Would telling him about what was going on steal that ease from him? I didn't want to break whatever was growing between us.

So instead, I changed the subject. "I have classes until six tonight, but after, I was thinking that maybe after school you could come with me and Dragon to the shelter and pick out a dog?"

He raised our joined hands to his lips. "I would like nothing more."

We returned to our respective places of business. The afternoon flew by, a busy wave of young girls practicing for an upcoming regional competition. The competition would be Alina's first showing and our students needed to be as ready as they could be. Little Mikaela was rocking it, sticking every landing as though her feet were superglued to the floor. A few of the others had wrinkles to iron out, but otherwise, I felt as if we were going to show up in a big way.

My mother and Dragon appeared at ten after six, and I waved to Alina that I was heading out. "How's garage sale prep coming?"

"There's still so much to do," My mother flapped her hands. "I can't believe I agreed to this."

Neither could I. She wasn't an animal person, had never liked the mess or the demands required of pet owners. I'd never had a pet as a child. With gymnastics, there had been no way I could have convinced her that I would be able to give an animal all that it required. Grammy B always had cats and I liked dogs. Maybe this would be okay.

"I asked Robin to come with us," I said.

"Is it true you two are engaged?" Dragon asked.

My gaze whipped to her. "How...?"

"Mrs. Beasly, the lady who works the lunch line, said to pass on her congratulations."

Of course, she did. Darcy hadn't been kidding that the

whole town was abuzz with the gossip. Well, one thing was for sure. Rain or shine, the garage sale was going to be a huge hit tomorrow because every gossip for fifty miles would be popping in to get the skinny on the happy couple.

"It's complicated," I told Dragon.

"Mrs. Beasly said that the electrician was coming out to wire the cottage so that you and Robin could live out there together after the wedding."

"Mrs. Beasly needs to get a life and stop speculating on mine." It amazed me how quickly the winds had shifted. In less than a month I had gone from being an object of pity—that poor Joey Whitmore who'd washed out of her gymnastics career before she'd ever taken off—to the woman who was engaged to a handsome stranger.

Emphasis on the strange.

We strode across the street. Robin was seated in Edith's chair. He grinned when he saw us and stood to retrieve his coat. "Ladies. Are we ready for a new adventure?"

"What's going on?" My father emerged from his office. He and my mother exchanged a long look. She blushed and looked away while the rest of us pretended not to see.

Except for Robin who stared in open fascination.

I elbowed him in the ribs.

He shook himself. "We are off to look for a dog. I thought a bit of security was in order. Three beautiful women living on their own ought to have some security."

"But you're living there, right?" My father frowned at Robin.

I winced. This was why I hadn't wanted my family to hear about our phony engagement. It would be up to me to explain why Robin was gone to all of them after he got his magic back and headed for the hills.

I hope that day never comes. The thought was there and gone in an instant. That didn't count as a wish, did it? I hadn't wished it. Hopes and wishes were two different things. And I wasn't even sure what I was hoping for. That I wouldn't have to explain. Or that Robin would never leave.

Oblivious to my distress, my family continued to debate about the reason for our outing.

"Extra protection." Robin clarified. "Would you care to come with us, Paul? I'm sure the ladies would appreciate your insight."

"Well, I'd have to close up the office…." My dad hedged.

"Your calendar is completely clear." Robin winked at me. "Why not be a rebel, just this once."

"I guess I could…just this once. If you would like." My father cast a look at my mother.

"That would be nice." She smiled shyly.

"Then it's settled," Robin nodded. "Lamb, let's take your car and everyone else can take Paul's."

"I saw what you did back there," I said to Robin when we were on the road headed out to the animal shelter.

He feigned innocence. "I have no idea what you're talking about."

"Extra protection? For a couple of women who typically leave the door unlocked?" A habit my father detested and griped about constantly. But he was originally from a city where my mother and I had been small-town girls for our entire lives.

"You told him what he needed to hear to get on board with the plan."

He flashed me a grin. "That obvious, was it?"

Only because I was beginning to recognize his methods. "Out of curiosity, how did you spin it to my mother?"

"That it would be good company for Dragon."

I shook my head. "So manipulative."

He cast me a devilish smirk. "I only use my powers for good these days, lamb."

My heart lurched. I desperately wanted to believe him. When he wasn't being the sly fae prince always on the lookout for a bargain, Robin Goodfellow was the kind of guy a woman could fall for.

To distract myself from that dangerous line of thought I asked, "Is there anything special I should be on the lookout for when it comes to picking a familiar? And why do I need a dog instead of a cat?"

Robin chose to answer the second question first. "Mostly because cats are notoriously self-sufficient. You need a companion who will ruthlessly protect you."

I slid him a sideways gaze. "We're not going to sacrifice the poor creature, right?"

He let out an exasperated sounding breath. "Just when I believe I'm making headway with you. No, Josephine. We are not doing any sort of ritual sacrifice. That's dark magic."

"We need to ground and siphon off some of the magic that's coursing through you. To do that you need a familiar and a purpose."

"I have a purpose. I'm a gymnastics instructor."

"A magical purpose," he clarified. "To be a force for good."

"Wait, aren't you trying to figure out how to get these powers *back*?" I don't know that I wanted to set up a shingle as a full-time faery godmother. Teaching Dragon to drive was about the extent of my public service capacity.

He shrugged. "These things take time."

I was about to argue but the shelter was up ahead on the left.

"As for the canine, your familiar will choose you." Robin popped the car door and unfolded himself from the seat.

My hands clenched on the steering wheel. How had this happened? A week ago I was happy. Well, more or less. Sure, maybe I dreaded Robin's return and lost a little sleep wondering what sort of vengeance he would extract. Now here I sat, about to let a shelter dog choose me so I could siphon off magic I didn't want and had nocturnal visits from pissed-off fae queens and was being semi-stalked by one fae prince while living with another.

Life was just weird.

Robin opened my mother's car door for her and offered her his hand. I saw my father frown as she smiled and took his hand. That sort of gallant gesture usually sent my mother into a full-blown feminist rant. When Robin handed her off to my dad though, Paul Blackthorn didn't question it, simply took shameless advantage of her docile acceptance.

Dragon was already on the pavement, bouncing up and down on her toes, her enthusiasm markedly childlike.

"Coming Joey?" My mother called over her shoulder.

"Here goes nothing," I said and got out of the car.

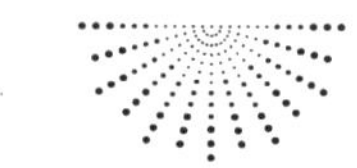

CHAPTER TEN

"You can't squeeze water from a stone. But sure as shootin', you can find a new place to dig your well."

-Notable quotable from Grammy B

"You've got to be kidding me," I grumbled as Georgia —aka my ex—sashayed up to us. Her smile was wide as she took in the motley crew that made up my immediate family, plus one fae prince.

"Joey, so good to see you," Georgia said in her trademark husky voice. She wore a blue smock over an oversized gold sweater and stylishly ripped skinny jeans. Her size eleven feet were encased in Ugg boots which didn't seem practical for either an animal shelter or the spring mud but looked hella comfy.

"Hey," I mumbled. It was weak, but seeing Georgia unexpectedly always threw me for a loop.

"Word around town is that you're getting married again." Her grin stretched ear to ear. "And this must be the lucky fellow."

She turned her full thousand-watt smile onto Robin, who took her hand and brought it to his lips. "What a charmer."

No, there was nothing at *all* weird about watching my phony fiancé, kiss my ex on the hand.

"What are you doing here, Georgia?" My mother offered her a warm smile.

"I volunteer several days a week." Her gaze was still locked on Robin, a frown marring her delicate brow. "Have we met?"

"I'm positive I would remember an enchantress such as yourself." Robin laid it on thick.

I scowled. I knew for a fact I'd introduced the two of them in one very awkward encounter at the diner. So why couldn't Georgia remember Robin from before the way Dragon could? Must be part of the whole cosmic checks and balances thing having to do with alternate timelines.

"We're here to adopt a dog," Dragon said to Georgia.

"You've come to the right place. Let me check in the office and I'll see who we have that's ready." My ex clapped her perfectly manicured hands together and grinned. "Joey, why don't you come with me. I know Ruby Sue would be delighted to see you."

"I seriously doubt it." Ruby Sue had been part of Ursula's gang back in high school. I knew she worked at the animal shelter but hadn't seen her since she returned to town a few months ago.

Robin bumped his shoulder against mine. "Go on, lamb. We'll wait here."

Not having much of a choice without being outright rude, I followed Georgia through a door labeled employees only.

The office was mostly a warehouse of crates and a bookshelf that held a ton of file folders. A battle-scarred table was shoved up against one wall with an ancient PC perched atop it. The thing even had a tower that was plugged in via a bright orange extension cord that snaked around the far wall to the nearest outlet. The ground was the same dark gray concrete as the rest of the building. Cold with a few cracks from where the ground had shifted and the foundation had given way.

Ruby Sue was on the phone and, to my surprise, her face lit when she caught sight of me. She held up one finger, indicating that I stay put while she dealt with whoever was on the line.

Georgia nudged me in the ribs. "I am so thrilled for you. He is absolutely dreamy."

I shifted from foot to foot, unable to meet her gaze. "Thanks."

"I mean that accent," she fanned herself dramatically. "To die for!"

"Let's hope not." My hand wrapped automatically over the bandage on my arm.

Georgia wasn't listening, a trait that had carried over from before. "You don't even know how great it is to see you with someone. I didn't think—" Her bubblegum pink lips pressed together.

"Think what?" I tilted my head to one side.

"Never mind. It's not important." One hand flitted up in the air as though to dismiss whatever thought had barged in.

It clicked. Her ecstatic gushing and air that smacked distinctly of relief. "You never thought I'd find someone else."

"No, no," she said. Maybe I had been spending too much time with Robin, but I recognized the lie for what it was.

That stung. I tried to come up with something to say that would make the situation less awkward. Nothing came to mind so we stood together in uncomfortable silence and waited for Ruby Sue to finish her call.

She set down her phone and closed her eyes. When she opened them once more she wore the look of a woman who had been given a bitter pill that she would be forced to swallow but still had to soldier on. "Joey, it's been ages."

She surprised me when she extracted herself from a dilapidated office chair that was more duct-tape than padding and wound through the clutter in the office, dirty blond ponytail swaying with each step. I spotted fine lines around her eyes and mouth. The kind that a woman developed from laughing with her head thrown back and spending plenty of time outdoors. She looked healthy as opposed to stylish and there was an air of contentment around her.

Then her strong arms drew me into a hug that felt one hundred percent genuine for all that it was a first.

Ruby Sue pulled back, her gaze sweeping me from head to toe. "How have you been? You know I saw you in the market a few weeks back. I was in a rush so I didn't get a chance to say hey. And I hear you're getting married. How exciting! When's the wedding?"

"Um, we haven't really made any plans yet." Crap, I hadn't

considered the depth of this fib. Weddings required things like dates and venues, guest lists, and cake. I was on board with the cake but the rest, not so much. To take the attention off me I asked, "Is something the matter?"

Sadness filled Ruby Sue's brown eyes. "That was the county budget commissioner. We're being shut down."

"What?" Georgia's hands flew to her trim hips. "How can they do that?"

"Lack of funding." Exhaustion wafted from Ruby Sue as she rubbed a hand over her face. "The writing was on the wall. Tourism is down, which means many of the small businesses are struggling, which means a smaller tax base. And we're not a top priority."

"I'm sorry about your job," I said, though I didn't know why Georgia was so upset since she was only a volunteer.

"It's more than just the job," Ruby Sue leaned on her desk, ignoring the hodgepodge piles of paperwork that teetered ominously. "This is the only no-kill shelter in the county."

"Without us, all the animals will most likely be destroyed." Georgia's tone was grim.

I sucked in a sharp breath. "Can't we find them homes?" The question sounded painfully naïve.

"Even if we could place all the dogs and cats here, which would be nothing short of a miracle, what about in the future? Strays, people who are forced to surrender their pets due to circumstances and relocations," Ruby Sue shrugged. "It's a huge job, even in a small community. And it's one no one wants to pay for."

"Half the time, Ruby Sue spends her own paycheck buying food and medicine for our animals," Georgia said.

That didn't sound like the stuck-up cheerleader I remembered at all. Then again, I wasn't the same stuck-up gymnast I'd once been either.

"I'm sorry." It seemed like the only appropriate thing to say. "Please, if there's anything I can do to help, let me know."

"Well, you can do what it is you came here to do in the first place." Georgia nudged me. "Adopt a critter. Was it a dog you said you wanted?"

I nodded mutely and Ruby Sue turned and went fishing on her desk. She handed me a blank form that had **Pet Adoption Agreement** printed across the top in bold font. "Why don't you fill out what you can. If you need a good vet I'll recommend one down the mountain who volunteers here twice a month. Volunteered." She corrected, but the slip didn't seem to upset her as much as it did me.

"Not Pete Green?" I asked.

"Hell no," Georgia huffed. "Not only does Pete overcharge for basics, but then you have to deal with the gorgon in the front office."

"Ursula's not so bad," Ruby Sue said diplomatically.

I just snorted. "Do you have a pen?"

Fifteen minutes later, we stood in front of the cages of the most ragtag group of animals I had ever seen. It wasn't as depressing as some of those tear-your-heart-out ASPCA commercials where all the pups gave the camera sad eye while that Sarah McLachlan song shredded your soul. But it wasn't much better.

My father and mother stood in front of one cage where a small white terrier mix stood on her hind legs turning herself inside out. Dragon was practically glued to a big black dog of indeterminant breed whose tongue lolled out in ecstasy as she scratched his ears. And Robin….

Robin was looking at me.

"What's wrong, lamb?"

"I can't choose." How could I, when by doing so I would be leaving all the rest to their fate? And never mind the cats. There were at least ten of them and we weren't even considering a cat, a fact which the felines seemed to sense. Their little glares bore daggers into my back.

Robin put a hand on my shoulder. "You're not supposed to choose, remember? Let the animal familiar choose you."

"How?" My emotions were volatile, my hormones rocketing out of control. Any second I would burst into tears and run sobbing out into the street.

"Close your eyes," he prompted. "Feel their auras."

"What does an aura feel like?" It sounded almost as though I were setting myself up for a lewd joke.

"Close your eyes."

I did and then sighed as Robin's hand moved up to the back of my neck. I shivered slightly as that spark sizzled through me when our skin touched. He seemed oblivious as he gently massaged the tense muscles as he continued to explain. "Each aura is different, unique. In humans, the aura is oftentimes confused. It gets muddied by more earthly concerns, but animal auras are pure. Find one that says protector or defender to you."

My head bobbed in rhythm with his ministrations. I tried to do what Robin advised. Nothing happened. "I don't think it's working."

His hand fell away. "You need to look outside of your own feelings of being judged by others."

My lids lifted and turned to face him. "What are you talking about?"

"Joey, come see this guy." Dragon was clearly in love with the big lummox dog who was drooling all over her jeans.

"In a minute, sweets." I dragged Robin into the corner and rounded on him. "Tell me what you meant."

His sapphire eyes searched my face. "Exactly what it is I said. You allow the perception of others to color your reality. You fret over what your mother thinks, and Alina and even your ex." He cast a speaking glance to where Georgia and Ruby Sue stood conferring with one another. "It's time to grow up and see things for yourself, with none of the shadows others cast. Your vision is clear, Joey. Trust yourself to see."

My lips parted. Was Robin right? I had promised myself that I would move forward with my life, to stop hanging my identity on who I had been. But had I fallen into another sort of trap? One where I let other people tell me who I was instead of being myself?

The thought of Ursula in the gym, calling me a lazy fat ass popped into my head. Yeah, okay, I totally did that. And why? Ursula was clearly unhappy, so why would I give her the power to undermine my confidence?

I squeezed Robin's hand and then whispered, "Thanks."

His smile was dazzling. "My pleasure."

My eyes slid shut once more and I listened to the animals around us. Each was unique, original, one of a kind. Behind my closed lids, I saw colors. Red for anger and frustration, a sickly yellow tinged with fear, blue for loyalty, green for trust….there.

With my eyes still closed, I allowed my feet to take me forward until I stopped before the sheer white light. My protector, my defender.

I opened my eyes and crouched down. "Well, hello there. You want to come home with me, boy?"

A steady thump of a tail. I smiled. "This one," I called out.

"You have got to be kidding." my mother said. "That creature looks like he's on his last legs. And a mutant to boot."

True, the dog who lay sprawled on the concrete floor before me was of indeterminate origins. One eye was brown, the other blue. He had long, floppy ears and jowls that went on for days.

"He doesn't look like much of a guard dog," my father muttered.

"This is Benji," Georgia came up beside me. "He's a mature seven-year-old mix who was surrendered after his owner passed away last month. Neutered and in good health, though he could stand to lose a few pounds."

"That makes two of us." I stood back and allowed Georgia to unlatch the cage. She looped a blue nylon leash over the dog's head and encouraged him to come out where I could get a better look at him. He flopped down by my feet and sighed.

Georgia hesitated. "He's not the liveliest creature in the bunch, but he's a great companion animal. Though he doesn't stand much of a chance of being adopted."

"Why not?"

"He's old." When I looked to Georgia she continued, "People want puppies. Something young and fun. Benji is a sweetheart but he would rather snuggle on the couch than romp through the woods or play ball."

I looked back to the dog, who laid his head down on my sneaker and stared mournfully up at me. Slow, sweet, and overlooked. "I'll take him."

"But," my mother gazed over her shoulder to where the terrier waited. I swear her lip trembled.

My cousin's eyes rounded in horror at the thought of leaving the slobber-pus behind. Ruby Sue had taken him out of the cage as well and his whole body quivered with pent-up energy. Dragon's arms went around him and she squeezed. He licked her whole face in one swipe.

I crouched down and scratched Benji behind the ears. "This is my dog. Mine. You guys can pick your own."

Georgia grinned up at Ruby Sue. "I think we're going to need a few more forms."

"I CAN'T BELIEVE you adopted three dogs," Darcy said as we sat on her front porch. The sunset was spectacular and Benji, who had enjoyed the walk from the Victorian down to her house, snoozed comfortably at my feet.

"Don't forget the cat we convinced my father to get. Who knew he was a cat person?" I sighed, enjoying the peace I had felt ever since I'd laid eyes on Benji. "You sure you don't want a pet for your boys?"

"It would just be something else for me to chase after," Darcy's tone became shrewd and she dumped the rest of the wine bottle into my glass. "Speaking of chasing after the kids, how about you babysit them at your place tomorrow?"

I groaned. "Garage sale day. I can't, Darce. I shouldn't even be here now. The rest of them are going to realize I've been shirking the drudge work and give me hell for it."

From our perch on the stairs, we could clearly see the activity in and around the Victorian. Robin and my father were moving the heavy items. Dragon with Bluto, the big black goofball of energy, running in and out of the house with pens and stickers and other assorted items. My mother with her yappy little terrier, Snowbelle, in one arm, the other busy arranging items on a table.

"Joey, I need this," Darcy whined.

"I have yoga, the garage sale, and then an afternoon class. Plus, Aunt Hannah will be in for dinner tomorrow night." I sipped my bribe wine, not feeling at all guilty at either the calories or the fact that I wasn't available to herd Darcy's kids. "Never mind coming clean with Robin about his family stalking me."

"They can help with the garage sale." Darcy was more persistent than I had ever seen her.

"Robin's family?"

"No, the boys."

I snorted. "Are you kidding?"

"You know as well as I do that garage sales always make more money when they look crowded. It's human nature to see a busy event and want to be a part of it." She clasped her hands together and begged, "Come on, just watch them for an hour or so. That's all I need."

She was right. Mom's biggest worry was that the garage sale would be a ghost town and we would then have to make arrangements for what to do with all that stuff. "I guess I could take them between ten and eleven-thirty. Dragon will be there."

"Yes." Darcy knocked back her wine and then reached for me.

I held up a finger. "One condition."

"Anything," my bestie promised.

"I'll watch the boys until I have to leave for work and then unload them on Dragon in the afternoon."

Her blue eyes sparkled with the thought of all that child-free time.

"In return, you'll go to the shelter."

Darcy's jaw dropped. "You know as well as I do that if I go to the shelter, I'm not leaving without at least one animal."

"There's a cute little beagle mix that would be perfect for you. Female, eighteen months old, already fixed." I would have taken the dog myself for Darcy if it had been allowed. And if we had been able to fit another soul into our cars. "Those are my terms. Take them, or leave them."

Benji sighed in his sleep, his tail dusting the boards of the porch. She glanced down at him and a soft smile stole over her lips. "Okay, I'll do it."

"Good." My gaze returned to the Victorian and a sigh escaped, though it was not nearly as content as Benji's. "In that case, I need to go home and face the music."

"What are you going to say to him?" Darcy asked.

It was something we had done since we were kids, rehearsing a difficult conversation in advance to feel better prepared.

"I don't know, maybe that your mother is a psycho who invaded my dreams and sliced my arm open. Oh, and your brother stopped by and wants your help to kill her."

"The blunt approach, I like it. So why are you stalling instead of getting on with it?"

Because he didn't have his magic. I had it. "What if he gets hurt?"

Darcy smirked. "Sounds like you care about him."

I thought of our picnic earlier, and his support at the shelter. "I'm starting to."

"And?"

I snorted. "I would be an idiot to fall for Robin. He doesn't intend to stick around. All he wants is…"

"Is…?"

"Look, if I tell you something, you have to promise not to freak out."

Darcy stuck out her pinky. "Promise on the pinky swear."

I took a deep breath. "Robin doesn't have his magic because I have it."

Her eyes rounded. "Are you serious?"

When I nodded she said, "Show me."

"I can't."

"Lame," Darcy sniped.

From inside the house, there was a crash, followed by a scream.

Darcy rolled her eyes. "I've got to go. Whatever you do, get plenty of sleep tonight. You're going to need it. And probably some 'magic'." She made air quotes with her fingers.

"Some friend you are." I finished my wine, handed her the glass, and then stroked Benji along his side. "Come on, boy, time to face the fae music."

"There you are," my mother was in full-blown dominatrix mode, issuing orders to anyone unfortunate enough to meet her gaze. "It's your turn to cook."

"It was my turn yesterday. Besides, I need to talk to Robin."

"Yes, and I know you cheated yesterday by going out for pizza." Her tone was disapproving, though I wasn't sure if that was about the cheating or the pizza.

"That was Robin's idea." I glanced around, hunting for the fae.

My mother noticed. "He's out back. Dan Fogle showed up early to run the power to the cottage."

"I thought Dan couldn't come until sometime next week?"

"I have a feeling Robin and your father incentivized him to get his rump out here sooner rather than later." The hand not holding Snowbelle rubbed together in the universal sign for money.

Robin had money? That was news to me. The pizza had gone on my credit card. "And what about his rent?"

"Paid up for the next three months. Much more than I had planned to ask him for too, probably double what that place is worth." Her eyes met mine. "Looks like he's planning on sticking around."

Not wanting to discuss my complicated relationship, I focused on the squirming beastie in her arms. "You know she can walk."

"I know that." Her other arm went around Snowbelle and she half turned away as though I would snatch the creature from her.

"My precious," I hissed.

"What?" Mom wasn't a big movie buff.

"Nothing. I'll go get dinner started." After I figured out what we had on hand. I couldn't remember the last time any of us had gone to the store.

Benji padded after me to the kitchen and then proceeded to flop on his side in the middle of the black and white tile to take up as much space as possible.

To my surprise, both the fridge and pantry were fully

stocked. Robin must have done it. But when? He'd been with me or my father all day.

I looked out the kitchen window to where he stood, hands-on-hips, surveying the electrician as Dan worked. A long black cord snaked between the side of the house and the cottage. My enchanted lights had faded, but the cheery glow remained.

I would tell him about the dream, the scratches, and Andreas after I made dinner. We needed to get on the same page as soon as possible. Deciding on a three-bean salad and potato soup, I pulled out the vegetable peeler and set to work.

An hour later, the kitchen was full of the scent of dill, the soup was ready and Dan Fogle's truck had just pulled away from the curb.

Benji's paws twitched as he dreamed doggie dreams. I decided to leave him where he was and headed out the back door and through the garden path.

Robin met me in front of the cottage. "There you are. Happy with your familiar?"

I nodded. "It's funny, he's only been here for a little while, and yet I can't imagine him not being here, you know?" A blush stole over my face as I realized what I said applied to more than just Benji.

Robin tilted his head. "You look…different somehow."

"What, how?" My hand flew to my hair. Had I gotten something in it?

His hand caught mine. "More relaxed and at peace than I've ever seen you."

I couldn't hold his gaze. "We need to talk."

"Sounds ominous." There was a teasing light of mischief

in his eyes and he stepped back from the door to wave me inside. "Come inside."

I crossed the threshold and my jaw dropped. Gone was the ratty sheet-covered pull-out, and the stacks of Rubbermaid bins. In its place sat a king-sized bed. It sported pale blue sheets and a red comforter along with an assortment of red and blue throw pillows. My squishy reading chair and the standing lamp with a funky shade sat in one corner. Darcy's handmade sparkly blue curtains covered the small window. A card table sat adjacent to the kitchen, with newly hung open shelving displaying plates and glasses in even rows. The new wine fridge held an assortment of fruit, cheeses, and yes, even wines. I walked into the bathroom and discovered the place had been cleaned and scrubbed to a fine polish and smelled faintly of something spicy.

On feet I could barely feel, I returned to the front room. Glanced at the woodstove and the rag rug that would be a perfect spot for Benji to snooze. "When did you do all this?"

A shrug. "I don't sleep much."

I took it all in again, unable to believe the transformation. "You used my stuff."

His finger curled under my chin, forcing my gaze to meet his. "Do you mind?"

Maybe I should mind that Robin had gone through the souvenirs I had bought when I had a different vision for my life. That he had helped himself to whatever worked in the space and instead of making the cottage his own, had glommed onto my vision for a cozy love nest. "No."

His lips feathered over mine in a sweet brush that was no less intense for its lightness. A spark of something zipped up my spine.

Magic.

The word drifted through my mind and settled like a puzzle piece clicking into place.

His hands cupped my face and I could feel the callouses scraping lightly against my skin. He stole my breath, my train of thought, everything. His effect on me was just as potent as it had been the last time. He made me yearn, made me crave more.

Out of reflex, my arms went around his neck so I could pull him closer. Pressed my body into his and relished the way my curves fit against his hardness. His fingers threaded through my hair and pulled it free of the messy bun that had all but fallen apart on its own. He tugged my head to the side, lips grazed along the column of my throat. I barely stifled a moan.

It was nothing short of perfect. And I craved more. My fingers traveled down to the waistband of his slacks and yanked on the shirt tucked into them.

He grabbed my hands, preventing me from touching him. "Joey, wait. We need to talk."

"I don't want to wait. Or talk." He'd been teasing me from the moment we met and somewhere along the line, I'd made up my mind that if we were going to keep this ruse up and be around each other, I was going to have some sex.

"There are things you don't know." His voice was low, insistent. "Things I've intentionally kept from you."

"That's what you always do." I tried to pull out of his vice-like grip with no success.

He transferred my wrists to one of his hands and curled a finger under my chin. "This is important."

What could possibly be so important that he would rather talk than get naked with me.

Unless….

Andreas's words came back to me. *You're not his usual type.* No, I wasn't young, long-legged, or empty-headed. I could take a freaking hint.

I let out an exasperated huff. "You are full of it, you know that?"

His brows drew together. "What are you talking about?"

This time when I jerked my arms out of his grip he let me go. "You know, just for shits and giggles, I wish you would be upfront. And stop with all your teasing."

"What truth? Joey, I don't know what you're talking about."

"That you don't really want me. It's all about the magic. How do I keep forgetting that? That you're *playing me again* to get what you want. This is what you do. God, I am *so* stupid." Embarrassment coursed through me. I had to get out of there, away from him. "I wish—"

"Stop!" Robin barked. A hand reached out and covered my kiss swollen lips. "Do not say what it was you were about to say because you're having one of your tantrums."

My jaw dropped. "I *do not* have tantrums."

"Fits of insecurity then." His hand fell away and he turned his back on me. In the distance, thunder rumbled. "You believe what you want to believe, Joey. But just because you believe it, doesn't mean it's the truth."

"Then what is the truth?" I challenged, hoping he would say something to explain his rejection.

Sapphire eyes held mine. "You aren't ready for that, not

yet." Then almost to himself, he murmured, "Maybe not ever."

I shook my head and walked to the door. With every step across the lawn, I wished that he would follow.

He didn't. Probably because I couldn't see that happening.

CHAPTER ELEVEN

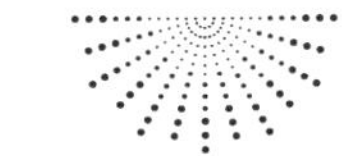

"Experience can make a world of difference."

-Notable quotable from Grammy B

I sat curled up in the window seat and watched the rain come down. Tried my best to ignore the twisting sensation in my chest.

Robin didn't want me. He wanted something from me. Namely his magic back. Why was I even surprised? I shouldn't be. Hell, he'd told me that was why he had come.

But what was with the picnic? And the way he held my hand and looked into my eyes and told me I was the only person he had ever felt genuine affection for? What was the point of that?

My head thunked back into the wall as realization

dawned. Affection. Like one might have for a younger sister. Not lust or desire. That was all coming from me. Just because I craved him didn't mean Robin wanted me back. He was a world-class flirt. And all the talk about marriage and phony engagements had muddied the waters even further. Stupid fricking middle-aged hormones.

Stupid fricking fae prince.

A knock sounded on my bedroom door. Benji picked up his head and tilted it, waiting for my response.

"Who is it?" I called.

"It's me," my mother replied.

"Come on in."

She did, Snowbelle trotting at her heels. Benji laid his head down again and closed his eyes.

"Aren't you going to have any dinner? The soup was delicious."

I turned my head back to stare out at the rain. "I'm not hungry."

"Well, Dragon and I are going to bring the dogs to meet Grammy and bring her dinner."

"Okay."

Mom hesitated. "Is everything all right, love?"

"Sure." There was no color to my response, just a flat word.

"Robin didn't come in for dinner either."

I made a non-committal sound.

"Did the two of you have a fight?" she probed.

I closed my eyes. It was too much to explain.

Her hand brushed across my forehead. "You feel warm. Do you think you're coming down with something?"

I heard the worry in her tone and forced a smile. "I'll be fine, Mom. I'm just tired."

She scowled. "I'll get you some Advil. And a glass of water. You should take a nice hot bath and get a good night's sleep."

I took the Advil, drank the water, and said a polite thank you. My mother brought a chenille throw from the trunk at the foot of my bed and tucked it around me. I stayed where I was until I saw her car, with Dragon behind the wheel, back out of the driveway. Though she almost took out the mailbox, Dragon managed to right the car and I watched the taillights disappear around the bend in the road.

Then, I uncurled from my position and wandered into the bathroom. One look at the tub and I knew there was no way a bath would help me feel any better. All it would do was serve as a reminder of the first night Robin had popped into my life.

"Stupid," I muttered though I wasn't sure if I was talking about the fae or myself. My feet took me down the stairs and into the kitchen. The soup pot had been cleaned out and the leftovers stowed neatly in the fridge. The thought of taking everything out seemed like more trouble than it was worth.

Back down the hall and to the stairs. I looked up them, to where Benji stood and wagged and didn't have enough energy to head up them. I sank onto the steps in the hallway and put my head in my hands. So pathetic. Darcy had been right. I did tend to glom onto men. Especially ones who didn't glom back.

Fits of insecurity, Robin had dubbed it. A tantrum.

Just because you believe it, doesn't mean it's the truth.
What is the truth?

You aren't ready for that. Maybe not ever.

Fae speak. How I detested it. Not so easy as a lie, but a word puzzle designed to make up seem like down and wrong seem like right.

For a moment I was tempted to use the watch and go back to before I had made an idiot out of myself with him. But that wouldn't change the fact that I knew what had happened.

And what did happen? The sensible shrew asked. *What really happened?*

He stopped me from touching him. Didn't want my hands on him.

Just like….

I'm sorry, Joey. My husband's eyes had brimmed with tears. I don't want you that way. Not anymore.

I let out a huge breath. Benji whined and padded down the steps to sit at my feet. I petted his soft fur. Georgia. Maybe that was my major malfunction. I'd trusted George, opened up to him, and shared things I hadn't with anyone else. And then he went away and I was alone again. The old tearing pain in my chest was back and I rubbed it, trying to ease the ache that had never really abated.

I picked up the phone, intending to text Darcy. But my hands froze. There was someone else I needed to talk to first.

After a steadying inhale, I dialed the familiar number she hadn't bothered changing.

"Joey?" Georgia's whiskey voice was full of gravel and thick from sleep.

"Sorry," I sniffled. "I didn't mean to wake you."

"It's okay." There was a click and I could picture her, rolling over to snap on a light. "Did you break down again?"

"No, I don't need a tow." I cleared my throat. "I think I need something else."

She cleared her throat. "Like what?"

"Closure."

She sucked in a breath. "I was wondering when we would have this conversation."

I closed my eyes and admitted the truth that still haunted me in the darkest shadows of the night. "You hurt me."

"I know." Remorse coated those two words. "I was a mess back then and you were such a sweetheart. So accepting and warm and funny and I thought maybe that would be enough."

I knew all that. Knew that my mate had been struggling much the same way I had been, to embrace a destiny that seemed so far out of our reach.

"Did you ever love me?" I whispered because I needed to know. At the same time, I feared the answer.

"I did. Or thought I did. But maybe it wasn't the right way." She let out a breath. "Hell, I knew it wasn't the right way because *I* wasn't right. I wanted to love you, wanted to be right for you. You made me feel good. But I wasn't being honest, not with you and not with myself. And I needed that more. You know I needed that. And I don't know how to make it up to you."

That stabbing ache eased, as though the instrument of torment had finally been withdrawn and the wound could bleed freely. "You weren't the only one who was playing pretend," I admitted.

"What do you mean?"

I let out a long breath. "I got married because it felt like the only thing I hadn't tried to make myself happy. Jobs never stuck and I was getting older and more bitter. I wasn't okay with who I was then either. So when you came to me and told me that you needed to be true to yourself, I felt like I had screwed up both of our lives. That you had only married me out of pity or desperation."

"Oh, Joey, no. I did want us to succeed. It just wasn't in the cards."

My voice rang with conviction I felt all the way down to my bones. "I am so, so proud of you. I admire you. The strength you have going about every single day like it's not a huge deal to be trans in a backwoods mountain town. It must take so much courage just to get up and face the world every day and know you are going to have to deal with stupid people."

"That's true for anyone," Georgia said. "But yeah, some days it is harder than others. Having good friends help."

"Like Ruby Sue?" Maybe more than the dogs and Ruby Sue were going to be missing out on a safe place when the shelter was shut down.

"Yeah. And you."

Though I appreciated her saying so, I hadn't been a good friend to Georgia. Not after we separated. It had been too painful and awkward to extend myself beyond a topical layer of support.

"I know it was hard for you to call me and admit all this," Georgia murmured. "Can I ask what prompted it?"

"Robin," A stray tear slid down my face. "He hurt me earlier."

"Do I need to kick the shit out of him?"

A laugh escaped. "No, not physically. And not on purpose, but…."

"But just because it's not intentional doesn't mean the hurt is any less."

"Yeah." I blew out a shaky breath. "When did you get so wise?"

Humor laced her voice. "They were handing it out with the C-cups. A package deal."

I laughed. "I've missed you, you know."

"I've missed you, too. I hate that you've been avoiding me."

I opened my mouth to deny it, but what was the use? She knew it and I knew it. "I'm sorry."

"I wish we could, I don't know, maybe try again. Meet up with no secrets and just be friends?" There was a hopeful note in her tone.

"I think we can totally do that. Margarita Monday is right around the corner. I'm going to need it too. My Aunt Hannah is coming to town. There might be bloodshed."

"Oh, you are so on," Georgia said. "I can't wait to hear all about it."

"Bring Ruby Sue too. If she's available. I want to let her work on Darcy in case she doesn't adopt that Beagle mix."

"The way you're going, we won't have any animals left in the building. You always were a crusader looking for a cause."

"You think so?"

"Hell, yes. And I can tell that, whatever your squabble was about, Robin's been a good influence on you."

I snorted. "He'll get a kick out of hearing that."

There was a pause and then she said, "Joey?"

"Hmmm?"

"Talk things out with him. He's right for you."

My throat felt tight with some unnamed emotion. "How do you know?"

"Because I saw the way he was looking at you earlier. What I wouldn't give to have a man look at me that way." She let out a dramatic sigh. "He doesn't happen to have a brother, does he?"

The doorbell rang and I hefted myself off the step and shuffled over to answer it. "Actually, he does," I said and stared up into the glittering leaf green fae eyes.

"WHAT ARE YOU DOING HERE, ANDREAS?" I asked even as I hung up with a baffled Georgia.

He should have been soaking wet since the rain was coming down in buckets, but he was perfectly dry. He wore a long black duster and black leather pants. Quintessential bad boy attire.

"Have you spoken to Robin yet?" He moved as though he planned to step past me into the house but I body blocked him.

"No," I said. "We have enough to deal with without—"

A growl sounded from behind me. I half turned and a blur streaked past me. Next thing I knew Andreas was lying flat on his back on the walkway, Benji looking more like Cujo as he snarled down at the fae.

Around the dog was that same blaze of white light that I had seen earlier. Protector. Benji was my guardian, my familiar, a conduit for magic.

"Looks like the dog has good taste," Robin sauntered around the side of the house, his hands stuffed in his jean's pockets. His feet were bare and the flannel shirt he had thrown on in haste hadn't been buttoned. I tried to catch his gaze but his focus was all on the other male. "Was it you spying on us last night?"

In all the turmoil, I'd forgotten all about the presence outside the gym.

Andreas didn't answer. Benji snapped a half an inch from his nose.

"I'd start talking, before he decides to rip your throat out, just for the fun of it. He's very protective of his mistress." Robin examined his nails as though he had no greater concern at the moment.

"Yes, it was me." Andreas sputtered. "I wanted to know if she could be trusted. That's why I felt it was safe to approach her with my offer."

"What offer?"

Andreas turned his head to face me. "You didn't tell him?"

"I was going to—"

Robin said something in a language I didn't recognize. A command, it must have been because Benji backed off, though all his hackles stood on end.

Robin reached down and grabbed Andreas by the lapels. "Go protect your mistress."

Benji shook once and then trotted up the steps and sat his wet hairy butt on my feet.

"Give me one reason," Robin's tone was deceptively mild. "Why I shouldn't kill you where you stand?"

Before I knew what was happening, a blaze of green light erupted from Andreas. Robin flew back and landed in the mud.

"I'm not here to fight with you, little brother," Andreas

huffed the words out like whatever had caused that flash of green light had exhausted him. "As I told your female earlier, I need your assistance."

Robin blinked as though stunned. I wanted to run to him, to make sure he was all right, but Benji sat on my feet.

Slowly, Robin pushed himself up to his hands and knees. "And why would I help you?"

"Because, we want the same thing. You know you'll never be free as long as she's in power."

Robin spat and a trail of crimson made his lips shine. "You've gone mad. She is too strong. Find your own loophole."

"And leave everyone else behind, as you have?" Andreas spat. "Unlike you, some of us have formed connections. But not you. You were always her perfect little weapon. No attachments, no feelings. What it must have been like for you these past two hundred and fifty years, unable to serve your purpose. I would have thought that the lashings would have made you see our mother for the vile creature she truly is."

Robin rose and shucked off the shirt that was spattered in mud and blood. "Believe me, Andreas, I know exactly what she is capable of."

Andreas frowned, though he wasn't looking at Robin's face. He held up his hand and a green ball of light appeared. I tensed, expecting him to attack Robin again and before I knew it, was half forming a wish.

But Robin wasn't looking at Andreas. Those sapphire eyes fixed on me and he slowly shook his head back and forth.

The green light expanded and, in its glow, Robin's skin

began to twist and stretch, almost as though something had melted away.

In its place…there was nothing but a mass of scars. Layer upon layer of damaged and healed and re-damaged skin. There was no flesh unmarked by the same jagged cuts that were hidden beneath the bandage on my arm.

My hands flew to my mouth. "What did you do to him?"

"Revealed the truth," Andreas breathed. He sounded as horrified as I felt. "He was hiding it behind his glamour."

"Not my glamour." Robin turned, presenting his back, which was more of the same, from the nape of his neck to where the waistband of his jeans hid his lower half. "Hers."

"It looks as if she peeled you." Andreas shook his head.

"She did," Robin sounded tired as he turned back around.

"And she hid all this with a glamour?" His brother sounded incredulous. "She could have healed you."

"She likes the damage beneath the perfect façade." He replaced his shirt and looked at his brother. "There's nothing I or anyone else can do to stand against her. She's too powerful."

"Maybe for one of us, but not both." Andreas insisted.

Robin laughed but the sound was bitter. "And if she catches wind of what we plan? She's destroyed members of her immediate family before for a perceived insult. To stand against her is to court death."

"Perhaps in our land, but not here." Andreas looked at me. "I can sense power from your female."

"Leave her out of this." Sapphire eyes blazed.

Shoeing Benji aside with the toe of my sneaker, I headed out into the rain before the two started fighting again. "Look,

Andreas. This is a lot. We need a little time to digest the information."

Andreas stared between us. "I'll give you twenty-four hours. But by this time tomorrow, I'll need an answer."

Robin opened his mouth but I cut him off. "We'll see you then."

Andreas nodded once. Thunder rumbled and then lightning struck. So close it nearly blinded me. When my vision returned, Andreas was gone.

Robin's shoulders slumped with exhaustion. "Why didn't you just tell him no?"

"Inside," I said and snagged his hand, leading him back into the house.

He stopped at the foot of the stairs while I shut and locked the door and then moved past him. "Stay," I said to Benji when the dog made to follow me. He whined but obeyed.

I hurried down the hall to the laundry room and retrieved a few of the freshly folded towels. After draping one around my neck, I bustled forward only to find Robin standing exactly where I left him.

I tended to the man first, seeing as how he looked too dazed to dry himself. I stood on the step behind him and scrubbed the moisture out of his blond locks, then swiped over his skin, careful to touch him only with the towel. Without the green glow from Andrea's light, the scars appeared more silver, but just as intense. The sight of them made my throat close up.

When I finished, I knelt on the hall runner to dry Benji. The dog rolled over, exposing his wet belly and I couldn't help but smile at his groan of satisfaction.

"He knew you were in trouble," Robin murmured. "You picked your familiar well."

"He picked me." I gave the dog one final pat then turned to the fae.

"You didn't tell me you spoke with Andreas." His tone was flat with no accusation.

I collected the towels to give myself a minute. "I was going to, but the day has a habit of getting away from me."

I looked at his chest and stomach, at the twisted, gnarled flesh and a lump formed in my throat. "Is this why you didn't want me to touch you?"

He turned his face to the side and a muscle jumped in his jaw. "A glamour works only on visuals. You would have felt the scars."

I moved into his line of sight and looked up into his eyes. "You could have told me."

He didn't say anything, so I reached out a hand. "Come on."

"Where are we going?"

"My room. Mom and Dragon will be back as soon as the storm clears. I don't want to be interrupted."

I waited for a quip or a smart remark but he remained blank. He did let me thread my fingers through his though.

Benji followed on our heels as we headed up the stairs and down the hall to my bedroom.

Robin stared at the bed for a full minute. "My jeans are all wet."

"Then take them off."

His gaze lifted to mine.

"That's not an invitation." I tossed him the last dry towel and forced a smile as though the earlier awkwardness hadn't happened. "Put that on if you want to preserve your modesty."

Without waiting for an answer, I headed down the hall to my bathroom where I shucked my wet clothes, draped them and the damp towels over the edge of the tub to drip dry, and then pulled on my bathrobe. I took a few minutes to brush my teeth, wash my face and comb out the tangles in my damp hair. Mostly I was giving Robin and myself a few minutes apart to collect our thoughts.

I reached for the doorknob but then spotted the bandage and hesitated. I'd already kept the truth about Andreas from him to my detriment. It was time to be completely honest. Even if it scared the shit out of me.

Maybe especially because it scared the shit out of me.

I padded back down the hall and opened the door to my room. The low lamp on the dresser still burned, casting shadows over Robin's inert form. He had burrowed beneath the thick comforter, his back to the door. The towel I had offered him was draped neatly over the foot of the bed.

His eyes were closed.

"Robin?" I asked.

He didn't stir and his breathing patterns remained slow and deep.

I took a moment to study the few visible scars on the back of his neck. From what I had seen after Andreas broke the glamour they covered his body, though his face remained unmarked. Moving closer, I compared them to the ones on my forearm. The spacing between the individual lines harder to distinguish because the scars on his skin were layered where I only had one swipe.

The way he slept, curled in on himself. So different than

the everyday Robin Goodfellow I thought I knew. Confidence that tipped into arrogance. *I don't sleep much,* he had said. Was that because he feared an attack while he lay defenseless?

"So much pain." I breathed through the tears that clogged my throat.

Part of me wanted to climb into bed with him. To snuggle deep and share warmth and comfort. I didn't understand his world but I recognized evil when I saw it. Robin had been hurt. Repeatedly. By his own mother. Why?

I'd been glad of all the trickster's pacts I had undone. But Robin was right. Magic always came with a price and instead of hurting and enslaving others over the past two hundred and fifty years, he had been the one hurt and enslaved.

My heart hurt for him. I had learned more about Robin tonight than I had when we had traveled through time. Imagining what he had endured made me want to vomit. And Andreas wanted more from him. From both of us. Were either of us up for such a challenge?

Then there was our relationship. We had things to work out between us. Confidences that needed to be shared, admissions that had to be made. Misunderstandings that needed to be straightened out.

So instead of climbing into bed, I retrieved the chenille blanket and resumed my position in the window seat. Benji padded over to me and after a few minutes of petting, hopped up onto the long cushion beside me.

He was still damp and smelled like wet dog, but at that moment, I was more grateful for him than anything in my whole life. He'd been so incredibly brave. Steadfastly loyal to attack a magic-wielding fae. Had he understood the danger he had put himself in?

Maybe, maybe not. But Robin had.

Seeing Andreas hurl that ball of green light at him had scared years off my life. For the first time, it dawned on me how helpless Robin was against his own kind. As defenseless as I had been when I'd first encountered him.

The rain slowed to a drizzle and then transitioned into a light mist. It was about ten when I spied my mother's car pull up to the curb. The front tire rolled up onto it before quickly righting itself. Dragon popped out from behind the wheel. I heard her say something to my mother before she retrieved Bluto from the back seat. My mother, Snowbelle still under her arm, exited the car and they made for the house.

I could go down and chat with them. Ask about Grammy and how she got on with the dogs. Knowing Grammy, the answer would be famously. Grammy was an animal person through and through.

But I stayed where I was, turning to look, not out into the night, but at the deeper mystery that was the sleeping figure tucked up in my bed.

"Robin Goodfellow, who are you?" I wondered out loud.

"Lamb?" Someone put a hand on my shoulder and shook me lightly.

A grunt escaped my lips followed by a sound like fatback bacon hitting a griddle. "Ouch."

The hand withdrew. "Are you hurt?"

I blinked up and saw Robin standing over me. The sky

had begun to pinken though the sun hadn't yet topped the hills to the east. "No, just have the mother of all cricks in my neck from sleeping at a right angle."

"Why did you?" His hands twitched but he made no move to rub my neck as he had the day before. The way I desperately wanted him to. And not just because working out a spasm on one's own was close to impossible without three Advil and a shot of espresso.

"You looked very peaceful and you said you hadn't been sleeping well. I figured it would be better if I let you be." I winced and barely stifled a groan when I swung my legs down from the window seat and felt the prickling of the pins and needles sensation. This was going to hurt like hell.

Before my feet hit the floor, Robin scooped me up, blanket and all and carried me back to the bed, and laid me out flat. "Turn over and I'll give you a massage."

I blinked up at him. He wore the damp jeans from the night before and nothing else. I wanted to make a joke about how a massage was never just a massage but didn't feel as though we were in the right place for levity. I turned over.

His hands swept my hair off my shoulders. Strong fingers dug into the meat of my back at just the right spot and an involuntary groan escaped. It was painful but in the very best way. He worked me like bread dough for a few silent minutes and I let him, glad to have the calm before the storm.

"I've made mistakes," he murmured.

"We all do. It's part of being human," I mumbled.

The fingers spaced out, finding new pain points, dipping beneath the collar of my robe. "You know I'm not human."

I let that one slide. "What mistakes are you talking about?"

The rubbing paused. "I'm honestly not sure. You've ripped the ground out from under me until I don't know where I stand."

I turned my head to the side so I could see his face. "Are you talking about our bargain?"

He didn't answer, just kept working on my neck. His expression was tightly locked down.

I thought about what he said, then struggled to sit up. This wasn't a conversation I was prepared to have while lying flat on my face. "Tell me what it is you want."

His lips parted. "I want to be with you. Here. To stay with you as we have been."

"Exactly the way we have been?" I raised a brow.

In answer, his heated gaze fell to where the fabric of my robe gaped open, revealing the outer swells of my breasts.

My heart sped up at that look. There was no way he was making fun of me. Or bargaining. That look was full of lust, pure and simple. But before I could say or do anything he glanced away, his jaw tight. "I have no right to ask anything of you. Not with me being so…damaged."

I reached out and laid my palm on his chest, over the steady thrum of his heart. His head swung to face me and his brows furrowed.

"You were hurt. Badly. That doesn't make you damaged."

His brows pulled together as he stared down at where I touched him. "You would still want me? Even as I am?"

The flash of vulnerability I saw in his eyes…how many times had I witnessed that exact emotion in the mirror?

Because I was older. Softer. Less than what I had been before. Less than I wanted to be.

But I was also brave. Strong. And I finally knew what I wanted.

In answer, I maneuvered until I was upright on the bed and untied the robe, and shrugged out of it. And then I knelt there, exposed in the early morning light in front of a man who was far from flawless but somehow even more perfect. "Do you want me as I am?"

"Gods, yes," he growled and reached for me. His hands were everywhere at once. Cupping. Kneading, not to alleviate pain but to bring pleasure. His lips blazed a hot trail from my mouth to my jaw, and down the side of my neck.

I touched him lightly on his shoulders, afraid that even the slightest contact would sting. But the scarred tissue was hard. "Does this hurt?" I whispered.

"Only when you stop," he breathed in my ear.

I giggled and reached for him again.

But Robin froze. "What's that?" He was looking at my arm.

Shit shit shit. "I was going to tell you about that."

Ardor was forgotten as he rolled off of me and pulled my arm closer for his inspection. "This looks fresh. When did you see her? And where?" His words were laced with panic.

And so much for the early morning orgasm. I could feel it slipping away into the ether. Talk of mothers killed the mood like nobody's business. "It was a dream. At least I thought it was but when I woke up, I had these scratches and my arm was bleeding."

Robin closed his eyes. His face was pinched tight as though he was in pain. "And you didn't tell me?"

My lips compressed together. What could I say? No, I hadn't told him about the dream. "I was spooked and trying to come to grips with it on my own first."

His lids lifted and he stared at me for a long moment. "How are you feeling?"

I shrugged. "Fine. Last night I was a little lethargic but that's understandable because things have been so crazy lately."

"Damn it." Robin ran a hand through his hair.

"Look, I'm sorry," I said. "Don't be angry with me. I was freaked out and—"

"I'm not angry with you," he cut me off. "You're sick, Joey."

"I told you, I'm fine."

He took a deep breath and then uttered three damning words. "She poisoned you."

CHAPTER TWELVE

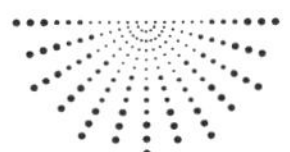

"Desire is fleeting. Stretch marks are forever."

-Notable quotable from Grammy B

Surely I hadn't heard him right. I yanked the robe back up, not wanting to have a conversation about the psycho fae queen while bare-breasted. "What do you mean?"

"Her thorns—nails. They're full of poison. Her own special blend." He made it sound like a coffee house special.

I looked pointedly at the mess of scar tissues on his chest and arms. "But, you're fine. She scratched you all to hell and you're fine."

"That's because she gave me the antidote. *Fuck.*" Robin slid off the bed and began to pace.

A chill wracked my body even swathed in my robe. "This poison. It's not…fatal, is it?"

Sapphire eyes, so full of pain it stole my breath, bore into me. "The queen plays for keeps. She knows you're my anchor and without you, I have to go back to her."

My brow furrowed. "But it was just a dream."

"That's probably the only reason you're still alive. If you had been given a full dose directly from her hand in person, it would have stopped your heart."

"Are you sure I'm sick?" I wet my lips. "I told you I wasn't great last night but I really do feel fine now."

"It'll come in waves. First bouts of fatigue. Then painful muscle spasms leading to paralysis. Eventually, your whole body will freeze up as the toxin works its way through you, system by system, shutting everything down. She's perfected it to leave her victims frozen in agony, begging for her to end them with their eyes."

What he was describing. No one could be that evil, could they? "How long?" I whispered, staring at the scratch marks in horror.

"I'm not sure. My magic protected you. That and Benji. He's helping to dilute the toxin, aren't you, boy?"

"It's not hurting him, is it?" The thought made me dizzy.

"No, he's fine. The poison is in your bloodstream." He knelt down and scratched the dog behind the ears. "Let's hope he helps for long enough."

"Long enough for what?"

Robin let out a breath and closed his eyes. "For me to go back to her."

Back to her. Where she would torture and torment him even more? "No,"

"Lamb—"

I shook my head vehemently. "No, Robin. Don't you lamb me. There has to be another way."

He shook his head. "I'm what she wants. Me back in line, making bargains and trades and siphoning power for her. She always hated that she couldn't control me. And if you die, I must return. If I bargain to go back now and to release you as my mortal anchor, she'll trade for the antidote. If I go now, I can help you."

"Is that what you want?" I asked quietly.

"You're what I want." He gripped me by the elbows, careful not to touch the scratches. "And if I don't give in to her, you won't survive. I can't let that happen. Not when I'm the one that brought you to her notice in the first place."

"What about Andreas?" I asked. "He wants you to join him, to overthrow her."

"I don't trust Andreas. Especially not with this." His hand rose to my face and he smoothed his thumb over my cheekbone. "And besides, I don't have my magic."

Because I had it. "What if I help? No one else knows I have magic. And Andreas seems interested in recruiting both of us. We won't tell him that I've got your magic."

He shook his head. "You don't know what you're saying. You can't control magic well enough to wield it in battle."

"Maybe not a battle, but how about a sneak attack? We bring the fight to her, only she doesn't know it's a fight. Maybe she thinks it's a bargain. You said yourself she put down uprisings before. But if she doesn't see it coming, we can catch her off guard, get the antidote for me and let Andreas take her down."

Something that looked a lot like hope dawned in his eyes.

But there was also a healthy dose of fear. "It's too risky. She could kill you outright. What if we don't get the antidote in time?"

"I don't want to think about that." Because I would be dead and Robin would be back in her clutches. "Listen, this is the only way we both get one for the win column. I'll be alive and you and all of your people will be free of her."

He closed his eyes. "I've learned that hope is a dangerous thing to try and hold on to."

I reached for his hand and curled my fingers around it. "We're a team now. You don't have to face her alone anymore."

There was so much longing on his face as he knelt before me. "Is this really what you want, Joey?"

I pressed my forehead against his. "We can beat her. I know it."

He exhaled slowly and pulled back far enough to look into my eyes. "Then I'll go look for Andreas. Tell him we'll help."

"What should I do?" I asked as he got to his feet and reached for his shirt.

"Go about your day, the way you normally would. We still don't know who might be spying on you. And keep Benji nearby. The watch as well."

I nodded and reached for my last clean set of work-out clothes. "Okay. I'll see you soon."

"That you will, lamb." He smiled and then opened my door.

Revealing my mother, hand poised to knock. At her feet, Snowbelle growled, showing off her slightly crooked teeth.

Robin glanced back at me in a panic.

"Act normal," I mouthed the words silently to him. Mom hadn't caught sight of the scars marring Robin's open shirt. The last thing I wanted was to try to BS my way out of answering her questions.

"Good morning, Ms. Whitmore. Shall I make you some coffee before I leave?" His charming fae prince mask was back in place.

She narrowed her gaze on his face. "I already made some."

"Excellent. Then I will have a cup before I go." He nodded once and then headed down the stairs.

"Josephine Louise Whitmore!" my mother snapped.

Oy with the three-naming thing already. "It's not what it looked like."

"It looked like you were half-naked and he was half-naked the morning of my garage sale."

Nothing got past her. "Okay then, it was exactly what it looked like."

"Joey, do you really think it's a good idea to have him sleeping in your room with you? You were in tears over him just last night."

"It was a misunderstanding." Clearly, my mother wasn't going to give me the luxury of leaving while I got dressed. I moved past her and shut the bedroom door. "And I'm a middle-aged woman. I'm allowed to have sleepovers with men."

"Why must everything with you be so high drama?" my mother asked.

"It's not." It kind of was, what with me being poisoned by his vindictive mother and all. But better if she didn't know about that part. I yanked my pants on beneath my robe as I said, "Look, Mom. We didn't have sex. Does that make you happy?"

She folded her arms over her breasts. "No, it doesn't. Better you have sex with him and get him out of your system than to get involved emotionally. That man will devastate you. Honestly, Joey, I thought you were smarter than this."

First Darcy and now my mother. What was with everyone telling me what an idiot I was when it came to men? Sure, I had made plenty of mistakes but that was a woman's prerogative. Men were like shoes, try them on until you find the right fit.

Mine just happened to be a scared fae with a psycho hose-beast for a mother. "Mom, I'm not discussing this with you."

She didn't hear me. "I mean you know better than to get married again, because—"

I had just dropped the robe and was in the process of tugging on my sports bra when something inside me snapped and I whirled to face her. "Because marriage isn't for me? That's what you were going to say, isn't it, mother?"

She blinked, though I couldn't tell if that was because the girls were banging out in the breeze or because I had called her on her crap.

"Yes, I made a mistake with Georgia. But that doesn't mean I can't or won't ever get married again. *I am not like you.* I don't want a thrice-weekly shagfest and then to come home and sleep alone. I want to find someone to share my life with on an intimate level. To wake up with every morning, and make dinner together at night. To laugh with and just enjoy being together."

Her chin jutted up. "And Robin is that person?"

"I don't know. Maybe."

"I raised you to be self-sufficient. To stand on your own two feet and never depend on a man to pay your way. You're not just some doll to be taken out and played with whenever the mood strikes him."

The bra was getting uncomfortable so I stuffed the girls into it even as I said, "That sounds like exactly how you've been treating my father."

She blanched but recovered fast. "We had an arrangement that suited us both."

"Had, mother. It doesn't suit him now. He wants more from you."

She shook her head.

I pulled my tank top on and then reached for my hoodie and a pair of socks. "Maybe you need to worry a little less about where my relationship with Robin is heading and a little more about how you want to move forward with Dad. Come on, Benji. Let's go get breakfast."

I left her standing in my room as I made my way down the stairs.

Being poisoned by a fae queen really ought to come with a get out of yoga free card. But Robin had told me to proceed with my day as though nothing was wrong. So I had my ass in the air, face smooshed into the yoga mat, and was sweating buckets. Again.

"And now move forward to your plank pose," Pam wore a sheer black gauzy ankle-length wrap today. I could see it swirling around her bare feet as she walked between the mats.

My arms shook and my hair was sticking to my face as I leaned my weight forward.

"Don't forget to breathe." Pam reminded in her soft voice.

Somehow, I had. I'd been holding my breath, waiting for the moment to pass. Or for me to pass out, whichever came first.

"And now down to your belly."

I collapsed in a heap.

"And push up into Cobra."

Nothing was working. I lay there, nose pressed to my yoga mat, and huffed and puffed like the big bad wolf intent on pork for dinner.

Why was I doing this to myself? It wasn't getting any easier. I didn't feel better for doing it. I was too old and out of shape to be a yoga instructor.

So how do you think you can beat a fae queen if you can't do forty minutes of yoga? the sensible shrew whispered.

I didn't, not really. As much as I wanted a happily ever after here, with me and Robin scoring the antidote and then celebrating with a week naked between the sheets, I didn't think that was how our story would play out. Better false hope than to have him bargain himself for the antidote. After seeing what that evil bitch had done to him, there was no way I would let him trade himself for me.

"Joey, can I talk to you a minute?"

I looked up to see the rest of the class had rolled their yoga mats and were heading for the exit. Pam stood over me, her purple leggings hugging her trim thighs.

"Sure," I huffed and then forced myself to get up. Here it

came. *I don't think you're cut out to do yoga, never mind teach it. Don't quit your day job.*

With my yoga mat neatly rolled and stowed on top of my gym bag by the door for a hasty escape, I followed her into her office. It was a soothing space with cream-colored walls and a little Chinese tea service that looked odd beside her state-of-the-art computer.

"Green tea?" she asked as she poured bottled water into a kettle.

I was sweating like a whore during Sunday service so tea was the last thing I wanted. But it seemed rude to refuse. "Sure."

I took in the tranquil space. It didn't look much like an office, other than the computer. The colorful crystals hanging at different lengths to catch in the sunlight, the prisms refracting the beams to make rainbow patterns on the white tile floor. Lots of leafy green plants flourished by a South facing window. Very clean and fresh and peaceful. A nice reprieve from the chaos of my life.

"How long have you been doing yoga?" I asked as she arranged the tiny teacups.

"Oh, almost ten years now." From the way she smiled, I could tell my face had detailed my surprise. "Not the answer you were expecting?"

No, but it seemed rude to say so. "What got you interested in it?

"My husband passed away. Heart attack." The kettle began to sing and she removed it from the hot plate and poured the steaming liquid into the little cups.

"I'm so sorry." I accepted the cup and wrapped my still sore palms around it, barely stifling the flinch.

"I was devastated. We hadn't even reached retirement age. There were so many things I still wanted to experience and my other half was gone. There were days I didn't want to get out of bed. It all seemed so pointless without him."

My heart went out to her. "What changed?"

She shrugged. "Me. I had to find a new path for me to follow on my own. Yoga soothed something inside me that nothing else managed to touch."

Not knowing how to respond to such a personal revelation from a woman who was essentially a stranger, I lifted the cup to my lips and took a sip. Surprisingly, it wasn't half bad.

"I can tell that you've been struggling." Pam eased herself down into the seat with a fluid grace that I both admired and envied. "I wanted to let you know that you're going to be a fabulous instructor."

I blinked. "Come again?"

"Listen, yoga isn't just for the young or the fit. All of your classmates, they're here because they like showing off their bodies or because they think they can make easy money with this certification. But you're different. What made you sign up for this course?"

"I work in a gymnastics studio in the high country. I wanted to convince my boss that we ought to hold yoga classes in the space. Maybe expand our business and help more people add some activity to their lives. But she has no interest in it."

"So, you thought if you got certified as an instructor, you could help people." Pam smiled. "Do you know why I think you'll make such a good instructor? Because it doesn't come easy to you. You have to work for it. And because of that, you'll have a level of respect for those students who maybe would be too intimidated to go into a class with the young and the fit. You, more than anyone else, can truly help people. But you have to keep at it. Practice in your free time to improve your stamina and flexibility. You do that and pretty soon this will all come together for you."

"Thank you," I whispered. "You always know exactly what I need to hear."

She shrugged. "Yogi's intuition. Yours will come in time."

I finished my tea and rose. "I better get home."

"I'm sure we'll be seeing each other again soon."

I headed out to the main area and picked up my gym bag. I was about to push out through the doors when I hesitated a moment. "Do you have any pets?"

Pam tipped her head to study me. "No. Why do you ask?"

"There's a shelter up the mountain that's about to close. All the animals there need homes. I thought maybe if you were in the market, you could take a little trip up there."

She grinned. "I will have to talk to Raul about it first. Make sure he's not allergic."

"Who's Raul?" I asked just as a blue Beemer pulled to a stop beside my VW.

"That's Raul." Pam waited for me to exit the studio, locked the door, and then strode over to the car and slid inside. I watched shamelessly as they shared a passion-filled kiss.

Raul didn't look a day over thirty and judging by the way his hands roved over her supple body, he didn't much care that Pam was twice his age.

"You go girl," I whispered and vowed right then and there

that I would stop using my age as an excuse to not go after what I wanted.

DARCY APPEARED the instant I emerged from my car, kids in tow. "You look like hell. I don't think yoga agrees with you." She set the urchins loose and they swarmed around the tables, picking up various items and making noise the way only young boys could.

"It's growing on me. My instructor is my new personal hero. Seriously, I want her to meet up with Grammy B and they can fight crime or reverse climate change or something." My eyebrows went up as I got a load of what Darcy had on. "You're wearing a dress. Can't remember the last time I saw that."

"Easy access. I'm not wearing underwear either." Darcy winked and behind her Reverend Phillips's wife Emily, dropped a snow globe she'd been inspecting while eavesdropping on us.

"That'll be ten dollars." My mother bustled over with a broom and a dustpan, studiously ignoring me.

"For a snow globe?" Emily scowled.

"It was an antique that my father picked up in Zürich."

Emily's eyes went wide and she fumbled with her coin purse. "Oh, I'm so sorry. Of course, I'm willing to pay for it."

Darcy giggled and turned away. "Nosy old bag, serves her right. Where did it really come from?"

"Either the airport gift shop or the dollar store. One of those for sure. My grandfather never went to Switzerland." I shook my head. "So, where are you and Mike off to?"

"Not sure yet. Probably some hotel."

"A hotel? I thought money was tight."

"For the ambiance. We like to meet at the bar and pretend we're strangers and hook up in the bathroom. I really appreciate you taking the kids."

I snorted. "Like you didn't beg."

"We'll be back by dinner, for sure." Her blue eyes narrowed and she studied me a moment. "And why is your mother giving you the cold shoulder? Did your dog chew up her favorite shoes or something?"

I glanced around for Emily, saw she was several tables away examining an old mirror, and then lowered my voice. "She caught Robin coming out of my room this morning."

Darcy's mouth dropped open. "No way. Did you guys boink?"

"Close your trap before you start catching flies," I told her. "No, no boinking, though we sort of fooled around a little."

I could hear her teeth forcibly click together. "*Ohmigawd!* I can't believe it. How was it?"

"Life-altering." I wanted to lay the whole poison scratches thing on her but couldn't bring myself to do it any more than I wanted to talk about Robin's scars.

"When you say life-altering, are we talking some fifty shades action?"

"No, perv. I mean emotionally terrifying."

Darcy nodded. "Is he a crier? A screamer? A premature ejaculator?"

"None of the above. Now go have some sex so you can stop thinking like a man and be reasonable again." I shoved at her shoulder.

"Yes, ma'am" Darcy threw off a jaunty salute, kissed each of her boys on the top of the head, and then power-walked up the street to her house.

"And don't sit on any cold benches!" I hollered after her. If not for the van load of church ladies who pulled up to the curb, I was sure she would have flipped me off.

Dragon had rounded up Darcy's boys and was playing some sort of blindfolded tag game with them, Bluto bounding in between them like a big idiot pony. I took the opportunity to sidle up to my mother and test the waters.

"How's it going?"

"Fine." She didn't look at me, her attention was focused on counting a stack of singles.

I looked around at the items that we had dragged out of the garage and lined around the sidewalk. There were several noticeable gaps. Grandpappy's record player was gone, as well as the armoire that had been hidden away in the canning shed. An old push lawn mower that we didn't use had vanished along with a few boxes of kitchenware. "Looks like some stuff has moved."

My mother slammed the bills down into the lockbox and snapped the lid shut.

"Mom, look. I'm sorry about earlier—"

She held up a hand. "I don't have time for this right now, Josephine. Some things need my attention."

"What things? Maybe I can help." I didn't want to fight with her. Robin could return with Andreas at any moment and I would be off to the final showdown with the fae queen. A trip that I might never return from. The last thing I wanted was to die while having a tiff with my mother.

"Just man the cash box, Joey." She shook her head, clearly not in the right mindset to forgive and forget.

I watched her disappear into the house, my stomach in knots. And I hadn't even gotten a chance to snag a cup of coffee before she abandoned me to the town.

I poked through a few odds and ends that Mom and Dragon had dragged out of Grammy's attic. Boxes full of hats. Bowler hats, baseball caps, fedoras. I tried and failed to imagine my gruff Grandpappy wearing a fedora.

There was a rack of clothing too. Old suits and dresses that smelled like mothballs. I smiled as I found the charcoal double-breasted suit he had worn to my wedding, then frowned when I felt a lump in the inner pocket.

Seriously? No one had checked the pockets of the clothing we were selling? What if there was money in there? It would be just like Grammy to stuff a fistful of twenties into her dead husband's suit pocket and then forget all about it. I had once found two hundred dollars in a Tupperware at the back of her freezer.

It wasn't a wad of cash though but a pocket watch. Smaller, and more worn than the one Robin had given me. I slipped it into the cash box, intending to give it to Robin. He would get a kick out of having something of my grandfather's.

At least I hoped.

Irma Getz, her big patent-leather purse dangling from one arm, bustled over to me. "Joey, dear. I hear you are getting married again. Where is that young man of yours?"

Staging an insurrection with his brother. "Hi, Mrs. Getz. He's spending some time with his family today."

"Well, be sure to bring him around the book shop when

you get the chance. I can't wait to meet him." She pawed through a cardboard box. "You got any of them super dirty romance novels?"

I do, but they are all loaded on my e-reader, not out in the open for the town busybodies to inspect. "Afraid not."

"Darn. I do love me a good smutty story. Especially the butt stuff. Mr. Getz never went in for any of that you know." She winked at me. "Make sure you and your young man experiment plenty because before you know it you'll be married to a boring old fart that don't know whether to scratch his watch or wind his butt."

"Mercy," I murmured as she shuffled off to inspect some bric-a-brack a few tables over.

"Sound advice," a lyrical voice said from behind me. "I hope you are planning to follow it."

I flushed to the roots of my hair. "Of course that's when you pop back in, just in time to overhear that particular conversation."

"Butt stuff. I wonder if she was talking about herself or—"

I put my hand over his lips. "Do *not* finish that sentence. I will never get the image out of my brain."

His eyes sparkled with mischief as he pressed a kiss to my fingers.

"I could have lived a long and happy life without knowing that about Walter Getz. Or Irma for that matter." With a final head shake, I removed my hand. "Did you find Andreas?"

Robin's expression sobered. "He's going to meet us at your gym later this afternoon. Her being in the mortal realm has afforded us a unique. opportunity."

"What sort of opportunity?"

He glanced at a nearby table of people who weren't even pretending not to stare at us. "Not here. When are you leaving for work?"

I checked my phone. "About twenty minutes from now. Why?"

His grin turned wicked. "Good. Come with me."

"What? Where are we going? If I leave the cash box unattended my mother will skin me alive." I clamped my lips together as I realized what I just said and to whom. "Sorry, I wasn't thinking about—"

A finger covered my lips as he cut off the apology I was in the middle of burping up. He reached down, collected the cash box in one hand, then snagged my arm with the other. He led me around the corner of the house, behind a rhododendron and away from prying eyes.

The next thing I knew, my back was pressed up against the house. His lips devoured mine in a hungry kiss.

"Andreas said you prefer your women younger with long legs and empty heads," I gasped when we paused to draw breath.

He wrapped his hand around my hair and pulled gently, tipping my head to the side so he could rain kisses along the column of my throat. "Andreas was trying to seed doubt."

I put my palms against his chest. "Are you saying that's not the kind of woman you prefer?"

He released my hair and cupped my face. "I'm saying that when it comes to the fae, you always need to look for the angle. Andreas wants you for himself. But he can bugger off. He can't have you. You're *mine*." Another soul-searing kiss scrambled my thoughts.

"You don't get to make a decree." It was hard to think while he touched me that way.

"I'm a fae prince," he murmured. "Decrees come with the territory."

"I'm not a toy you get to own, ah—!" My protest cut off as he nipped my earlobe.

"Please, don't ask me to share you though." He pulled away and his eyes begged.

"That wasn't what I meant."

"Then what did you mean?" He searched my face and I realized we were having one of those cultural miscommunications again.

He wasn't a controlling bastard. But he was a manipulative one, something that had proven to be far more dangerous. How easy it would be to keep going, to let him kiss and touch me until all of our problems vanished. But coming to a meeting of the minds on the issue of ownership was far more important. As much as being with Robin made me feel like a randy teenager, I wasn't one. Time to draw the line.

"I want you. No one else. Are we clear on that?"

"Crystal."

I put my hand on his chest. "That doesn't mean you own me or gives you the right to tell me what to do."

He frowned. "Why would I want to tell you what to do when you are so much more capable than I have ever been?"

I drew up short. He meant that, I could see it on his face. I took a moment and retrenched. "Or maybe what not to do? Like, make wishes?"

"That's for your safety—"

"And I'm in charge of that. Me. Not you. We clear?"

He didn't like it, I could see it in his face.

"In return, I won't tell you what to do either. But I will make requests. I will talk to you and share my thoughts with you because I value your opinion. That's how a real adult relationship works. Are you okay with that?"

"Can I request that you get naked?"

A laugh bubbled out of me. "Robin we can't do that here." It was a token protest. He might have figured out a way to actually make a garage sale fun.

"Then come to the cottage with me," he breathed in my ear following it up with a playful nip. "I have several more requests to make of you."

The cottage that he had fixed up, that held that luscious king-sized bed. I was sorely tempted. Too much making out, not enough seeing things through. An orgasm lurked somewhere out there with my name on it.

"What about Dragon. And Darcy's kids? I can't leave her to watch the boys and handle a busload of garage sale seniors on her own. Especially when she'll have to deal with her mother later."

He sighed and rested his forehead against my own. "Has anyone ever told you that you have too much going on?"

I shrugged. "This is my world."

His hand rose to cup my cheek. "Thank you for letting me be a part of it, even for a little while."

I didn't like the air of resignation that seemed to cling to him like mountain mist. "You're not giving up on me, are you?"

"Experience has taught me that no one can win against her. But when I look at you, my lamb," his thumb brushed over my kiss swollen bottom lip. "You have a knack for making the impossible happen."

I could become addicted to the way his gaze consumed me. Tenderness, awe, pride, hope. All because of little old me. It boggled the mind. "I wish I could see myself the way you do."

"Have more confidence, Joey. You have done more in your short mortal life than many immortals ever accomplish. Wear that experience like the badge it is."

"I'll make you a bargain," I began.

His eyes lit up. "I'm listening."

"I'll do my best to wear confidence like a badge, even if it is ill-fitting. If you promise you won't trade yourself to her for the antidote."

I'd shocked him, it was clear from the way he blinked at me.

"Why would you ask that of me?"

I threaded my hand through his. "Because I couldn't go on knowing you were being hurt because of me. I don't think you get how sick I have been since I found out what happened to you. All because I agreed to be your anchor. If I could go back and spare you that pain, I would. Trust that we'll find another way. Don't ask me to live with knowing that you're suffering because of me."

His lips parted but before he could answer the screech of tires and a piercing scream shattered our bubble.

"Come on." Gripping my hand in one of his, Robin hauled me toward the street where a crowd had gathered.

"What happened?" I called out. "Is someone hurt?"

"Hit and run." A woman's voice, one I didn't recognize. "Did anyone see who was driving?"

"Who was hit?" I asked Robin. His height gave him the advantage of being able to see.

"Someone call an ambulance!" A man cried out. "She's not breathing."

"Robin?" Fear twisted my insides in an icy grip. I put a hand on his shoulder. "Who is it?"

He turned and I caught a glimpse of black fur and a pain-filled whine. Bluto. And beside him the crumpled form of a teenage girl.

My hand flew up to cover my mouth, to keep the scream from flying out. No. *No no no no no. It couldn't be.*

Her eyes were open, sightless. Blood trickled from one ear and pooled around her in a growing crimson puddle.

"It's Dragon," Robin's voice fractured as he whispered, "she's gone."

CHAPTER THIRTEEN

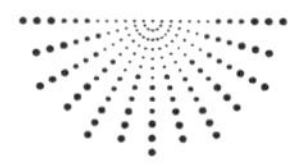

"Don't take my word for it. Some things a woman needs to experience herself."
-Notable quotable from Grammy B

Gone.

Voice filtered in past the ringing in my ears.

"The boy threw the ball into the road. The dog went after it." Someone said.

"But the car didn't slow down. In fact, it looked like it gunned it for them."

Words swirled around me as I stared at the still forms.

Get up, I thought the words at her. *Be okay.*

It wasn't a wish. It was a psychic shriek from the depths of my shattered heart.

"Joey." Robin shook me. "Joey, where's the watch?"

I could barely hear him. Couldn't tear my gaze away from the two still forms of girl and dog lying on the pavement.

"The watch, Joey." Robin gripped my face and forced me to meet his gaze. "You can undo this without using magic that will cost you something dear."

I blinked.

"I know you're in shock but the longer you wait, the harder it will be. Now, where is the pocket watch?"

"My car," I exhaled the answer. "Gym bag."

"Come with me." Robin gripped my hand and dragged me to my vehicle. Out of my periphery, I saw my mother fly down the front steps and barrel toward the road. Darcy's boys stood silent for once, all big-eyed and terrified.

They'd be traumatized. How would I explain it to Darcy? Or Aunt Hannah? Oh, Dragon, no.

"Joey, focus!" Robin dropped my hand long enough to toss open my car door. He rooted through my bag and pressed the watch into my hands. "Use it now. Spin time around you back. Benji will go with you so you can use your magic."

Was it possible to hear your own heart beating? Blood pounded in my ears, muffling all other sounds. "What if I can't stop it? What if it's fated?" The way my career-ending accident had been.

Robin took the chain and draped the watch over my head. "You won't know until you try. Now wind it back."

With trembling fingers, I gripped the dial and spun in in reverse. The minute hand moved back five minutes and then ten. Robin was gone. I glanced around and saw him standing among the crowd. Then it dispersed, everyone, running backward. Some to their homes across the road, others to the overflowing tables of our garage sale. Robin walked backward and disappeared behind the bush.

My attention turned toward the street, to where a black sedan with tinted windows was driving in reverse. I saw the moment the car hit Dragon and Bluto happen in reverse. With bodies lifting up off the pavement, into the air, and then down, where they stood on the street.

I didn't wait for time to resume. I ran for the road, put myself between them and the oncoming car. She was still alive. I could do this. I had to do this. Benji moved up beside me and stood at the ready to do whatever the hell it was a familiar did.

Coldness seeped into me. It felt as though malice radiated from the car and was directed at us. No way to see the driver through those tinted windows.

In my mind's eye, I imagined the four of us on the lawn, well out of the car's path. Saw that reality. *I wish we were safe.*

Golden sparkles effervesced like champagne bubbles around us.

An engine roared. Tires screeched. I could feel the tug of displaced air pulling at my clothes as the car zoomed past. It blew through the stop sign and then vanished, but not before I got a good look at the vanity plates.

Beeyotch1.

"Slow down!" Someone hollered. "Jesus, God in heaven. Someone could be killed."

Behind me, Dragon shrieked.

I turned to face her. "Are you all right?"

"Joey?" She asked, eyes huge as duck eggs. "That car. How…?"

She'd been dead. And now she wasn't. I reached for her and pulled her into my arms. Relief swamped me. I would never forget those sightless eyes, the way her skull had been caved in.

It took her a minute to let out a shaky breath and another for her to hug me back. Bluto licked her hand and she reached down to pet him, though she shook from head to toe.

"You're in shock." She wasn't the only one. "Maybe we ought to take you to the hospital."

She shook her head and swallowed hard. "No."

"At least go inside. Have Aunt Prudence make you a cup of tea." I pointed to the house.

"We were in the road," she said. "One second we were right in the path of that car and the next…."

I wasn't about to deny it. She was smart, she knew where we'd been. No way would I blow smoke at her and make her question what she'd seen. Dragon had enough betrayal in her young life already. "Not now."

I gestured to where patrons milled about, oblivious to what had almost happened.

What had happened. What I had undone.

A chill skittered down my spine. It was her. The faery queen had been in that car. I'd felt her presence.

And though I didn't see the driver, I recognized the vehicle.

"Joey?" Robin called my name and I spun and saw him emerging from behind the bushes, a puzzled expression on his face.

"Here." Gripping Bluto by the collar and Dragon by the arm, I towed them back towards the Victorian. Loyal Benji followed right behind me.

Robin's gaze dropped to where the watch hung between

my breasts. When his sapphire eyes lifted to study me, I nodded once, letting him know I had used it.

My mother met us on the steps. "What's going on?"

"Dragon had a close call." Too damn close. What if Robin hadn't given me that watch? She would have died.

"Make her some tea. I need to go check on Darcy's boys."

When they were out of earshot, I grabbed Robin by the arm. After scanning the crowd to find the boys grubbing in the dormant flower beds looking for earthworms, I made sure no one else could overhear. "I just undid something kinda major. And I think your mother was involved."

Robin stilled. "What do you mean?"

I told him about the accident, the loathing that radiated from the vehicle, and how I had shifted us out of the car's path. It was an effort not to check between my legs and make sure I hadn't wet myself.

"She was dead, Robin. Your mother killed her." My gorge rose and I barely bit back the urge to vomit. "Why would she hurt her?"

He pulled me into his chest. Didn't say a word as he held me and I shook and fell apart as much as I could. That woman was evil. I knew it when I'd dreamed about her. Seen the reality of it on Robin's skin. But to mow down an innocent girl and her dog that way?

"Why Dragon?" I sniffled.

"She might have thought she was you."

Though I didn't want to lose the feeling of being enclosed in his arms, I pulled back so I could see his face. "How in the world could she mistake a teenager for me?"

"She doesn't know much about you, lamb. Other than

where you live because I'm here. But she knows only that you are my bride to be, not that you tricked me."

"But she saw me," I insisted. "When she scratched me in that dream. I know she looked right in my eyes."

"My mother doesn't know what you are. Many people can change what they look like in a dream. No magic involved. She probably thought your physical appearance was meant to hide your true face."

"But why a car?" I shook my head. "Why not attack me with magic?"

"Again, she doesn't understand your abilities. She probably figured a sneak attack was best. Easier to weaponize her mortal anchor's flesh and belongings."

That sounded ominous. "How though?"

"Through compulsion." He shot me an uneasy glance. "Fae use their anchors for more than simply grounding magic in this plane. They get us whatever we require. And we can take over their bodies for limited amounts of time."

"Take over?" I staggered back from him. "Like body-snatching?"

"It's nothing I would have tried with you," he hurriedly tagged on. "For one thing you're too stubborn and strong-willed. You would fight that sort of control."

"You bet your fae ass I would." I closed my eyes and tried to get a grip on this latest revelation. "You mean she made Ursula try to run me over?"

His blond brows pulled down. "Ursula?"

"It was her car. I couldn't see her face, but I recognized the plate."

Robin nodded slowly. "If Ursula is my mother's anchor,

it's a recent development. Have you noticed her situation has changed at all lately?"

"Well, she's gotten herself engaged to one of the level ten fathers. He's an investment broker or something. They live outside of town in a huge compound. She was at the gym the other night, being difficult, insisting that her soon-to-be stepdaughter got preferential treatment and generally giving me crap."

Robin nodded as if in thought. "That might have been her trade. She anchors my mother in exchange for an improvement in her life situation."

I blew out a breath as I thought it through. "If Dragon had died and Ursula was the one behind the wheel, she would be the one who was arrested."

"That's exactly her style. Dragon, Bluto, Ursula. All collateral damage."

I stared down at the scratches on my arm. "But she's already poisoned me. Why would she waste her time trying to run me over?"

"She doesn't know where your magic comes from or how strong you are. Maybe she thought you healed yourself or were somehow immune to her poison."

I wrapped my arms around myself. "She'll try again." It wasn't a question.

He scrubbed a hand over his face. "Right now, she's going to be investigating you, trying to find out every last little thing about you. We have a bit of time. And knowing who her anchor is, is a huge advantage."

I couldn't follow his train of thought. "In what way?"

"Because, if we kill her anchor, she must return to the fae realm."

My lips parted. "Kill? You want to kill Ursula Green?"

He gripped my upper arms. "Listen to me, Joey. I will do whatever I have to to make sure that you and your family are safe."

I stepped back and shook my head. "I can't even discuss this with you."

Robin ran a hand through his disheveled hair. "She has been awful to you for years. I don't understand why you feel the need to protect her."

"Maybe because she didn't know what she was in for with the fae any more than I did."

He flinched.

I wasn't done. "Or how about the fact that killing someone, no matter how convenient it is for you or how much you dislike them, is wrong. How do you not get that by now?"

"And what if it comes down to a choice between her life or yours?" Robin's tone grew quiet. "You want me to allow my mother to murder you when there is anything I can do to stop it? You said your safety was your responsibility but you can't go it alone, not in this."

My lips parted but before I could think of a suitable retort he pushed on. "What if it comes down to Ursula or your mother? Or Grammy B? Would you still fight so hard to protect the woman who made her bed and might very well die in it?"

A heartbeat of silence passed before I cleared my throat. "I need to get to work."

"I'll ride with you."

"I don't think—"

He spun me to face him and then his lips were pressed

firmly against mine. A dark, hungry sort of kiss that addled my brain. He stole my breath, my thoughts and made the world around me spin even farther out of control.

When he finally broke away, I stared up at him, at a loss. "What was that?"

His lips twitched. "My way of going back in time. To before everything went to absolute shite."

Both my palms rested on his chest. "I don't want to fight with you."

His expression sobered. "Don't ask me to leave you unprotected. If anything happens to you…."

"You'll have to go back." I nodded in understanding.

But Robin shook his head. "You still don't get it."

"What?"

"I'll go start the car." He turned and walked away.

Leaving me wondering what I had missed.

ROBIN WASN'T ALONE when I exited my gymnastics class through the back door to the parking lot. Andreas stood beside him, hands in the pockets of his leather trench coat.

I nodded to Andreas and he smirked and gave me a slow once over, emerald gaze locked on the mounds of my breasts. "I'll tell you now, Robin, I will gladly do as you ask in exchange for a night with your lovely fiancée."

Robin's right hand clenched into a fist at Andrea's indecent proposal. Judging by the way the muscle jumped in his jaw, their conversation had been less than productive. And now Andreas was using me to bait Robin. Again.

I sighed and plunked my gym bag down. "Okay."

"What?" Both their heads whipped to me, identical expressions of shock on their handsome faces.

"I said okay, I'll spend the night with Andreas."

He grinned and Robin looked as though I had gutted him with a rusty spork.

Andreas strode forward and looped an arm over my shoulders. "I'll take good care of her for you."

"Lamb—"

"So, it's a bargain?" I didn't glance Robin's way, all my attention on Andreas and dusting off my underdeveloped feminine wiles. "I promise to put you to good use."

"One night with you in exchange for sneaking into the mortal anchor's home. A bargain well struck," Andreas grinned down at me and offered his hand.

I gripped it in mine and magic swirled between us making all the small hairs on my arms rise. Golden light shimmered around the dirty alley, cementing our bargain. When it dissipated I released him and stepped back toward Robin who looked ready to puke his guts up.

"So, when are we going to do this?" Andreas practically purred.

In an innocent tone I offered, "How does Thursday sound? I promised to watch Darcy's boys while she and Mike went out so I could definitely use an extra set of hands. Just FYI, the oldest is a bit of a firebug."

"That's not—" he sputtered.

"Ah ah, you agreed to one night. You said nothing about what we were going to be doing."

Andreas's lips parted. "You set me up."

Robin didn't bother to hide his satisfaction. "You never see her coming. She's a wolf in lamb's clothing."

I rolled my eyes at him. Obviously, he wanted to pretend that he'd been in on the bait and switch from the beginning. I decided to let him save face in front of his brother.

Andreas scrutinized me more carefully. "And what if I had included sex with our bargain? Would you have still taken me up on it?"

I shrugged. "The world may never know."

"At the very least I ought to be annoyed about being so easily duped, but I find myself unable to muster the proper resentment since her…handling is so masterful." He tossed me a wink.

"You better get going before someone sees us together." Robin pulled me in close to his side.

"See you at midnight." With a final kiss blown at me, Andreas vanished.

"What's happening at midnight?" I turned deeper into Robin's embrace. The wind had picked up and in the distance, the clouds stacked up with dark underbellies. I shivered against the cold.

"Now you ask," Robin tugged on the lapels of my coat. "But not before you agreed to spend the night with him?"

I shrugged. "You wanted me to own my confidence. I knew I could handle him and that you needed his help."

"You're beautiful when you're handling my brother," he murmured.

My nose wrinkled. "You might want to rephrase that."

A chuckle escaped.

"So, midnight? What's happening?"

"Andreas is going to see if he can enthrall Ursula."

I frowned. "What good will that do?"

"If my mother is residing inside the mortal, his essence

won't be able to enthrall her. But if he can, he'll lure Ursula back to the fae realm. And that will give my mother no choice but to return there because she will be without an anchor here."

I let out a breath. "Enslaving Ursula for a year and a day."

"I know how you feel about that, Joey. But honestly, isn't it better than ending her life? She did make a bargain with a fae. Magic always has a price."

"I'm so sick of hearing that," I groaned and then pulled out of his grip. "Come on, we need to get going if we're going to make it to Grammy's by seven."

Hand in hand, we walked to where my car was parked.

"Tell me about your aunt," Robin urged. "What do I need to do to impress her?"

"Money and lots of it." I took the turn out of town that cut through the industrial district but took a good ten minutes off the commute. "Power, influence, the usual suspects. Why do you care anyway?"

"Because I was hoping she would let us adopt Dragon."

I nearly crashed into a mailbox. "Say what now?"

"When I spoke with her earlier she made it clear that she's unhappy at the prospect of her mother being in town. She deserves to have the same sort of loving home you come from. As long as her mother is in the picture, she won't have that."

"Yes but, Robin. You can't just adopt someone else's kid on a whim."

"Why not?"

"Well, for one thing, there's the fact that you are barely employed and practically homeless."

He waved that away. "Your father will write me a letter of

recommendation. And she has a home with your mother while we can live in the cottage."

"Um…." My hands tightened on the steering wheel. "Haven't you forgotten the teeny tiny fact that I've been poisoned? And that your mother—aka the faery queen—wants to kill me? Dragon was almost collateral damage earlier. And—"

"And?" he prompted.

There was no way I could continue to drive and have this conversation. I pulled over into the cheese factory lot, threw the car into park, and turned in my seat. "Let's face facts. Even if we deal with the whole homicidal mommy issue, we don't know if we are going to last."

He threaded his fingers through mine, a look of pure concentration on his face. "We will."

"How can you be so sure?"

He stared out the window for a long moment. "After our bargain, the one where you became my anchor, I felt nothing but humiliation. I was the best at what I did and a mortal female had tricked me. I hated you but more importantly, I hated myself for allowing it to happen. For not asking more questions about who you were and why you offered yourself up to be my anchor. I swore that I would make you pay for my loss."

The bleakness on his face plucked my heartstrings. I wanted to apologize again for putting him in that position, but Robin wasn't finished.

"I didn't know if my torment would ever end. I had no idea how to find you if you were dead or alive if you had trapped me as some sort of punishment for past deeds. And I started to notice things that I had taken for granted before.

Things like the enslaved mortals we used and discarded like so much rubbish. I found myself comparing my situation to theirs. What made me any different from them? I was a prince but yet I was also a prisoner, unable to escape my mother's wrath."

"Why was she so angry?" It was such a foreign concept to me, a mother who would hurt her child.

"I was the most promising of her offspring. The one who would secure her reign, her legacy. Power drives her. Accumulating it, controlling it. She surrounds herself with it. I was to marry a powerful fae heiress who would trade her magic for a royal husband."

My hands clenched into fists at the thought, but I pressed my lips together and didn't say a word. So not the time for jealousy.

"When it became known that I couldn't bargain or trade with mortals, couldn't leave the fae realm, my intended forsook me. All the queen's carefully laid plans were in tatters. Her wrath is bottomless. Sometimes she'd gouge me and would let me twist in agony, let me feel the poison spreading through my body almost to the point of death before administering the antidote. There were times I wished she wouldn't be fast enough and that all the pain, the degradation would end. She hid the scars to keep others from seeing what she had done even as she taunted me for my ugliness. My weakness."

"Robin." A tear slipped down my cheek.

He reached for it, caught it on his fingertip, and studied the drop of moisture. "Days stretched into years, years into decades. Things started coming back to me. Odd, pieces of the puzzle. The sound of your laughter. The brush of your skin as you touched my arm. The scent of your hair." His fingers tangled in said hair which was once again, slipping free from my ponytail. "I'd wake from dreams that darted away the moment I awoke. Dreams of a kiss that changed everything, that made me see beyond my own selfish existence. Your memory haunted me, lamb. I felt sure you were a powerful mage sent to ensorcell me completely. It was madness and I embraced it because it offered me an escape. It was mine and she couldn't take it from me.

"Even though you had caused my torment you were my only reprieve from the hell that was my life. I hated you and loved you by equal turns. And then it came back. The pieces coalesced and I could see the whole picture. I remembered who I had been, the life I'd lived, and how I had met you. And I realized the only one to blame for my suffering was me. I realized that what you had done was nothing, *nothing* compared to the pain I had caused and would have caused again if you hadn't stopped me."

His thumb traced my cheekbone. "We are going to last because you are my light in the darkness. My moral compass. My reason for being more than I was born to be. You told me that real love means that no word or deed would change those feelings. We are going to last because even if you tire of me, I will *never* stop loving you."

Stunned, I tried to absorb what he had just done, essentially baring his soul to me.

He sighed. "It was just a thought."

It took me a moment to connect the dots. "You mean about Dragon?"

He nodded. "I knew you weren't ready to hear the full truth. You want something simpler, easier, right?"

I want you. Why couldn't I say the words? They were right there, on the tip of my tongue.

Sapphire eyes searched my face. "You know the thing I love most about you, Joey? That even though you can lie, you don't do it. Not when it matters. There is no comfort in pretty lies. Not for someone who has been discarded."

Wordlessly I nodded.

"We better get going," Robin brushed his lips lightly over mine. "We're going to be late."

So, like a coward, I reached for the gear shift.

And doubled over as invisible fire raced up my arm. The pain paralyzed my vocal cords and I turned my horrified gaze to face Robin.

"The poison?" His eyes were wide, his hands reaching for me.

I screamed when he made contact. The soothing touch he normally offered was hotter than a brand. He drew back immediately.

I couldn't speak, couldn't breathe. The world faded to a cocoon of white-hot agony.

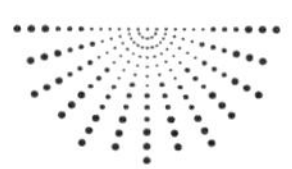

"There are three sides to every story. Your side, my side, and the truth that lies somewhere in between. Up to you what you want to believe."

-Notable quotable from Grammy B

"Lamb? Wake up."

I blinked my eyes open to see Robin hovering over me, his sapphire eyes anxious. A comforting warmth was pressed into my right side. Benji.

Robin let out a relieved breath and his shoulders relaxed. "That was too close."

"What happened?"

"The pain took you down fast. Faster than I thought possible. I shifted you out of the driver's seat and brought you back here. You were apart from your familiar for too long. It's my fault, I should have insisted you stay here." Guilt radiated from his every pore.

"We agreed. You're not the boss of me." It might have been more impressive if I had the energy to sit up.

"No, I'm not." Strong arms came around me and I realized I was lying on the rug in the front parlor of the Victorian. "Even so, you shouldn't go anywhere without Benji until after Andreas enthralls the fae queen's anchor."

My thoughts were cobwebby and barely holding together but there was something there, like an itch between the shoulder blades that I just couldn't reach. "Is anyone else at home?"

Robin shook his head. "They've gone to see your aunt."

"I should be there." I tried and failed to get to my feet. Benji whined. "Dragon needs the support."

"You need to rest." Robin heaved out a breath. "I think you ought to use the watch."

Twice in one day? "No way."

"Listen to me. You can use it to go forward. If Andreas succeeds in enthralling Ursula, we'll have leverage with my mother. We need to get you that antidote. Once we do, you are free to come back and relive this dinner you and Dragon are both dreading but insist that we attend."

Though I wanted to argue, what he said made sense. And I really didn't want to experience that blinding pain or the accompanying fear that went along with it ever again.

Robin pressed the watch into my hand, then dropped a kiss to my forehead. "I'll see you soon."

The feel of his lips against my skin brought it back to me. The confession Robin had made right before the poison had taken root. *I will never stop loving you.* "Robin, about before—"

"Later," he murmured. "Go now."

I didn't want to, but the fear got the best of me. The thought of experiencing that pain again, of not waking up....

Taking a deep breath and placing a hand on Benji, I wound the watch forward, to midnight.

When I looked up, Robin was nowhere in sight.

"Robin?" Stiff from being sprawled on the floor, I got to my hands and knees and crawled over to the chaise, and used it to heft myself up.

Since I'd never traveled forward through time before, I didn't know what to expect. But Robin had known this was the plan, that I was going to skip a few hours ahead. So why wasn't he waiting here for me?

Mental forehead smack. Robin was meeting Andreas at midnight over at Ursula's place. I should have come back at 11:30 to intercept him before he left.

Screw time travel loops and the horse they rode in on.

I had to get myself to Ursula's house to oversee the enthralling. And I had to take my familiar with me, to keep the poison at bay until Andreas could get me the antidote.

"Want to go for a ride, boy?" I reached down and scratched Benji behind the ear.

The dog got up, stretched his front legs and back, and sauntered to the door. Even though he normally stuck to my side like glue, I clipped a leash on him and then headed out into the darkness.

No cars in the driveaway. Robin must have taken my ride. Weird though, I would have thought Mom and Dragon would have been home hours ago. After all, Aunt Hannah wasn't exactly their favorite person.

I called Darcy. She answered on the first ring with a breathy, "You are a goddess and don't let anyone tell you otherwise."

In the background, I picked up the distinct whirring of a sewing machine. She must be working. "Did you have a good time?"

"It was exactly what I needed, Joey. Got all of my creative juices flowing again. And speaking of which, why aren't you getting busy with your live-in lover instead of calling me in the middle of the night?"

"I was wondering if I could borrow your car."

"Girl, after what you did for me today, you could ask for a kidney and I would snip it out with my pinking shears."

"Just the car, Darce. I'll be up in a few to snag the keys." I hung up the phone and then Benji and I trotted up the road to Darcy's house.

She met us on the front porch, clad in oversized jeans and a white cardigan. "So where are you headed?"

I had to tell her since she needed to know where her car was and all. "Ursula's house."

Darcy blinked. "You're shitting me, right?"

"I shit you not." I didn't want to freak her out about the incident from earlier or tell her the fae queen had poisoned me but she deserved an explanation. "Robin thinks Ursula is the fae queen's anchor. Robin's brother is going to enthrall her."

"Oh, this I've got to see." Darcy shut the door behind her and scurried down the steps.

"Darcy," I began.

"Nope, no way am I letting you do this without me." She strode purposefully toward her minivan.

I hurried to catch up with her. "Technically, it's kidnapping. I don't want you involved in this."

Darcy paused with her hand on the driver's side door. "Listen up babe because I am only going to say this once. I know you. I know that you have a damn good reason for whatever the hell it is you're helping them do. And I am completely and totally one hundred percent on your side. Plus, I'm married to a cop. If shit gets real, Mike and I can make sure your ass is not left billowing in the breeze."

My lips parted but no words came out. What could I tell her that would convince her to stay behind and keep herself out of the fae skirmish? Nothing came to mind and we were wasting time.

As though sensing my upset, Benji whined. I took a steadying breath and then nodded. "Okay. Just promise to keep your distance. The last thing I need is to try to explain to Mike how you got yourself enthralled to a fae prince."

Darcy nodded and I slid open the rear compartment letting Benji scramble into the back before climbing into the passenger's seat.

"So, catch me up," Darcy seemed more her usual self, confident and ready to take the world by storm. I guess a little bit of nookie will do that for a girl.

"Robin told me he's in love with me." I hadn't meant to say it. The words just tumbled out.

"And...?" Darcy took a turn too fast and I slammed into the door.

"And what?" I asked. "Slow down."

"And what did you say back?" she prompted.

I sighed. "Nothing."

She faux winced. "Poor Robin."

Her tone got my back up. "Look, it's a really shady situation. He's been through a lot and I don't think he's viewing things clearly."

She cut her gaze to me. "Maybe you're the one who isn't thinking clearly."

I frowned. "What do you mean?"

"Nothing. Is it this left?" Darcy had paused by a stop sign.

"Next one I think. Pretty sure they have their own gate." Ursula's fiancé didn't live in a part of town that I frequented very often, but I had driven by once or twice.

Darcy nodded but didn't say anything else.

I blew out a sigh. "You totally suck, you know?"

"What?" she asked all innocent-like.

"You're sitting over there, obviously not saying whatever the hell is on your mind and squirming like a toddler who has to tinkle because you can't keep it in."

She shot me a sideways glance. "Okay, fine. The thing is, I know you. You're afraid of what comes next after the I love yous."

"And what comes next?"

"You, if he's any good."

"Darcy," I moaned.

"Seriously, you are terrified of intimacy. You always shut people down at a certain point. You only let them in so far. Who is closer to you than me?"

Good, an easy question. "No one."

"And do you think the same is true for me?"

I considered it. "I don't know, maybe?"

She made a disgruntled sound. "If someone asked me

who my ride or die was, I would say you, no question about it. But as close as we are, Mike is my best friend. He knows me in ways you never could, the same way I know him. We're one hundred percent honest with each other, even if it takes us a while to get there. "

"Are you saying you're not a hundred percent honest with me?"

"I am. But it's different. You make me stronger, bolder."

I snorted. "Don't go blaming me for that."

"It's true. And I know I do the same for you. When we are together we can be our true and honest selves. But in a relationship, there's this layer of vulnerability. You worry over things like how that person sees you because there's no bravado anymore. All the masks get stripped away leaving you exposed. And that is a layer you have never been comfortable with."

I swallowed. "How do you know that?"

The corner of her mouth kicked up. "Because I've been paying attention. You only date safe people, ones that don't make it past the first few layers. Georgia was the closest you came to a real connection."

Because I'd forced our relationship to fit the mold I'd wanted. "Being intimate isn't just about sex, though."

Darcy cut her gaze to me. "Right. it means you have to risk being rejected when you are at your most vulnerable."

The way Robin had when he'd confessed his feelings.

The lines on the road disappeared and the incline increased. Darcy focused on the road ahead of us and then asked, "Do you believe he loves you?"

"He can't lie."

She blew out a breath. "That's not what I mean. Do you

believe, deep down in your heart that he genuinely feels the same way about you that your father feels toward your mother? Or the way your grandparents felt about each other?"

His heartfelt confession about what had been done to him, how he would go back and endure all that again to save my life. That wasn't some trick or a ploy. He hadn't asked me for anything in return. No bargain, just sacrifice. Why else would someone do that if not for love?

"Yeah," I put my head in my hands. "You're right. But I've made so many mistakes. And I feel like the rules are constantly changing with Robin. The bargains, the magic, it complicates everything even more. When I'm so muddled, how can I know if what I feel is real or I'm just seeing what I want to see and forcing it?"

She shrugged. "You need to get out of your head. Knock a few back and jump on him."

That sounded suspiciously like Grammy B's dumbstick advice. But coming from two women who made long term relationships look easy…maybe I ought to heed it.

Later.

The white mansion stood glowing brilliantly under the full moon. My car had been pulled off the road, well away from the house. Darcy parked in behind it and we stared up at the house.

"Now what?" she asked.

I popped the car door. "Stay here. Let me see if I can find Robin."

At that moment all the lights went out, including her headlights.

"What the hell? Darcy asked.

I blinked, waiting for my eyes to adjust to the natural darkness. "It's Andreas. Tech doesn't work around the fae. Remember?"

The wind picked up, blowing my hair back away from my face. I slid open the rear door letting Benji out, then turned to face Darcy. "Stay here."

When she nodded, I shut the door as softly as I could. The magic would have taken out any cameras, but who knew if Henry St. John had flesh and blood security.

"Let's do this," I said to the dog.

He wagged his tail and we headed up the hill to the darkened mansion.

I FOUND Robin crouched behind a box hedge that had been trimmed into the shape of a tiger. As Grammy said, some people had more money than sense.

I studied the fae prince as I approached. He wore head to toe black and his face was illuminated by the pale moonlight. The strain showed around his eyes. His focus was intent on the dark house.

"Hey," I touched his arm and he jumped. "Sorry. Didn't mean to startle you."

"How did you get here?" he snapped.

I blinked. "Darcy gave me a ride."

"Fantastic." He turned his attention back toward the house.

I tried not to be stung but his curt dismissal. There I'd been stressing about opening myself up to him and now it seemed like he couldn't wait to ditch me. "Wasn't this the plan all along?"

"Things change," Robin muttered.

"In four hours?"

"Look, it would be better if you had Darcy take you home. I'll meet you there as soon as we finish up—"

A scream pierced the night.

I stiffened. "What's going on, Robin?"

He blew out a breath and rose from his crouched position behind the hedge. "Damn it. Go home, Joey."

He made to walk away but I snagged his arm. "Is Andreas hurting her?"

"I don't have time for—"

"Answer the question, Robin. Did you tell your brother to kill Ursula?" I searched his face even as I dreaded the answer.

"Only if he has to."

I let go of him.

"This is exactly why I didn't want you here."

"We talked about this. We said if she couldn't be enthralled, we would have to find another way."

"Yes, and then I watched you in the grip of that poison and decided that we didn't have the time to find another way." He gripped my hand and tugged me forward. "Since you're here, you can provide magical backup. Come on."

We ran across the gravel drive and around the side of the house.

I struggled to keep up with his long-legged stride, my mind still reeling. What if Ursula was dead? Would I even be able to look at Robin the same way knowing he had orchestrated it?

He pulled me up against the side of the house, beneath an open window.

My heart was beating out of control. It had been bad enough knowing she would be enthralled and abducted. But dead? Damn it, if Robin sanctioned some sort of mob-style execution on Ursula I would never forgive him.

"Hey?" A male voice called from up above. "You there?"

I craned my neck up in time to see Andreas's emerald gaze, peering down at me from the second story.

"What the hell happened?" I hissed. *Is Ursula still alive?*

"Nothing I couldn't handle," Andreas winked. "Meet me around the side door."

Robin huffed out a breath as the window slid shut. "He's all about the dramatic flair."

"Those who live in glass houses," I muttered.

A moment later, Andreas appeared and I was relieved to see Ursula's red hair bobbing along behind him. She wore a see-through satin nightgown with loose sleeves and a sweetheart bodice. Her eyes were glazed over as she stared up at Andreas adoringly.

"Any sign of mother?" Robin asked.

Andreas shook his head. "Not a trace."

"Who screamed?" I asked.

"The daughter." He chucked his thumb at the door where we saw Ursula's soon-to-be stepdaughter watching intently. "I mistook her room for Ursula's. Once we got that straightened out, she was happy to help me dispose of the slag. Her words."

My lips parted. "Veronica St. John just handed her stepmother over to you? You didn't enchant her, did you?"

"Nope, she's fairly resistant to my essence."

"That's because you're old," Veronica called.

Andreas turned to look at her and she shrugged.

"Teenagers," I muttered.

"Hey, Ms. Whitmore. Say hi to Dragon for me." Veronica called out.

"You know Dragon?" I blinked.

"She's pretty cool." Even in the low light from the candle she held, I could tell Veronica was blushing.

"I think that's why she's resistant," Robin muttered.

I shook my head. No way was I going to steer Dragon toward Veronica. She deserved so much better, especially because she was helping us with Ursula's abduction.

"It's thirty degrees out," I stared down at Ursula's bare feet. "She'll get frostbite."

Andreas sighed and turned to his thrall. "Go get yourself some shoes, dove."

I shook my head in wonder as Ursula headed inside to grab a pair of pink and purple snow boots. I had never thought I would see her so passive. It felt…wrong. Icky, like I had helped the two of them slip her a roofie. "She needs a coat, too."

"She won't need it where she's going," Andreas smirked.

I glared at him and he heaved a put-upon sigh then ordered "Ursula, grab a coat." When she did, he refocused on me. "Anything else? Should I have her pack for the weekend? How about a good old-fashioned steamer trunk full of wide-brimmed hats?"

"Don't be a dick," I snapped at him. Though I was glad to see Ursula was still alive, I seriously doubted having Andreas look after her was in her best interest.

"Did I look that zonked out when I was enthralled?" I asked Robin.

He didn't answer. "Quit screwing around. We need to get her out of here before anyone catches us."

I didn't know if he meant Ursula's intended or his mother, but neither sounded like a stellar option.

Clad in her boots and coat, Ursula reemerged from the house. Veronica gave a little finger wave and then slammed the door behind us.

"She's going to cover for us. Tell her father that Ursula left with a ruggedly handsome stranger and that she would be back in a year. Sometimes the truth is stranger than any fiction."

No arguing with that.

Robin led us across the property and down the hill, past the tiger hedge and to the open security gate. The second Andreas crossed through it the power came back on.

Robin stopped at the line of trees where we had left the cars. Darcy's blonde head popped out. "Holy crap, did I look that stoned when he used his mojo on me?"

"No," I told her, but had no doubt that she would have if I let her hang around Robin any longer in her hard-up state.

I stared hard at Ursula. What would it be like to be out of your head for a year and a day, to be passed around like a party favor in the fae realm? I touched Robin on the arm. "Are you sure this is the only way?"

He nodded. "She has to cross back so that the queen will as well."

I looked up at Andreas. "Please, don't hurt her."

His green eyes softened. "I have no intention of hurting

her, Josephine Louise Whitmore. She will be my guest and no one will lay a hand on her the entire time she is with me."

"You better go," Robin said to him.

Andreas nodded and then winked at me. "I'll see you Thursday for our date."

Looping his arm through Ursula's, he snapped his fingers and the two of them vanished.

Robin closed his eyes. Beside me, he tensed.

"What is it?" I asked.

"She's still here."

She. As in his mother. "How can that be?"

He shook his head. "It shouldn't be possible."

"What's going on?" Darcy called.

I shook my head. "We made a mistake. Ursula wasn't the anchor."

But then the question remained, who was?

CHAPTER FIFTEEN

"Marry in haste. Repent at leisure while doing twenty-five to life."

-Notable quotable from Grammy B

Darcy dropped me off in front of my house. "You okay, Joey? You look a little pale."

"It's winter, I'm always pale." Damn, I was practically fae the way I could twist the truth.

The truth was we had sent Ursula into the fae realm for nothing. And unless I could come up with something else quick, the faery queen's poison was going to kill me.

I opened the door and Benji leapt out onto the lawn.

"You know, I think I will get that dog tomorrow," Darcy said as she stared down at my familiar.

"What changed your mind?"

She shrugged. "It's nice to have someone around who always appreciates you."

I reached for her hand and squeezed. "I appreciate you, babe. Never forget that."

"Boy, you're usually not this sentimental unless you're a few shots of tequila in." She yawned. "We're still on for Margarita Monday, right?"

"Georgia is coming. For real this time. And she might bring Ruby Sue." Another misleading statement because I desperately didn't want my best friend to know that I might be dead by Monday.

I was already feeling colder than the balmy night warranted.

"Awesome." She yawned again. I shut the door and turned away before she could see the tears in my eyes.

I trudged inside, Benji padding at my heels. The lights that I'd left on in the kitchen were still on. My mother's art studio was dark. Probably just as well they stayed over at Grammy's. I had a murderous fae queen to deal with. Maybe I should rent them a little cabin on a lake for a week, so they would be safely hidden from the queen until after….

Shoving that thought away, I went into the kitchen, filled Benji's bowl with food, and checked his water. Canine happily settled, I hunted until I found the tequila in the back of the snack cabinet. Finding a vessel was tougher. Mom had really gone to town with clearing the house of excessive bits and bobs. Finally, I discovered a little shot glass Grammy had won from a trip to Dave and Busters. After cleaning the dust out of it with the hem of my tank top, I poured myself a shot. By the third, my eyes burned and my throat felt borderline raw.

Outside, a car door slammed and a moment later Robin appeared.

"What's going to happen with Ursula?" It had been tormenting me since Robin discovered his mother was still in the portal plane.

"Since she isn't the anchor, Andreas will return her to her life and encourage her to act normally. Though I doubt Veronica will like that."

I poured another shot. "And the car that hit Dragon? I know for a fact it's Ursula's."

"It was probably my mother's favor being cashed in to throw us off the scent."

"It worked," I muttered.

"What are you doing, lamb?"

"Liquid courage." I raised the glass in a toast before knocking it back.

"Courage for what?"

"For this." I pushed myself up and staggered over to him.

He caught me before I could face-plant onto the floor. Damn, how long had it been since I'd done tequila shooters? Twenty years?

For good reason, too.

"Tequila makes my clothes fall off," I informed Robin as I looped my arms around his neck and pulled my body even tighter to his. His scent invaded me down to my core. I needed this, needed him. And tonight, I would have him.

"Joey, no." His expression appeared pained.

"Why not?" I traced my tongue along his collarbone, right above the line where his scars stopped.

He swallowed and I could sense his resolve wavering. "Because I don't want you to regret this."

"You know what I regret?" I whispered in his ear. "That I didn't kiss you the very first time you asked me to. That I was too scared of being hurt again to take you up on what you've been freely offering. I regret hiding from life instead of living it."

His gaze roved over my face. "What's changed?"

I was going to die. And all the things I thought I would have more time for were never going to happen. No proficiency in yoga. No more walks to Darcy's with Benji. No more dinners with Grammy, Mom, or Dragon.

No more Robin Goodfellow.

"Everything," I said and molded my lips to his.

Just FYI, this is the part where I sully the hell out of a certain fae prince. Oh, don't act surprised, you knew it was coming. Imminent death plus liquor plus hot guy…can you blame me? If reading about what's to come—or as Darcy would say, who—isn't your jam, skip on over to the next chapter. I'll meet you there.

Consider this your fade to black.

Seriously.

The author's been doing tequila shooters too and isn't about to hold back on any detail. We're too seasoned to pussyfoot around.

Don't say I didn't warn you.

The kiss was hot, hungry, and held nothing back. I demanded his absolute surrender to my drunken will. His hands hovered and I could sense his internal struggle, the battle of self-denial. But deep down, he was a hedonist, a pleasure seeker and he desired the same thing I did.

Robin had changed, but not that much.

A groan escaped him and he scooped me up and carried

me toward the stairs. The gesture was extra hot because he didn't stumble or wheeze as he made his way to the second floor, then down the hall to my bedroom.

He set me down long enough to shut the door. That gave me enough time to do the not so sensual removal of my tank top and sports bra. The gods of carnal lust were with me because it came off in one relatively easy tug. I toed off my sneakers and yanked on one sock, then the other. Robin turned around and saw that I was in the process of shoving both my pants and underwear down past my knees

Hot sapphire eyes slid over me and I could feel the look like a grazing touch. "You weren't kidding about the tequila."

"Stronger than your average fae essence, it is the ultimate aphrodisiac." Of course, the man in front of me was no slouch either.

I reached for the hem of his long-sleeved t-shirt but he was already tugging it off. Beneath the scars he was perfect. Not an extra ounce of fat anywhere. If I hadn't been in such a hurry, I would have sighed and stared.

Another fun side effect of tequila, while under its influence, I had a hard time keeping my hands to myself. Or my lips. I was busy following the goody trail that ran from his navel to where it disappeared into his jeans when he caught my face in his hands. He knelt before me and slid his hands into my hair until our gazes locked.

"Are you really sure this is what you want?" His eyes searched my face.

"You're what I want." I stroked him through his jeans so there would be no mistaking my intentions.

He kissed me then and I let him because, yes, he was exactly what I wanted, what I craved. His lips left a slow-burning trail from my mouth to my jaw and down across my breasts.

The room spun and I gave myself up to the pleasure, the liquor, and the need to not overthink the shit out of life anymore.

Sometimes it was better to live it.

His mouth closed over a tight nipple and a wicked shiver went through my body.

He released me long enough to ask, "Cold?"

"Aroused," I corrected.

"Then we should do something about that." With a sinful smirk, he returned to lick and suckle the other breast. They weren't perfect, had never been perfect. I'd gone from a tight bodied undernourished elite gymnast only to catch up on puberty in a big rush when my training ended. Perky tits hadn't come with the package. Age hadn't done them any favors.

Robin worshiped them with his hands and mouth as though he'd never seen anything more glorious.

Heat built in my core, the spool tightening almost to the point of pain. "Robin, I wish…"

His hand covered my mouth. "Don't say it."

A giggle effervesced out of me. Right. Wishing equaled bad.

Damn, I was drunk as a skunk as Grammy B would say.

The hand vanished. "Lamb, how much of this will you even remember tomorrow?"

"We can always do it again, can't we?" I suggested. "Just as a refresher."

For a moment he looked crestfallen.

"What? Did I say something wrong?"

He shook himself and pasted on a smile. "If that's what you want."

I sat up, the growing heat between my legs momentarily displaced as my number one concern. "Hey, talk to me. Tell me what's wrong."

"Besides the fact that you've been poisoned by my mother?"

I let out a long breath.

"And now I've killed the mood."

"Come here." I reached out and wrapped my arms around him. He came willingly and snuggled his head onto my shoulder. I stroked his hair and hummed, doing my best to soothe him. He'd known so much hurt and loss. But there was good in him. I'd seen it myself the way he interacted with Dragon, my mom, and Grammy. The way he respected my father.

The way he loved me.

After an untold amount of time, he lifted his head. Those sapphire eyes glowed in the dimness. "You deserve the world, my lamb. You deserve perfect."

"How about perfect for me?" I whispered. "Because that's what you are, Robin. We fit together. Two jagged-edged halves of a whole."

I rose up and kissed him, once, twice, and a final time. Then I lay back down and waited.

He followed me down, the way I'd hoped he would. His hands grew bolder, skimming up the inside of my thighs to touch the damp curls at the juncture. We both hissed out a breath when he pushed deeper within and touched my sex.

I rolled my hips up with abandon, glad for the tequila

because, for the first time in my life, I wasn't worried about what I looked like. I just let it go and enjoyed it.

Best friend plus more, Darcy had said. Now I knew exactly what she meant. Robin wasn't judging me, wasn't comparing me to anyone in his past or rushing to get to the endzone. He was beautiful and vulnerable and all mine.

His gaze grew hooded as he explored me, delving deeper with first one finger and then two.

"That feels so good," I moaned.

"I want to taste you," he breathed.

"Like I'm going to say no to that?"

He raised a brow, as though surprised.

I curled one finger and beckoned him forward. "Let me tell you a secret."

When he leaned down, I nipped his earlobe and then whispered, "You can do whatever you want to me, Robin. I trust you."

"You do?" he sounded shocked. And maybe it was shocking, considering how we'd begun. But I knew he'd do everything in his power to protect and even cherish my body.

In answer, I parted my legs wider, eager to see his broad shoulders fitting between them. To feel what he could do to me with his mouth down there.

He didn't hesitate. After withdrawing his hand from me he moved so that he could lie between my legs. My knees were bent and he wound his arms through them before setting to his work.

I gasped at the electric jolt that went through me as his tongue touched me right there.

It was magic.

The room swirled around me. Blame the bed spins or the

wicked fae doing equally wicked things to my nether region. Each heartbeat took an eternity. My fingers gripped his golden locks. I might have been hurting him, but he didn't slow to complain.

I breathed his name as he slid a finger back inside and curled up in the same beckoning motion I had used on him earlier. Everything crystallized as he found that spot inside me at the same time as his teeth dragged along my most sensitive bit.

My back arched and I detonated on a wordless scream. Colors danced before my eyes for what felt like an eternity before the pleasure finally began to recede.

When my awareness returned, Robin was pressing a kiss to the top of my mound. "You're the most incredible thing I've ever seen."

I smiled down at him. "You're not so bad yourself."

He leaned back against my bed.

I scowled when I realized he still had pants on. "Lose the jeans."

"I don't have any of your human contraceptives," he said.

"I'm on the pill. For the hormone regulation."

He blinked. "What about diseases?"

"I haven't been with anyone since my marriage and that was over two years ago. How about you?"

"Two… hundred and fifty-one," he admitted.

I laughed and threaded my fingers through his. "Is that what you meant when you said you hadn't had any complaints?"

"It's not my fault I was enchanted," he murmured.

"I think we're good. Lose the pants."

"You're so bossy. Who would have thought?"

He stood and unzipped the jeans and pushed them down. My lips parted as I got my first look at his naked body.

He was scarred everywhere, the marks silvery beneath the dusting of golden hair. I skimmed my hands along his legs, feeling the horrific marks that must have been inflicted over hours, days even, to heal so poorly. He was hard everywhere, the male part of him eager for release yet he held back.

Our gazes locked. He stood silently, awaiting my judgment.

"Perfect for me," I whispered.

And then he let go. Whatever thread of control he had been clinging to snapped. He moved atop me, fitting his body against mine. It was even more delicious than in my dirtiest dreams.

My legs parted and he reached between our bodies, lining himself up at my opening. He thrust forward hard and fast and I cried out. Then his mouth was on mine, swallowing my scream of delight as I felt the two of us joined.

He withdrew a few inches and then pushed further in. My nails sank into his back and my legs wrapped around him. My spine was digging into the floor. I would have a bruise there come morning. Couldn't be bothered to give a damn.

I rolled my hips up, meeting his thrusts as they grew more aggressive. I'd expected smooth and practiced skill, something that fit the taunting, teasing fae prince. But this was Robin, raw and desperate for me. It was the hottest thing I had ever known. Pleasure curled and spiraled, the spring coiling ever tighter.

"I'm so close," I breathed.

He caught my face between his hands. "Look at me. Don't close your eyes. I want to see you."

And no way could I refuse him. My back arched, my muscles seized and I held his gaze as my second release swept over me.

"I love you," he said and then let me see his own slice of heaven as he followed me down into the abyss.

We caught our breaths, clinging to each other, limbs entwined, hearts beating in sync. He withdrew from me and lay on his back and I immediately curled into him, my head fitting perfectly into the contour of his shoulder. "We fit this way too."

"In all the ways that matter." He sighed and repeated his earlier declaration. "I love you."

I remember reading once that if a man said I love you before you slept with him, he just wanted to get in your pants. If he said it during, he might be caught up in the moment.

But if he said it after…you could take that to the bank.

I wanted to say it in return, but a yawn stretched my jaw.

He chuckled and rested his chin on my head. "Sleep, my lamb."

I put my hand on his scarred chest and fell asleep listening to the steady thrum of his heart.

CHAPTER SIXTEEN

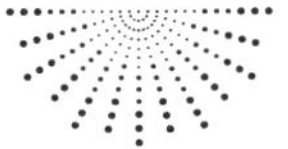

*"Life is like a middle-aged woman. Just when you think you've got
her figured out, she kicks you between the uprights."*
-Notable quotable from Grammy B

I woke up with the worst case of cottonmouth in the
history of the world. My tongue was glued to the roof
of my mouth. Slowly, I worked it free. It felt like I had
been snacking on the lint trap. My head throbbed in time
with my heartbeat. If the poison had struck me down at that
moment, I would have considered it a favor.

Three things occurred to me at once. I was still naked and
sprawled on the floor with only the chenille blanket draped
over me. Benji had been let into the room at some point and
had curled himself up on the window seat. And Robin was
gone.

I waited for the regret to set in but felt none. The wrath of the tequila was worth the boldness it had helped me tap into. I had sullied the hell out of my fae prince.

Go me.

But where had he snuck off to? I'd expected Robin to be a snuggler. Especially with all the, I love yous he'd whispered, and at one point groaned, in my ear.

Probably best that he wasn't here to witness me in all my post-hangover glory.

Slowly, wary of my aching head, I sat up. Benji wagged at me, clearly ready to get up and be about his business. I padded over to the closet, snagged a robe, and pulled it shut. I shuffled into the bathroom and took care of the basics, including brushing my fuzzy teeth and combing the sex knots out of my hair. Downing three Advil, two for the hangover and one for sleeping on the cold floor which my wonky hip didn't appreciate. I couldn't keep the stupid grin off my face though. Hot damn had I ever needed that.

I could face a whole host of fae and their essence wouldn't affect me one bit because I was one thoroughly-satisfied woman.

Benji waited for me in the hall, his tail wagging. I scratched him behind the ears. "You need to go out, boy?"

We headed down the stairs and I pushed my way to the door, inhaling the scent of freshly brewed coffee. Hell yeah, that was what the doctor ordered.

After letting Benji out, I retrieved my Atlanta 1996 Olympics mug and filled it to the brim. The first sip was pure heaven. I closed my eyes and half turned away, making plans for the day. I'd take a badly needed shower, make breakfast for the household, find the damn fae queen, get my antidote and kick her ass back to her own realm. Practice yoga and then find Robin and….

When I opened my eyes I saw the piece of paper that had fallen off the counter. Frowning, I bent down and picked it up. Two words were written on it.

I'm sorry.

"What?" The word slipped out. Who was sorry and for what?

Outside, Benji started barking. I set the coffee and the note aside and then opened the kitchen door.

Andreas stood there, his hands glowing with green magic. All of Benji's hackles were raised as he faced off against the fae.

"Easy boy," I snagged Benji by the collar and dragged him into the house before turning my attention to Andreas. "What are you doing here?"

"Making a delivery." He handed me a vial of purple and gold-flecked liquid.

"What's that?" But I already knew.

I'm sorry, he had said. He had made me coffee, written the note and then left to….

"It's the antidote." Andreas's emerald eyes held sympathy. "Robin traded himself to our mother this morning in exchange for it."

ANDREAS WAS STILL in the kitchen when I returned, freshly showered and dressed. The antidote was where I left it, sitting as a reminder that Robin didn't have enough faith in me to wait for me to find another way.

Either that or the fae prince really did love me.

"Damn it." We were close, I could feel it in my marrow. "Why would he do this?"

"He wants you to live, Josephine Louise Whitmore."

I rounded on him. "What is the damn deal with using my full name all the time?"

He was quiet for so long I feared he wouldn't answer. Finally, he said, "Fae were badly used by humans in the past. That's part of the reason why old ones, like my mother, delight in enslaving and tormenting mortals. The only power we ever had over humans was that of the bargain. And to create a bargain, we needed information about the mortal we were bargaining with."

"So, you use our full names to show you know something about us?"

"In part. A name is connected to the self. By using the name, we can tap into the power of the self and approach a mortal without fear of the unknown. When I use your name, it makes you more real to me. It turns a being of power into a person with wants and desires who I can manipulate to fulfill my own wants and desires."

"So, what's your mother's full name?"

Andreas shook his head. "Anyone who ever knew it is dead. We simply call her mother or the queen."

I blew out a breath. That would have been too easy.

Andreas looked to the counter, to the vial. "You need to drink that or his sacrifice will be in vain."

"I know. But if I do, he'll be gone for good." Tears threatened but I held them back.

Andreas tilted his head to the side. "He told me you didn't love him."

"What?"

"Robin. He said that you weren't in love with him, but clearly, that's not the case." He frowned.

"I never told him that I loved him."

"But you made love with him?"

"That's none of your business," I snapped.

"I wouldn't ask if it wasn't important. Do you love him?"

A lump had formed in my throat. I couldn't say the words to Andreas. That would be a betrayal of Robin because he was the one who deserved to hear it. So, I nodded once.

"He lied," Andreas whispered.

"Not possible. Robin can't lie. He's fae."

Still appearing shell shocked, Andreas backed away. "No, Josephine Louise Whitmore, I don't believe he is any longer."

I stared up at him. "What are you talking about? He's your brother?"

"The fae are only different from the humans because of our ability to wield magic. The more power we accumulate through our bargains, the stronger and more alien we become. My brother was once the most powerful, aside from the queen herself. But he has diminished over the last two and a half centuries. If he wasn't making bargains, his power would continue to trickle away. And without magic, he would become fully human."

I was about to tell him that Robin's magic hadn't trickled away, just shifted to me. But I bit my tongue. Robin hadn't wanted Andreas or anyone else to know that I possessed his magic. Had he suspected that his brother was a spy for their mother? Or was he just being overcautious?

"So what you're saying is that all it takes is a few bargains to turn a human into a fae?" I asked.

Andreas shook his head. "No. Much like energy can't be created or destroyed, neither can power. That power is transferred to the fae throughout the bargain. Some we bring home and add to the clan's collective. The stronger members receive the most, which is why the queen never has to bargain herself. To put it bluntly, the better we screw over a strong-willed being, the more magic we obtain."

My bargain had screwed Robin over, hardcore. Was that why I'd inherited his magic? If that were true, all he would have to do to get it back was to screw me over in equal measure. There were a thousand different ways he could have done that. Economically, emotionally.

But he hadn't.

I stared hard at the magical antidote on the counter. "I'm going to save him."

Andreas shook his head. "It's too late. The bargain is already struck."

Ignoring him I scooped up the vile and put it in the pocket of my sweater. "It's a good thing I have a get out of bargains free card. Come on Benji."

I patted my leg and Benji fell into step beside me.

"Wait, where are you going!" Footsteps indicated that Andreas was following us out into the side yard. I let myself in through the garage door and flicked on the overhead light.

The cashbox my mother had used at the sale had been emptied. I slammed the lid and thought furiously. My mother would have taken the money out and put it directly in her purse. Which she had taken to Grammy's.

But money wasn't what I was looking for.

"What's going on?" Andreas asked as I strode past him

and went back to the kitchen door. "Joey, wait." He gripped my arm and held me still.

Benji turned and bared his teeth.

Andreas released me.

I half turned on the step to stare at him. "I've got this. Trust me." *Fake it till you make it.*

Andreas put a hand over his heart and bowed down. It was a curious old-fashioned sort of gesture that denoted respect. I would have to think about what it meant, later.

The object I was looking for sat on my mother's dresser. I pocketed it and then took the steps two at a time up to my room and then started shuffling through the dirty clothes on the floor. I found the watch tangled up with my sports bra. Benji pressed into my side in preparation.

"Here goes everything," I said and turned the watch back, once, twice, three times.

Then waited.

Benji panted away the seconds, even as Robin, still naked, sat up beside my unconscious form and peered into the shadowy corner where I stood.

I wish he wouldn't see us.

There was no way to tell whether or not the spell had worked. But Robin turned to face the woman beside him.

Frigging great, I was drooling in my sleep. Real class act.

Emotion played over the fae's face as he stared down at the drunken sot beside him. My heart thundered as he watched me sleep. For once, his expression was completely transparent. The masks were gone. Yearning. It was the real Robin Goodfellow looking down at me through brilliant sapphire eyes. How many women got the chance to see the way their lover looked at them in such an unguarded moment? It was something we all deserved to see at least once.

"I love you, lamb," he whispered.

I love you, too. The words were there, on the tip of my tongue. Any lingering doubts had been obliterated by that look. I yearned to step out of the darkness and reveal myself. But events needed to unfold. I wished I would have the chance to share my heart's very real truth with him.

And I would happily pay the price.

Robin rose from the floor, reached for the chenille blanket, and tucked it around me. He stabbed his legs into his discarded jeans and then retrieved his shirt, pausing to brush his hand across his scarred chest. He turned and looked at me again and I saw his jaw tense as his resolve cemented itself. He collected his shoes, then crept to the door.

A soft whine came from outside. Benji.

Robin opened the door and the dog came in. He moved, not to the window seat where I'd first seen him, but right to the corner where Benji and I stood. I gestured with my hand, trying to shoo him back before he gave me away.

Lucky for us Robin was also intent on his getaway. The door shut and a moment later I heard his light footsteps on the stairs.

Over on the floor, I let out a snort.

"I'm never drinking again," I muttered, then scratched past Benji behind his ear. "Go lie down boy. I'll see you when I wake up."

He obeyed, hopping up on the window seat, turning around once, and then plopping down with a contented sigh.

I headed to the door, my Benji in lockstep with me. I counted to one hundred, long enough to give Robin time to put on his shoes, make the coffee and scribble that note. Then I scurried down the stairs in time to see him depart through the back door. Quietly as I could, I crept out into the night.

It occurred to me that if he took my car to wherever he was going, I wouldn't be able to follow. But Robin strode past the car and headed down the street on foot. It was going to be a pain in the ass to follow him without revealing myself.

"I wish I had a way to track him," I muttered.

At that moment, a sapphire light blazed from Robin. Like the aura I'd seen around Benji and the other dogs that day in the shelter. Only this was a million times brighter. Robin didn't break stride, so I could only assume the light was viewable to my eyes only.

The wind picked up, blowing my hair back from my face as I strode behind him, wondering where he was going. Dread pooled in my stomach as we turned onto a familiar street.

Grammy B's house sat at the end. It was coated in a glimmering golden shell like it had been draped in a transparent bubble and dusted with glitter. A shield of some sort?

What was he doing there? Checking on my mom and Dragon? Wanting to say goodbye?

The fist in my stomach and the huge bubble of magic told me that no, it was nothing so innocent. He'd been jumpy and nervous at Ursula's house, freaked out even when I'd shown up. Had he known we were on the wrong path already? Had he discovered something while I was fast-forwarding through time?

I stared in horror as Robin knocked. The door opened

and my Aunt Hannah stared down at him through icy, sapphire eyes.

"Have you come to make a bargain, my son?"

I SHUT MY EYES. The fae queen. And she had inhabited my Aunt Hannah. Robin said she could do that with her anchor.

I emptied my pockets, stared down at the three objects there. The potion, the watch, and the item I had retrieved from my mother's bedroom. My grandfather's watch.

If you can see, it can be.

Good thing I had a guideline.

Over on the steps, Robin was moving forward, his lips parted. I had to act quickly.

"No, I have though." I emerged from my hiding place. They both turned and stared directly at me with identical sapphire eyes.

"Joey?" Robin's shoulders tensed. "What are you doing here?"

I didn't answer him, not wanting to take my gaze away from the predator that had been masquerading as my aunt for who knew how long.

"You want to bargain with me, don't you?" If what Andreas told me was accurate, my inherited magic was second only to hers, while Robin was no stronger than a mortal.

Meaning I was better bait.

"Yes," she hissed in a sibilant tone. "But I thought you were smarter than this."

"Lamb, no, you don't know what you're doing." Robin

reached for me. I held up a hand, freezing him in place like a statue.

"Where are they?" I asked the woman who looked so much like an aged up, frumped up version of Dragon it was painful.

"Your other loved ones are unharmed." She smiled and gestured for me to enter. "Come see for yourself."

"Stay," I told Benji, not wanting him in the line of fire.

He whined but then lay down on the lawn. I strode past Robin who begged me with his eyes and words, "Don't do this."

I reigned in my emotions the same way I had done countless times when performing gymnastics. I had to hide the nervous flutters, the anxiety over past mistakes, everything I didn't want my audience to see. It was all about perception. Fake it 'til you make it. I stepped onto the mat and I owned them.

"Not your call," I lifted my chin so I could stare down my nose at Robin. "She's messed with my family. This is between her and me."

He recognized my resolve and closed his eyes. "Be careful. You're bargaining for all of our lives."

I reached for his hand, grasped it for a moment, and then walked past his mother—who was also my aunt and how fucked up was that—and into the house.

"I'll deal with you later," she said to Robin. There was a tingle up my spine and I could feel that protective magic shell going back over the house, closing us all in. And I knew deep down that only one of us would leave alive.

For the sake of everyone I loved, it had better be me.

Grammy B, my mother, and Dragon were huddled on the couch, their expressions frozen in silent screams.

"What did you do to them?" I whispered.

"Showed them what I did to your aunt," the fae queen purred. "Then captured them at the moment."

"You killed her?" I had to be sure.

She shrugged and then…unzipped her skin. It was like watching a snake emerge and what was left behind was a bloody lump of flesh.

"It was time I found myself a new anchor anyhow." The fae queen, the same as I had seen her in my dream, turned to face me. Her cobwebby dress clung to her perfect body.

"Why her?"

She studied me intently, taking my measure. I knew what she saw, could see it reflected in her gaze. An overweight middle-aged mortal who had left her anchor outside.

Go ahead, I thought. *Underestimate me. That'll be fun.*

The queen turned her head and looked down at what was left of Aunt Hannah passionlessly. "She's served me well for the past forty-two years, but I've gotten tired of her constant demands."

Wait. "Forty-two years?"

"Oh yes. You see, I made it my business to learn all about my son's anchor. Where she came from, who she was related to and how exactly she managed to deceive the best trickster the world had ever seen."

I didn't interrupt. Let her monologue it out to my benefit.

"It didn't take long for me to realize that your aunt was an ambitious and easy quarry for a bargain. Anchors need to be strong as well as desperate. It was easy enough to twist her ambition until I got what I wanted from her—a direct line to you. Unfortunately, I chose the wrong relation, being as once your gymnastics career ended, she didn't bother to keep in touch with you."

The expressions on my family's faces were making me ill. Never mind the Aunt Hannah suit. I had to deliberately turn my back on all of it. "That's the trouble with fickle people. They skedaddle the second they realize the gravy train has ended."

"Yes, so I was forced to hunt down a new anchor, someone closer to you." Her lips curled up in a predatory smile. "Have you figured it out yet?"

My brows drew together. "Figured what out?"

Triumph radiated from her. "All the females in your family are so strong-willed. So which one has agreed to serve as my new anchor?"

My lips parted and I turned back to them once more. No. No no *no*. There was no way….

Was there?

The faery queen gestured to the couch. "Your grand-mother, well she's as the elderly often are, isn't she? Her body is slowly decaying. She's lonely and oftentimes feels like a burden to those around her."

Was that true? Grammy had been prickly when we went out for pizza, sniping about how the young didn't listen. The same night that Robin had felt his mother's presence for the first time.

"Then there's your mother and all of her financial woes. How easy it would have been to make a bargain with her for a sack full of cash."

A roaring sound filled my ears, almost drowning out her

words. I had intentionally kept them in the dark about the fae and magic. Had my inaction caused this scene?

The queen moved past me and laid her hand on Dragon's head. "And this one. She was a challenge. Had it not been for my close relationship with her mother, I may never have figured out that what she desires most is acceptance. And she would do *anything* to get it."

The fae queen leaned forward and whispered in my ear. "You know I need an anchor to stay here, Josephine Louise Whitmore. You know that destroying that anchor would send me away for good. The rest of your tribe would be safe. So will you destroy one, to save the rest?"

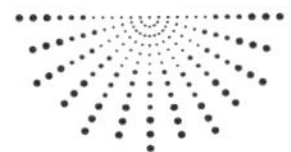

CHAPTER SEVENTEEN

"You need to live with yourself so make damn sure that you live for yourself first."
-Notable quotable from Grammy B

"No." The word escaped my lips as though it was a prisoner hellbent on a jailbreak. I stared at the three frozen women on the couch. The queen's proposition was a no-win scenario. At least with my way, we all stood a chance of surviving, no matter how minuscule.

"No?" She repeated the word as though she'd never heard it before.

I turned my back on them. "I want to bargain with you."

Her laugh made all the small hairs rise along the back of my neck. "You think you can fool me? I'm older than this mountain your mortal feet stand upon. I have seen humanity and know your uses and they are few."

Her words reminded me of Robin Goodfellow as he had been before I became his anchor. Arrogant, dismissive of humans in general. He had learned it from this creature and her wicked ways.

But I had fooled one fae royal. And dagnabbit, I could do it again.

Her laughter died away as she surveyed me from head to foot. "What is this bargain you propose to strike? I know what you want, to save the lives of your family. Mortals are so boringly predictable. But what could you possibly offer to entice me?"

I held up the pocket watch letting it dangle from my fingers.

She sucked in a breath. "Where did you get that?"

I ignored the question. "Do I have your interest? Or should I fast forward in time to see how this all turns out?"

Her breasts rose and fell as she stared at the item in my hands. "I'll trade one of your family members for the watch."

"No."

"Two," she snapped, obviously impatient.

I shook my head.

She made a sound that was half oath, half snarl. "Fine all three."

I waited.

"Well?" She barked.

"That's not the bargain I want."

"Well, what is?"

"Tell me your full name."

Her eyes narrowed. "My name?"

I nodded. "Your *full* name, in exchange for this watch."

She searched my face, obviously sensing a trap. "Give me the watch first and then I'll tell you my name."

"At the same time." The pocket watch spun on the chain and I held it out, wary of those deadly nails. "Is it a bargain?"

Her lips curled up in a satisfied smile. "A bargain well struck."

Magic swirled between us, engulfing us both in a column of gold and purple sparks. A mystical wind lifted my hair off my face, the same way it did hers. Her cold eyes seemed to suck at my soul even as the watch whirled between us.

Her face lit with avarice as a hand closed around the face of the watch even as I maintained my grip on the chain. "My name is Galina Ann Humphries."

She couldn't lie. I was banking on that.

I released the chain and staggard back. With the bargain fulfilled she was free to hurt or kill me. I narrowly missed a swipe of her deadly claws as I belly-flopped onto the floor.

Andreas was right. Knowing someone's full name made them all the more real.

"Galina Ann Humphries," I called out over the sound of a shitstorm of magic. "You've just been played." Reaching into my coat pocket, I held up the real watch. The one that created time loops for the bearer.

Her brows drew together and she frowned down at me. Then looked to the watch. Wound it.

The glamour I had placed on my grandfather's pocket watch faded away at the same time that the fae queen's body was replaced by Galina's true physical form. That of a middle aged-woman with sagging breasts and crow's feet.

"No," she breathed, gaze flying to meet mine. "It's not possible!"

She threw the watch at the wall and then rounded on me, raising her hand to do her worst. Then she stared at the appendage in disbelief when nothing happened.

Magic tingled through me from my gray roots down to the bunions on my feet. Magic always came with a price, but damn, if it didn't feel amazing.

In the distance, thunder boomed. Lightning flashed down, striking the dove gray carpet of my grandmother's living room, setting the place ablaze.

"It's mine," she shrieked in outrage and lunged through the fire toward me, claws bared.

I threw my arms up to protect my face and prepared myself for the agony of her poisoned scratches.

It never came. Galina's hands stopped inches from my flesh, held back by both arms, one by Andreas, the other by Robin.

"Joey," Robin called over the roar of the wind. "Get them out of here!"

I nodded and shoved myself up and stumbled on watery legs over to the couch. With her magic gone, the spell she had cast around my mother, Grammy B, and Dragon lifted. They shrieked like a nest of harpies, the horror of what they'd witnessed still buried in their minds.

"Come on," I snapped. "We need to go."

Grammy blinked up at me and then reached for my hand. "Joey? What in tarnation?"

"Grammy, I promise I will do my best to explain it all but we need to get out of here *now*." I gestured toward the fire which had engulfed half the living room.

My mother and Dragon leaned on each other for support as I half carried Grammy B out of the house and to the front lawn where Benji waited.

"Stay here," I said to Grammy then rushed back for the front door in time to see Andreas snap his mother's neck.

"For Gwendolyn." Andreas closed his eyes, his chest heaving.

My lips parted in shock. Gwendolyn? Who was that?

"Lamb, come on," Robin had appeared in front of me.

"But…" I had just witnessed a murder. Matricide. I had forgotten how to blink.

Robin tugged me away even as sirens pierced the night.

"The cops. How are we going to explain this?"

A dead body, a burning house.

"Andreas will handle it." Robin pressed something into my palm. "Drink it, now."

I stared down and saw the vial of antidote I had slipped into his hand and was now back in mine. After fumbling with the tiny cork, I popped the lid and then knocked the potion back, grimacing at the taste. "Yuck. What the hell is in this?"

"Goblin piss."

My head whipped to Robin. "What?"

"Kidding." His grin was lopsided, eyes full of amusement. "You ought to see the look on your face though."

"Kidding, you mean lying," I poked him in the chest.

He reached up and started rubbing the back of his neck. "Yeah, about that….I can explain."

But I shook my head. "You don't have to. I trust you, even if you are nothing but a pesky lying mortal now."

His hand fell to his side. "Really?"

I reached for him and put my hands on his chest. "I love you, Robin Goodfellow."

A look of wonder took over his features. "Well, what do you know? Are you sure you're not lying to get back at me?"

I leaned up and brushed my lips over his. "And I told you I wouldn't regret anything come morning." I waved toward the eastern horizon where the sky transitioned from dark blue to light pink to golden white.

"You were right."

I sighed and leaned against his chest. "Those three magic words."

How I loved making my fae prince-turned-mortal laugh.

"So which of you did it?" I paced in front of my bedraggled family. We had returned to the Victorian well after the point where the past me and Benji had turned back time. Or was that future me?

Seriously, time travel could go kick rocks.

Just like Robin had promised, Andreas had removed his mother's body as well as himself before the fire department had put out the blaze. Grammy's house was water-logged and in no way habitable. The shock still hadn't settled in. Too much had happened in too short a time.

"Did what?" My mother tried to sip her coffee but her hands were shaking too badly. She set it down on the end table.

"Made a bargain with the fae queen."

Robin cleared his throat. I glanced at him and he winked at me. "Correction, the former fae queen."

Who, deep down, had been nothing more than an insecure middle-aged woman. What had happened to her in her life to turn the tide? What had twisted her up to the point of being so ruthless that she had tortured one son and killed the other's lover?

Fear. Loneliness. Being dismissed by the world, shoved in a corner, and told to be a good girl and not to rock the effing boat.

She hadn't listened. Instead of rolling over and dying, she'd fought like a rabid wolverine to carve out a life where she held power. Part of me admired her for that, though I decided to keep that nugget to myself.

"Fae queen?" Dragon looked up at me and her eyes were haunted.

I glanced at Robin and after a moment of silent communication, he nodded. "Yes, she was my mother."

"Was?" My own mother looked between us.

"She was sick," Robin said. "You don't need to worry about her any longer."

"But I still want to know who made the bargain, because that's something we need to deal with." I folded my arms over my chest and waited.

My mother looked at Dragon and then at Grammy before turning back to face me. "We didn't."

"But she said that one of my family members bargained with her. She was unable to lie."

A car door slammed and then the sound of footsteps hurrying up the path and to the porch. A moment later my father appeared, eyes wild as he searched the gathered faces. "Prudence? I just heard. Are you all right?"

"I'm fine, Paul." My mother stood and my father went to her and wrapped his arms around her in a fierce hug.

"No." My jaw dropped. "Not him."

Robin pulled me back into his chest and rested his chin on my head. "Does it really surprise you, lamb? My mother wouldn't have wanted her anchor where he could be killed. She stacked the deck in her favor every time."

I blew out a sigh. "She wanted me to kill one of them. Hell, all of them, all the while knowing that it wouldn't do any good."

"And if you had been a different sort of person, perhaps you would have taken the easy way. And she would have won."

I swallowed, then cut my gaze to where my parents were still hugging. "All right, enough of this. Put the poor guy out of his misery and marry him already."

"But...?" My mother blinked. "Can we talk about this later?"

"No." I looked at my father, the desperate idiot. "You, will you promise that you won't lose interest in her once she agrees to marry you? Because that's what she's really afraid of."

My mother blinked. "How...?"

"Easy. It's the same damn thing I'm scared of. That I'll get old and boring and no one will give a shit."

"Josephine Louise Whitmore, language!"

I wasn't about to apologize for my language. Or much of anything else anymore. "So, Dad? You gonna throw her over for a younger model once she agrees to forever?"

He reared back as though I offended him. "Of course not."

I rounded on my mother and stabbed a finger in her face.

"That is the best you are going to get. He was willing to bargain with a faery queen to get your cantankerous hide down the aisle. You love him, he loves you. He won't smother you because he knows you'll hate that and all he wants to do is make you happy. Besides, I have had four-plus decades of being your bastard lovechild and I have had enough of it."

Her lips thinned but finally, she breathed a reluctant, "okay."

"One down," Robin whispered in my ear, his tone filled with amusement. "I love to watch you work."

"Grammy." I sat beside her. "You do know that you are my favorite person in the whole wide world, don't you?"

Her lip trembled. "You don't have to say that."

"Taking care of you is my privilege because it means I get extra time to learn from you. To hear your stories. I am so sorry if I ever once made you feel like you are a burden to me or that I don't listen. Please, be patient with me. Being middle-aged isn't easy."

She patted my hand. "Oh, I can remember that well enough."

"I'm sorry about your house," I murmured.

She shrugged it off like losing the home she had dwelled in for her entire adult life was no biggie. "I've got what's truly important. Though I'm not sure where I'll stay now."

"You'll stay right here, Mom." My mother stepped forward. "My room is on the bottom floor so you don't need to worry about the stairs."

"And where will you go?" I asked. "The guest room is pretty tight, especially for a married couple and a dog."

"I was thinking I could take over your room."

My mouth dropped. "You want to take over my room?"

"Well, yeah. Since you're going to be moving out to the cottage and all." She winked.

"I never said—," I began.

"It's only temporary." Robin cut me off.

I thought about the space that he had set up so beautifully. And I could see us there.

If you can see, it can be.

We were all getting shuffled around and forced to make concessions. And really, we were all going to be better off for it.

Amazing what could happen when you let go of fear and stubborn pride and love with your whole heart.

"And Dragon?" I glanced toward the other end of the couch. But my cousin was gone.

I FOUND her on the back steps. Her eyes red-rimmed as she stared out at the street. Bluto sat by her side, whining. I didn't touch her, didn't try to pull anything out of her, just sat beside her in silence. Dragon had been through a lot in her young life, more than many had by my age or even by Grammy's. The rest of us were content to settle in, settle down knowing who we were and having our place in the world. But Dragon had yet to carve out hers. Her mother was dead. She must feel so alone.

"Robin asked me if we could adopt you."

She let out a derisive snort. "I don't want his pity."

"It's not pity, Dragon. It's empathy. You saw what a horror show his mother turned out to be. He gets it."

"So what, my mom is dead and the two of you are going to drop everything to be my parents?" She sneered.

"Robin asked me yesterday before we found out about your mother. He wanted you to know you would always have a place where people loved you and wanted you, exactly how you are."

She turned to face me and I could feel her gaze roving my features. "So you and Robin are a permanent thing?"

"As permanent as it gets. It's like I told my mom, there aren't any guarantees. But I want to be with him and he wants to be with me. And look, if the adoption thing is crazy then it's okay to tell us so—"

She picked at a hole in the knee of her jeans. "It is crazy. But it's also…nice. To be wanted."

I gave in to the impulse and put my arm around her. "You will always have a place with me. I'm not much of a mom, but I will do my best for you. We all will. Heaven help you." My free hand gestured back to the house.

I got a laugh out of her and considering what she had been through, it was more than I could have hoped.

"Anybody hungry?" Robin stuck his head out of the screen door to ask.

"Starving. You?" I looked to Dragon.

"I could eat," she admitted.

"Waffles coming right up." Robin winked and then disappeared.

We gathered around the table. My whole family, most of us covered with ash and soot and passed a tray of waffles around the room.

"This isn't that crap fake syrup is it?" Grammy moved her

dentures around as she stared suspiciously at the little white jug.

"What do you take me for?" my mother huffed.

"Notice how she didn't answer the question?" I whispered in Robin's ear.

"She'd make an excellent fae," he whispered back.

The thought made me shudder.

"So, Robin. Are you going to continue on at the firm?" My father asked as he cut his waffle into precise bits.

"That depends," he hedged.

"On what?" Dragon asked.

"On whether Joey wants to take up residence in the fae realm."

Forks paused in mid-air and all eyes turned to me.

"Hell no," I said firmly. "They can have it."

"Are you sure, lamb? You haven't even seen it yet. If you stay here, eventually the magic will fade and—"

I covered his mouth with my hand. "I'm good."

He nipped my fingers playfully and then turned back to my father. "In that case, yes, Paul. I would be delighted to work with you permanently." Robin draped an arm over the back of my chair.

He fit in with our motley little crew, I realized. With my family and into my life. It wasn't a seamless transition for any of us. But it was right.

Later, fresh out of the shower and snuggled in the king-sized bed next to Robin, I let out a contented sigh. "Damn, I needed that." I hadn't meant to say the words out loud, but considering how utterly boneless my body was at the moment, it was little wonder I'd lost control over my impulses.

Robin chuckled, an action that shook my entire body since I'd collapsed on top of him. "I told you so."

I lifted my head and glowered down my nose at him. "Nobody likes a know-it-all."

"You seemed to like me just fine a few minutes ago." He tangled his fingers with mine and brought my knuckles to his lips in a tender kiss. "To think, we could have been enjoying each other this way from the start."

I rolled my eyes. "It doesn't work that way."

His brows drew together in that way that told me I was being too mortal for his comprehension. "What do you mean?"

"It means I didn't trust you then. And for good reason."

"That's because you are a clever little lamb."

A low rumble of thunder sounded outside our cozy love nest. The fire in the small wood stove popped and hissed. I shivered and curled tighter into his warmth.

Outside the door came a pitiful whine.

"Your familiar misses you." The cabin was so small that Robin didn't need to get out of bed to undo the latch and let Benji in. The door blew wide and the dog darted in. He circled the bed, stuck a cold, wet nose in a place where no cold wet nose should ever go, and then loped to the rug in front of the woodstove and plopped onto it before my yelp had faded.

"Should I peel you off the ceiling or can you get down yourself?" Robin asked from below me.

He wasn't being dramatic. Somehow, after the uncomfortable bonding moment with my new puppy, I'd floated up to the ceiling. It was a good thing the curtains were drawn or anyone walking by would have gotten an eyeful of one former gymnast and the effects gravity had on a middle-aged body.

"I feel like that woman from *Ghostbusters*." I flailed, naked in the air, and tried to ignore the fact that he wasn't even trying to contain his laughter. "When exactly is this magic going to dissipate?"

"You've got mine and now my mother's as well since you deceived her so beautifully. It'll take time. Take a page out of his book and try to relax and enjoy the good things." Robin nodded to where Benji had already started to snore.

I glared at him. "I was."

Robin lay back and folded his hands behind his head in an utterly scrumptious display of male muscle, beneath the webwork of scars. "You know I could get used to this view."

I struggled a moment more, trying unsuccessfully to navigate to where I could see Benji. After a moment, I gave up and then just glared at Robin while thinking, *Get me down, now.*

As usually happened with magic and wishes I hadn't thought through all the angles. Instead of drifting softly like a feather, I plummeted like a sack of potatoes. Robin's eyes went wide and he reached out to catch me before I flattened him completely.

"You all right, lamb?" he asked as he brushed a curl out of my face.

I couldn't respond, my heart was beating much too fast.

"You're not going to knee me in the ballocks again, are you?"

"Don't tempt me." I released a shuddering breath and then, cautious in case I went airborne again, slid to the side.

A self-satisfied smirk stole over his face and he waggled his eyebrows. "That good, am I?"

"You are such a guy, you know that." I rolled my eyes. "But seriously, how long until the magic goes away?"

"Well, if you can refrain from making bargains, maybe a year or two. Unless you've changed your mind about being a faery godmother."

I shook my head. "No way. I want back to my boring old life. No more prices I can't afford."

"Then it will drift away like smoke caught by an air current, a little at a time."

"Andreas told me magic couldn't be created or destroyed. So where will it go?" I asked.

"To someone who needs it." He shrugged and reached for me again. "You know what I need right now?"

I pretended to think, even as I couldn't contain my smile. "Give me three guesses."

Sapphire eyes lit with amusement. "Are you really *bargaining* with me?"

"Nope," I shook my head. "A girl doesn't bargain when she has everything she wants."

"Amen to that," Robin said and kissed me.

The End.

So where will the magic go? Find out in Mid-Century Modern Magic, *book 1 in my upcoming Witch Way After Forty PWF series. Preorder your copy now!*

My first thought when seeing the naked blonde riding my husband in our bed was, *Of course, the selfish ass insisted she is on top.* Never mind that those clearly artificial double Ds were bound to cause her slight frame serious back pain in a few years. He wasn't much for manual labor, old Kyle. His idea of getting a workout involved mowing the lawn or shoveling the driveway. Which he never did well and I was usually forced to go back over it to clean up the sloppy job.

In some shadowy corner of my mind, I recognized that it probably wasn't normal to feel sympathy for the woman boinking your spouse.

Then again, I'd known it was coming.

Just like Kyle was about to. I could tell by the way his face turned red and he bucked beneath her spastically.

The hell with that. He hadn't respected me enough to keep his side dish on the side, well, then he could just deal with blue balls.

The bedroom door was open so I strode in, doing my best to keep from snagging a heel in the filmy bits of lace that obviously didn't belong to me. Perhaps when I was three, I could have fit that size. Then again, I might have had a Barbie once that could wear those skivvies.

What was this woman even doing with Kyle? It seemed like a pertinent question so I tapped her on the shoulder. "You know, honey, you can do better."

She screamed and scrambled off of him, about two seconds before Kyle was about to nut. I reached down and grabbed him by the balls and twisted. I'd boil my hand later. Or maybe chew it off.

For his part, Kyle's groan turned to one of sheer agony. "Alys," he gasped.

"Who's this?" Blondie asked.

"His wife. I'd offer a handshake but mine are busy at the moment."

The woman's big green eyes went from me to Kyle, whose skin had flushed purple. His whole body shook. "You know it costs more for another girl, don't you?"

Her accent was clear New Jersey. That combined with the fact that I had never seen her before topped with her mention of cost had me turning back to the worm in my bed. "A prostitute, Kyle? Seriously?"

He made a gargling noise and I sank my nails in, just a little.

My sister had told me Kyle was a bastard coated bastard with bastard filling. I should have listened.

"You ought to leave," I nodded to the dental floss that passed for her undergarments.

"Nu-uh," Blondie folded her arms over her implants. "Not 'til I get my scratch."

I sighed. "How much?"

"Four hundred."

I raised a brow. "Seriously? For what, twenty minutes of work? Considering how he performs, you would have time for a shower after."

She reached for her bra and I had a moment of envy when her breasts didn't alter an iota as she snapped it on. "I charge double for the uggos. Plus, there's the drive."

The gurgling sound Kyle made when Blondie called him an uggo was worth four hundred bucks. My purse was downstairs in the hallway, but Kyle's Rolex was on the nightstand. With my left hand, I retrieved it and lobbed it to her. "Keep it."

"Do I look like a pawn shop to you?" I could see her assessing the watch and the gleam in her eye. The watch was worth a lot more than four hundred.

"It's the best you're gonna get. He's in no position to finish, so unless you want to wait around until he recovers...." I smiled sweetly at the puce color on my husband's face.

She pulled her micromini up and then threw on a jacket, over the top. "I'm good."

I released Kyle the moment the front door shut behind her. He curled onto his side in the fetal position. Fitting, since he was such a big baby.

I didn't say a word. Instead, I kicked off my heels and turned to the bathroom. I let the water run as hot as it could go, then used half a bottle of antibacterial soap. For the record, that was the last time I was touching that man's privates. The thought filled me with a giddy sort of relief.

The signs had been there for months. Internet porn had been constant throughout the marriage and easy enough to ignore. But then the credit card charges had popped up. Sites that were clearly shell companies with BS names to protect privacy. Phone calls to numbers I didn't know. Him never going to bed at the same time as me. I thought it had been a run of the mill affair, something middle-aged men did to prove they were just as young and virile as they had once been.

In Kyle's case, the bar wasn't set too high. It was probably even lower now. Between Blondie's dismount and my claws. I hadn't drawn blood, but the thought of leaving him emasculated was far too tempting.

If he had been discreet, I could have gone on feigning ignorance. But he'd forced me into this position, into being the victim, the foolish wife.

The thing that hurt most was my pride. And in my book, that was unforgivable.

I stared at my reflection, at the crow's feet lining my eyes, the streaks of silver in my short black bob, and winter pale skin which was even paler than usual. I pinched a little color into my cheeks, then turned to the medicine cabinet. After sorting through its contents, I scooped what I needed into one hand and then carried it out to the bedroom.

Kyle had extracted himself from the bed and pulled on a pair of sweats. "You can't honestly be surprised, Alys."

I didn't bother to look at him as I snagged my overnight bag from the top of the closet. My toiletry bag was inside and I took the time to separate the liquids from the pills, from the make-up brushes. *Everything in its place. Don't let him see the wound.*

"When was the last time we even had sex?" Kyle sounded triumphant, as though he had just scored a point.

I tapped my chin as though contemplating the question and then shrugged. "I really couldn't say, Kyle. Seeing as it wasn't all that memorable."

His brown eyes narrowed. "You're a frigid old bitch."

I went back to my packing, trying to figure out what exactly I would need for my new Kyle-free life. Clothes for work, both demo and client meetings. Jeans, sweatshirts, and work boots as well as twinsets, slacks, and heels. And it was fall now, heading toward winter. What about a coat and snow boots? Maybe I'd have to get another bag out of the attic. The thought made me tired. I just wanted to leave the house that I had lived in for twenty years and never really liked and not look back.

"I should have kicked you to the curb years ago." Clearly irritated that even his blatant act of defiance didn't get my undivided attention, Kyle began to rant in classic dipshit monologue.

No to the slog to the attic, I decided. I'd come back with Maeve at some point and get the rest of it. When I was in a better place to deal with this crap. Keep it simple. *Think capsule wardrobe. Black pairs with anything. Neutrals are good too.* I added two pairs of slacks, a twinset, and three different blouses along with the set of black heels I had been wearing and then crammed as many jeans and sweats on top as I could fit. Making swift decisions always helped fuel me so I zipped the bag, snagged my e-reader off my nightstand, my jewelry box from the top of the dresser, and headed for the door.

"Where are you going?" Kyle called as I descended the grand staircase to the bottom floor. He chased me down, looking none too healthy. I hoped he wouldn't have a heart attack. I didn't want to stick around long enough to let the EMTs in.

At that, I rounded on him. "If I'm so awful, why not just go file for divorce?"

His lips parted but he didn't say anything. We both knew why. He liked having money. Liked the lavish lifestyle my business had afforded us. He'd retired early and that was when the trouble began.

"You're not getting a dime." Thank god Aunt Jess had taught me to keep my finances separate from my spouse's.

"It's half mine," he snarled.

"Like hell it is. You spent every dime you made on the mausoleum." Done with him, I turned to the door.

He folded his arms over his chest. "Do you really want the entire town to know that I paid a prostitute for sex?"

I froze with my hand on the door and a sliver of fear ran down my spine.

He pushed on. "Think of the gossip. Alys Stevens can't hold a man."

My heart pounded and for a moment I was afraid I would be the one to pass out. "You can have the house. And your damn Corvette. But no money."

"We'll see." He looked smug and I was sorry I hadn't gelded him when I'd had the chance.

Preorder Mid-Century Modern Magic now!

ABOUT THE AUTHOR

USA Today bestselling author Jennifer L. Hart writes about characters that cuss, get naked, and often make poor but hilarious life choices. A native New Yorker, Jenn now lives in the mountains of North Carolina with her imaginary friends. Her works to date include the Damaged Goods mystery series and the Magical Midlife Misadventures.

Subscribe to Jenn's author newsletter, Hart's Hitlist.

Printed in Poland
by Amazon Fulfillment
Poland Sp. z o.o., Wrocław
22 April 2021

09dbfd40-8476-4fd8-a476-9700378ed536R01